RIDE

AND

DIE

RIDE
AND
DIE

RIDGEMORE BOOK 1

LUCÍA ASHTA

Podium

Cover design by Yoly Cortez

ISBN: 978-1-0394-7852-7

Published in 2024 by Podium Publishing
www.podiumaudio.com

Podium

For my husband and daughters

RIDE

AND

DIE

1

A Party Foul to End Them All

As I tipped back my beer, I strained to hear what Layla was saying to that jackass Rich over the noise of the party and the crackling of the fire pit between us. It wasn't as if Layla couldn't take care of herself. The girl was a spitfire who had no reservations about speaking her mind. But she was like a sister, and Rich Connely was a grade A prick of the highest order. He'd been chasing Layla's tail since the third grade. At least then he'd been better at taking *no* for an answer.

Wedging my beer bottle between the two cinder blocks I sat on, I stood just as "Uptown Funk" rang out of someone's portable speaker. The construction debris around us distorted the sound. What had once been a hoity-toity dining room was now a charred ruin thanks to an endless number of nights like this one. Fischer House sat at the edge of town, abandoned decades before when the family that was building it got caught up in scandal and was run out of Ridgemore. Half swallowed up by the encroaching forest, with long-range views of the surrounding rolling hills, it had been party central for teenagers since our parents used to drink here.

A hand landed lightly on my shoulder, stopping me in my tracks. I'd recognize Griffin Conway's touch underwater and blindfolded and didn't turn to see who it was, keeping my attention on Rich instead. I didn't appreciate the way he was smirking at Layla like he knew better than she did.

"She's fine," Griffin said in that deep bass that felt too much like a caress. "If he pushes her much more, she'll kick him in the balls."

Rich dipped his head to speak close to Layla's ear and I stiffened.

"We're not little kids anymore," Griffin reminded me, leaning closer.

"I know," I responded tersely. How could I forget when his touch all too often sent excited tingles rushing across my skin? But Griffin and I had grown up together too.

"I just don't like it. Don't like him," I said. None of this was news.

Griffin peered through the crowd before taking a sip of his own beer. "No one really likes him unless they're after the family money."

I tipped my head, studying Rich, though I could describe his features from memory. That was the downside of living in a small town, population under four thousand. You knew most everyone, whether you wanted to or not.

"I thought he had a girlfriend now?"

Griffin took another swig of his beer. "Nope. They broke up a few hours ago."

"So that's why he's sniffing after Layla like a hound dog with a boner."

"Yup. And he'll keep at it till he lands his next girlfriend. Like always."

"You'd think they'd learn. He treats them all like shit."

Griffin shrugged. "To each their own."

"Yeah, fine. But not when he's bugging Layla."

As if she heard me, Layla turned her back to Rich, pushed her way through a group of jocks and cheerleaders, and headed toward the balcony. Rich walked off in the opposite direction.

Griffin draped his arm over my shoulders. "See? She sent him packing. All's good."

But Rich grabbed a handful of Jell-O shots before fist bumping the captain of the lacrosse team and sauntering toward the balcony.

"Shit," Griffin grumbled when Brady, Layla's actual brother, popped out of the shadows and trailed after Rich.

Griffin didn't have to tell me to move; I was already in motion. Hunt Fletcher, the final member of our unofficial crew, stalked by us, apparently just as aware of what was going on as we were.

"Fight!" someone called out as Griffin, Hunt, and I converged outside the wide threshold of the veranda, designed for elegant French doors that were never installed.

"No fight," Griffin snapped over his shoulder, loudly enough to be heard over the music. "Nothing's going on. Just stay where you are."

No one listened. As well as we knew Rich's ways, so did everyone else. And they knew ours, too. Layla and Brady might be the only ones related by blood, but the five of us were family. If there was going to be a fight tonight, then we were all going to be in the thick of it.

By the time we got onto the balcony and shooed away the gawking, ready audience that had already been outside enjoying the warm night, Brady had Rich by the collar.

"Back the fuck off my sister, dude." His muscles and ink bulged as he leaned into Rich.

The prick sighed theatrically and rolled his eyes, knocking Brady's hands away before running his own through his hair, fixing it, as if a single strand could possibly break free of the thick gel he was sporting.

"I'm not doing anything, asshole. Layla and me, we're just talking. . ."

None of us needed the fresh reminder of how much more he was constantly pushing for.

Brady growled and reached for him again. Layla *tsk*ed and put a hand on her brother's bicep, exposed by one of the countless sleeveless t-shirts he lived in during the summer.

"Come on, Brade. I'm fine. He didn't do anything."

"Not yet he didn't," Brady snarled. "But he wants to."

Rich took a step back from Brady and pressed up against the railing. His stance was casual, one foot braced against a balustrade as if Brady were a puny freshman instead of six-feet-plus of angry muscle.

Rich shrugged, his traditionally handsome features twisting into feigned boredom. "You can't blame me for trying. Layla's beautiful."

Though his admiration was sincere, I pondered whether I could get away with punching him in the mouth. Yes, my friend was beautiful, but why was that the reason he pursued her like a hyena after a vulnerable gazelle? Layla kicked ass in a thousand ways that had nothing to do with her looks.

As if he could feel the intensity of my thoughts, Rich glanced my way. "I'd go after foxy Joss-y too—the more hotties the mer-rier—but I don't have a death wish." Chuckling, he flicked a look at Griffin, which I ignored as Griffin stepped closer to me so that there was no space between us.

"Watch it, Rich," Griffin said evenly. Not even Rich was stu-pid enough to miss the threat embedded in that simple statement.

"You okay there, buddy?" asked another voice from behind us. Ridgemore High's starting wide receiver. A nice enough guy but with poor taste in friends.

I glanced his way as several more members of the football team popped their heads out behind him.

"Totally fine," Rich said with a cocky smile that I was two seconds away from wiping off his smug mug. "We're just having a little chat, aren't we, Brady?"

Rich shot an arched-brow look at Brady, but Brady didn't respond beyond a murderous glare.

"Are we gonna have a problem here?" Rich pressed. "Because if so, maybe we should take this downstairs. I'm sure my friends wouldn't mind joining me in a little . . . exercise."

"Hell no, we wouldn't," a moron by the name of Pike Bills shouted too loudly. He flexed his muscles and cracked his knuckles like he was an extra in some gangster movie, proving our working theory that it wasn't the asshole's fault his momma had dropped him on his head as a baby.

After popping his neck to either side, he added, "I ain't had a good fight in ages."

Rich snickered. "You beat John B. to a pulp two days ago."

Pike grinned, exposing a broken tooth from said fight. "Yeah, I did."

I huffed and ran a hand over my face. "This has got nothing to do with the rest of you. We're just out here having a nice talk with our friend Rich about his manners."

Rich snorted, and a few of the members of his backup echoed the sentiment. "Joss Bryson. Teaching about manners."

I slammed a hand to one hip. "That's right, dickwad. Manners. You'd better get some or you're gonna wind up with my boot up your ass."

He waggled his brows. "Kinky. Me like-y." Then he shrugged. "Hey, if you're into the weird shit, for you, baby, I'd go there." He made a show of eyeing me up and down.

Griffin took a step toward him and I shot a hand out to stop him.

"He's not worth it," I said, even as I calculated how much room there was to jump him and pin him down on the crowded veranda.

"He's definitely not worth shit," Griffin bit out.

Rich smiled, a predatory glint in his gaze. "Jealousy doesn't suit you, my man."

"And what exactly would I be jealous of? The fact that your daddy would rather pay you off than spend time with you?"

That was a low blow, even for Griffin, which meant he was closer than I was to smashing Rich's pretty face in.

Rich lunged at Griffin, but Brady was in his way. Rich threw a wild punch. Brady dodged it, slipping behind Rich to lock his arms around him. Rich roared like he was some wild beast, straining to rip his arms free. Brady didn't let go, but he did stumble backward into the railing.

"Let me go right this fucking second," Rich snarled, his pretty-boy face screwed up as if he were a savage animal.

Brady grunted from the effort of holding on while Rich thrashed.

So many things happened at once that they distilled into separate actions, registering in slow motion.

Duncan, Pike, and several others shoved through our small audience to rush Brady. Griffin stepped between them and me, lining himself up so none of the guys could get to me or Layla without going through him. Layla and I shared an exasperated look and went to move around Griffin while Hunt squared up next to Brady, facing down the approaching football team.

Then a horrendous clap sliced through the caveman-like shouting and posturing. Spinning in place, I searched for its source, already gesturing and ushering the idiots standing around gawking to run inside.

"It's too much weight," I yelled, without being sure that was the problem—but it had to be, especially when construction on the house was never completed. Gripping Griffin and Layla, I dragged them toward the doorway, planning to snatch Hunt and Brady next. Then another clap split the humid air.

The floor tipped toward Brady, Hunt, and Rich. Instinctively, I released Griffin and Layla and reached for the others.

A crack raced across the balcony, cleaving it in two. The fissure widened until a third of the veranda detached from the rest and dropped fast. The chunk of terrace pitched until it was nearly vertical, then slid downward, taking Brady with it, Rich falling above him.

Arms outstretched, Hunt leaped for them, shouting at us, "Grab my legs," trusting that we'd catch him before he fell too.

Griffin, Layla, and I scrambled to grip Hunt's legs, and Duncan, Slater, and a few others grabbed us, holding on to our waists, thighs, and ankles.

"I got 'em," Hunt grunted, the veins in his neck popping. He was long and lean, but strong as a bull. "Hold me, hold me," he mumbled in a rush as he slid.

Brady probably weighed more than one-eighty, and Rich was about the same. I held on to Hunt like it was my life that hung in the balance, my thoughts suddenly still.

The balcony beneath us moaned and slipped farther, and a cacophony of shouts blended eerily as Eminem's "Lose Yourself" started playing, carrying from the house's open interior.

More grunts from below. Hunt screamed unintelligibly, before a nauseating crash and snap resounded from somewhere beneath us.

His breath hitched with a strangled sob that was utterly unlike my stoic friend. My heart stopped beating entirely for a few seconds.

Hunt twisted to the left, reaching both arms in one direction. One direction. Not two.

I could only pull in thick breaths that felt wrong. My pulse thumped in my ears.

Suddenly, *everything* felt wrong, like a limb had just been hacked off with a dull kitchen knife.

High-pitched screams that reminded me of a rape whistle rose from below, chilling me to the bone.

Hunt, breathing hard, heaved Rich up, swinging him toward the threshold behind us. The second Rich's friends grabbed him, Hunt army-crawled backward across the incline, then barked at us, "Go, go, go!"

His eyes, usually animated, were flat, dead. Even his voice sounded off, like it wasn't really his.

"Where's Brady?" Layla asked, the question garbled in her panic.

Shaking my head in a daze, I pitched inside, found my feet, and ran stumbling, jumping over a haphazard collection of cinder block seats, bottles, kindling, and camping chairs. I dodged people and the fire, blindly elbowing some girl out of the way before I slammed down onto the thick padding of decomposing leaves that covered the ground outside.

"Holy fucking shit," someone wheezed from the other side of the house, their stunned falsetto voice carrying. "Brady Rafferty, he's . . . he's . . . fuck, he's dead."

One thought consumed my mind and hung on my lips—*no, no, no, no, no.*

I circled the house, my fingers skimming brick to keep me upright, until I saw a crowd gathered.

I pushed my way through them, stopping short and gasping, hand over my mouth. Griffin ran into me, Layla piling up behind him. A second later, I shot off to the side, thinking I was going to empty my stomach, my arm trembling against the tree that held me up. I sank against it.

Brady and I had been tight since we were in diapers.

Now my friend was impaled on exposed rebar several inches thick. Stabbed straight through the chest.

No one could survive that. No one.

Not even Brady Rafferty, who'd always seemed larger than life, capable of living forever.

But he hadn't.

Brady was dead.

2

The Five of Us, Together Forever

Turn that fucking music off," somebody shouted, and Billie Eilish's broody croon cut off. The chirping insects in the trees surrounding us grew unbearably loud for the few seconds during which no one spoke.

I rubbed a hand roughly across my face, trying to spur myself into action.

For the dozens of us at the party, all future seniors and some juniors, the night was supposed to end in laughs, shenanigans, hookups, and finally, hangovers before the grind of school started back up. Nothing like this was supposed to happen, especially not to one of my own.

I swallowed thickly, blinking away images of Brady's body bent over a pillar, the foundation of some structure that never got erected, his arms and legs hanging down it like vines. The cement supported his torso while the thick rebar jutted through the entirety of his upper body. Pierced him straight through.

I hadn't seen his face. His head was draped down the back of the column, his usual skullcap beanie on the ground, jarred free upon impact.

"Ohmygod, ohmygod, ohmygod, what the hell do we do?" whined a feminine voice I didn't bother trying to place.

Usually our crew would take charge of a situation like this one, probably rushing forward to administer CPR or to check Brady's pulse even though there was no way he could have survived the accident. We'd be the ones to figure out the next steps and to move quickly through them, directing the others as needed.

My thoughts were sluggish when they needed to be faster than ever. Layla would be needing me. Hell, Griffin and Hunt would be freaking out too. The fact that none of them were checking on me was evidence that shock was racking them as violently as it was me.

"He's got no pulse," a classmate by the name of Zoe Wills announced, her voice even despite a panic so thick I sensed it vibrating against my bare arms, skimming the dip in my shirt across my chest, encroaching toward my heart. "There's not much blood. The steel must be holding it back."

"Jones, call your dad," our starting wide receiver snapped.

"I can't." Wade Jones's voice was tremulous in a way I'd never heard it before. "I snuck out. I'm not even supposed to be here. I'm already grounded for-fucking-ever. My dad'll kill me if he finds me at a party."

"Dude, seriously? Who cares if you're fucking grounded. Brady's *dead*. Do you get that?"

Still staring out into a darkness so deep it could swallow me up if I let it, I didn't watch the scene. Even with my back turned to them, I could feel the impact of Brady's fate slamming into Wade.

"Right, right. Yeah, of course," Wade said as if on autopilot. "I'm an idiot. I'll call my dad now."

"Leave it, man," Reed Carter said with his usual gravel. "Get out of here. I'll call my dad. He'll call yours."

"Okay, cool. Yeah," Wade stuttered, but it didn't sound like he cared about his punishment anymore.

But Reed's dad was a sheriff's deputy, and it wasn't like speed of response mattered. There was nothing that could be done to save Brady.

"Dad?" Reed's voice faded as he walked away. "I'm okay, Dad. Yeah, fine. But something real bad happened." A pause while Reed listened. "At a party at the Fischer House. Uh-uh. Nope. An accident. Brady Rafferty got hurt, and, Dad . . . he's dead."

Hearing Reed summarize the situation so succinctly yanked me out of my shock. Spinning, I scanned the scene quickly for my friends. Layla, face pale in the camping lanterns set up on the back porch, was staring blankly at Brady's body, a hand against the cement beside him as if it were all that was propping her up. I started walking toward her, searching for Griffin and Hunt.

Amid the big chunks of terracotta tiles, cement, and twisted rebar from the balcony, the two whispered harshly at each other. When Griffin flicked a homicidal glare at Rich, who sat, jaw slack, next to the broken pieces of the balcony, I knew what Griffin would do next. I changed directions, stalking toward them, stepping over more refuse from parties past and detritus from the forest. This place was half civilized, half savage.

In steps so quick that Rich didn't see the attack coming, Griffin jumped him, wrapping an arm around his neck and slamming him against the dirt so hard that the dull thump rang out over the sudden excited chatter.

Hunt was fast enough to interfere before Griffin threw the first punch, and he was definitely quick enough to stop the second. He didn't though, moving slowly, telling me that he also felt like punishing the prick who'd indirectly thrown Brady onto that rebar.

Screams and grunts marked my paces as I lined up next to Griffin, barely out of reach. He would never hurt me on purpose, but right then, with his mouth screwed up into a hateful sneer, I wasn't sure how much he was registering beyond his fury and loss.

"Griff," I said, forcing his name out even though I wrestled between the urges to pull him off Rich and to shove him out of the way so I could be the one to pummel the asshole instead.

Rich, for the first time since I'd known him, didn't fight back. He brought up his arms to protect his face but didn't retaliate.

"Griffin!" I snapped. Griffin didn't react, as if he didn't even hear me. I'd always been able to get through to him before. Even when the others couldn't, I could.

Griffin punched Rich in the gut, then pulled back, suddenly seeming to realize that Rich wasn't defending himself. Hunt finally swooped in to restrain Griffin, but his efforts were half-hearted. Duncan and some of the other football players helped Rich up but didn't say anything.

None of us were reacting like we usually would. I feared that Brady's death had broken us all. Already, I felt hollow inside. *Brady's dead* kept running through my thoughts in the background, like a disembodied chant turned low, but even so, I couldn't quite finish absorbing the truth of it.

Brady just couldn't be dead. *He couldn't.*

I felt Griffin's eyes on me and glanced up to meet them. They flashed with so much emotion, so much devastation, that even though they were as dark as the forest, they still somehow reminded me of a lightning storm. A lethal one.

A glance at Hunt revealed a hard jaw and even harder eyes. He didn't so much as blink as he stared back at me, his nostrils flaring a couple of times as he attempted to steady his breathing, his arms loose around Griffin as if he wouldn't bother stopping him if he were to pound on Rich again.

"Shit. Layla," I muttered under my breath. This time, though I spoke softly, Griffin reacted, shaking off Hunt's hands and stalking toward her, snatching my hand up as he passed me. Hunt was a step behind us.

Anyone standing between us and Layla slunk out of our way. People gathered in pockets toward the side of the house, behind Rich, and far away from Brady.

Reed appeared from the opposite direction, pocketing his phone. "My dad's calling it in now. Emergency services will be here in fifteen or twenty."

As if the Fischer House were cursed, no one had built in the immediate area after it was abandoned. There was still plenty of acreage to be had in Ridgemore, where no particular industry had claimed the town as its home. The fire department was located on the opposite end, beyond a short line of quaint boutique stores that catered more to the occasional visitor than to locals.

"He's gonna hurry them, just in case," Reed added, before casting a hopeless look at Brady, whose body hadn't so much as twitched since I'd been studying it.

I wanted to thank Reed for doing what we should have done, but no words came out. Hunt nodded at him in silent bro communication. Reed dipped his chin in response, then went to join the others, leaving us alone with Brady.

Griffin, Hunt, and I stepped closer to Layla. Sucking in my first deep breath since it all happened, I placed a hand on her back. She shook at my touch but didn't turn.

"Lay," I whispered.

Her shoulders trembled as she ran a hand along Brady's leg, her fingers featherlight on his jeans.

"I. . ." I started, but then had no idea what to say. That it couldn't be real? That I wanted to scream my lungs out until this stupid world delivered us a better outcome? One where Brady walked out of here with us tonight?

In the end, I leaned my head on her shoulder and said nothing. Griffin wrapped an arm around both of us, and Hunt did the same from our other side.

Huddled like that, with our backs to everyone, we stood for a long time, unmoving, weighed down by the heaviness of life . . . and death. The chasm that sliced through the balcony was nothing compared to the break pulling apart my heart, bit by wretched bit.

Eventually, Reed told the others, "Come on, guys. Let's leave them be. The troops should be arriving any minute. Help me stash the booze and weed so none of us get taken in. And if you're like Wade and aren't supposed to be here, now's your last chance to get out. No one'll know you were ever here, but you gotta leave right now."

People moved under the balcony, onto the porch that was nothing more than a cement slab, and into the house. Others went the way I had come, around the side of the house and in through the front door. Cars started peeling out, but not as many as I'd guessed would. Without bothering to count, I figured something like two-thirds of our classmates stuck around. Whether it was so we wouldn't have to face the awful reality alone, or whether it was due to lingering shock or a desire to be in the thick of things, I wasn't sure. We'd never had to rely on anyone outside of our circle of five.

Stepping out from under Griffin and Hunt, I walked around the rough cement, peering up at Brady's torso, at least a foot above eye level. Up close, the rebar was even more brutal, as thick as my arm with its twisted threads. It pierced him slightly off center and to the left, so that there was no escaping his heart. He almost certainly died on impact.

Trailing my fingers along the skin of his arm, through a tight throat, I whispered, "Dammit, Brady. This. . ." I sniffled. The last time I'd cried had been when he'd been teaching me how to skateboard and I'd come in for a rough crash landing after attempting a railslide on a handrail. I'd been nine.

I linked my fingers with his, running my thumb over his palm, still warm, back and forth. "This can't be." My breath was dense with tears I didn't know if I'd be able to hold back. "It can't be. Not over a stupid fight with an idiot asshole."

"Joss," Griffin said, my name on his lips a balm to the bloody pulp that remained of my heart, as messed up as Brady's, only still beating.

I shook my head at Griffin, at Brady, at whatever unseen force had decided to take Brady from us. *From me.* "No. Just no, dammit. I don't accept this."

"Joss." This time, Hunt's arm wrapped around my shoulders, trying to pull me to him. I resisted, jerking free.

"No, Hunt. No, no, *no*. Brady can't leave us. We're meant to be together. All of us. It's the five of us. Together forever, you remember?"

As I stared into Hunt's eyes, I saw my memories reflected there. The five of us swore a blood pact, scoring our grubby ten-year-old palms with a pocketknife, to have each other's backs until we were as old and gray as our parents, who were only in their thirties and forties then. We were born in the same year, and Layla and Brady were fraternal twins. Even before we came along, our parents had been close friends. Our friendship was destined, inevitable.

Sirens, still far away, finally made it that much more real. More final.

I squeezed Brady's fingers with the same force that clenched my heart, wishing that my touch alone could ground him here, tether him to me, and keep him in this world, in his body, in this life.

Dropping my forehead against the cement, uncaring that it scratched, I gripped his fingers with all my might. It was useless, I knew, but so was his death. Nothing made sense anymore, and I was certain that nothing ever would again.

We'd have to call Brady and Layla's parents, all our parents, and watch their hearts break too.

Gritting my teeth against the torrential shitstorm I was only barely holding back, I clutched Brady's hand so tightly I would have hurt him if he could still feel. It was the same hand he'd carved our blood oath into. A paper-thin scar was visible along his palm.

I growled like a beast, hearing myself come apart.

And then Brady's fingers twitched in mine.

I gasped, dropping his hand like it was on fire, jumping back and right into Griffin, who grabbed me to hold me up.

"What? What is it?" he asked as the sirens grew louder.

I couldn't answer. The only thing I could do was stare at Brady's hand and pray I hadn't imagined his movement.

Sirens wailed through a complete cycle. Once, twice, three times, then more, and Brady's hand was lifeless.

Then . . . his index finger jerked.

Griffin went rigid behind me, and when Hunt asked what was going on, drawing Layla to us, Griffin hushed him harshly and pointed.

Again, we waited, staring at Brady's hand. I didn't dare move a hair for fear I might interfere with whatever was happening.

This time, his thumb jumped.

As one, the four of us sucked in a sharp hitch of breath as hope, that cruel mistress, pressed in on our chests with the weight of an entire ocean.

3

Stealth Ninja

As the sirens shrieked louder, drawing close, I urgently wrapped my fingers around Brady's wrist, not even breathing as I waited for a pulse. Yes, Zoe had already checked. But none of *us* had.

"Well?" Layla prodded when not even three seconds had passed, her breath hot on my neck as she crowded me.

I didn't answer, my attention lasered on my hand and Brady's, searching for even the slightest thump that would indicate he hadn't left us after all.

"Anything?" Hunt asked, again too soon, and he was the most patient of us.

"Not yet," I muttered, willing Brady's heart to beat no matter how dead he looked, sprawled across a column that had done its best to break him in half.

But sirens consumed the night, and still . . . no heartbeat.

I shook my head, clamping down on my disappointment. "Nothing." I let my hand slide away, placing Brady's gently back against the cement as if being gentle with him now would change a damn thing.

Brady's entire hand spasmed before it settled back into that eerie stillness that had my nerves in knots.

For a few breaths, we did nothing more than stare. Then we rushed into action, Hunt and Griffin pacing the small diameter of the column like caged jungle cats.

"He's alive," Layla said. "He's gotta be."

"But he has no pulse," I reminded her gently. "It must be delayed nervous system activity."

Layla's gaze was trained on her brother as she addressed me. "Are you sure?"

"That he has no pulse? Yeah. Or, I mean, as much as I can be without a stethoscope. And obviously I don't know shit about medicine, so I have no idea about the nervous system thing, but it sounds right."

"We've gotta get him down from there," Griffin said.

Hunt was already dragging a spent keg toward the pillar. When Griffin noticed, he jogged over to grab a second discarded keg and lined it up on the other side of the pylon.

"Wait," I said even as the guys were climbing onto the kegs and eyeing Brady's body, trying to figure out the best way to free him. "You guys, you can't just un-impale him."

"Why not?" Layla asked. "Okay, he's got no pulse, but he's twitching, Joss. He's actually *moving*."

I stared at my friend, another reminder fresh on my tongue that if her brother's heart wasn't beating, he couldn't be alive. But the devastation welling in her eyes made me swallow it. Finally, I nodded.

"Okay, but then we've gotta think about what's gonna happen when he comes off that rebar. It might be the only thing keeping him from bleeding out."

It was, of course, an absurd consideration. His heart wasn't pumping blood throughout his body, hence no bleeding out. But

I'd watched enough TV to know you didn't remove the nasty foreign object blocking a severed artery. That was Hollywood Medicine 101.

"And what about his back?"

"What about it?" Layla asked.

"Well, look at him. Does that angle seem normal to you? He's bent the wrong way."

"Not really. He's flexible. He's no more bent up than if he were doing a wheel pose or one of those moves that makes him think he's a fucking ninja." She snorted, and I couldn't help but crack a smile despite the dire nature of our predicament. Brady loved saying he was a stealth ninja, though his pretending had grown less absurd over the years as he honed his fighting skills into something respectable.

"Okay. Fair enough. But he's gotta be hurt from that impact. We could do more damage moving him. Plus, the rebar and the bleeding out bit."

Layla, Hunt, and Griffin just studied Brady, foreheads scrunched in lines of anguish, obviously desperate to do something—anything—to help our friend.

I added, "The EMTs are almost here, and we could mess things up by trying to help. If he weren't stuck up there, we could do CPR, try to jumpstart him."

But that rebar was shoved straight through his chest. There was no way to do chest compressions. No way to do anything helpful, really.

"So, what? We just wait?" Griffin asked in a rough grumble. He made decisions quickly and moved on them even faster.

My shoulders softened with a sigh. "Yeah, Griff, I think so. If there's any chance of him coming back from this, then moving him could make things worse. Harder for him to recover." Though when I examined the unyielding steel skewering Brady's body, our conversation took on even more of a ridiculous edge. I ignored it, as desperate as the rest of them to get our miracle.

"Fine, then," Griffin grunted on a frown, already jumping down from the keg. "I'm gonna be waiting for the EMTs to rush them back here."

"Good idea," I said, not that Griffin would wait for my approval to do what he set his mind to. "And one of us needs to call his parents."

Hunt and Layla looked at me, Griffin already sweeping through the house to meet the emergency responders.

Layla's eyes brimmed with tears, and she wasn't one to cry either. "I just . . . I just can't, Joss. Please."

Swallowing my usual groan of complaint, I was already tugging my phone out of the pocket of the denim miniskirt I was wearing. I knew Celia and Porter Rafferty nearly as well as my own parents. But who wanted to be the one to call a mother and father to tell them their kid was dead?

Probably dead.

Almost certainly.

I exchanged a look with Hunt, confirming that he had Layla and wouldn't let anyone touch Brady who shouldn't. Then I hit the dial button and put distance between me and them. Layla didn't need to hear this.

4

It Seems Impossible, But There You Have It

Dawn was breaking outside the large windows lining the ICU waiting room. Layla, Griffin, Hunt, and I were bleary-eyed, staring blankly ahead or into the depths of our terrible vending machine coffees. The adrenaline had fled my body an hour into Brady's surgery; now every part of me felt as loose as overcooked spaghetti, though I knew there was no chance sleep would come, not until we received news.

The group of our combined parents, however, couldn't seem to sit still. Celia was surprisingly resilient, and once she got past the original shock of the news, she mobilized the rest of the adults. They almost beat us to the hospital, even though they'd been in bed already. Layla and Hunt had ridden in the ambulance with Brady, while Griffin and I followed in his Mustang.

Though I'd tried not to give anyone false hope with my description of Brady's twitching, their faces were animated with it, and every time the doors to the ICU unit swung open, all sets of eyes trained on whoever was exiting. So far, no one had come looking for us, and our parents seemed ready to jump out of their skins.

Griffin's dad, Orson, and Hunt's mom, Alexis, took turns playing musical chairs. None of the adults remained seated for long.
My dad, Reece, was pacing the length of the small waiting room,
back and forth, again and again. If I'd had any oomph left in me,
I would have told him to sit down before he drove us all crazy.

When the double doors next opened, a surgeon in scrubs
exited, his sneakers squeaking on the shiny tile floor. His eyes
were haunted, the skin beneath them shadowed. He pinned them
on us before he even walked through the open door to the waiting room.

My breath lodged in my lungs as those of us who'd been sitting
leaped to our feet.

He removed the cloth cap that was probably meant to keep
stray hairs from landing inside open body cavities, fiddling with it
in his hands as Porter rushed to ask, "Is my son okay?"

"If your son's Brady Rafferty, then he's the luckiest kid I've
ever seen."

A cold tingle swept through my body, leaving me lightheaded.
"He's going to live, then?" I eked out, sensing everyone holding
their breath as we waited for the surgeon to say it again, to make
it real.

"Yes, he is."

I groaned in relief and slumped backward, leaning into Griffin's arms. I was as far from a fainting belle as I could be, but hell
if Brady hadn't given us the fright of our entire lives. He was dead.
And then . . . he wasn't. A smile fought to rush forth, but I was
still too traumatized to trust the relief spreading through me.

Griffin held my back to his chest as Layla tumbled into her
mom's open arms, sobbing already. Even Hunt let Alexis pull him
against her side, though he was a head taller than his mom.

At our collective relief, the surgeon allowed himself an easy, albeit
tired, smile. "Brady's going to win the hospital's yearly luckiest survi-
vor award. I've never seen anything like this before and I've been an

ER doc for going on twenty years. I've seen a lot of crazy cases over that time, some that would blow your minds, but nothing like this, not even close. His injuries were so bad that he should've died. But somehow . . . he didn't."

Our parents exchanged a heavy look with each other.

"Doctor," Porter asked, "are there any"—he stopped to gulp back his fear—"lasting effects? Will he be . . . okay? Like his usual self?"

The surgeon nodded, but slowly, as if he were formulating some caveat to his response. Finally he just said, "Though his spinal column is bruised from the impact, there are no fractures. Not even a vertebra popped out of place, which seems impossible, but there you have it."

"And the puncture? His heart, lungs?" Celia asked, her eyes big as she waited for a response.

"The rebar pierced Brady's torso, leaving a hole the size of a grapefruit. It crushed or snapped several of his ribs, but it's possible they'll heal well enough if he abides by the indicated bed rest. His lungs weren't harmed."

"And his heart?" Celia pressed.

The surgeon made eye contact with every one of us there before proceeding. "The rebar sheared the mitral valve, leaving it all but irreparable."

Celia gasped softly, and Layla whimpered in her arms.

The surgeon held up a hand, silently asking us to wait before reacting. "His heart was tilted out of position, and it did stop beating. We had to piece together the torn valve, along with other tissue of the heart organ. And, well, I did a bunch of other things too that I can go over with you after I finish up in there. I just wanted to give you the good news first."

He met Celia's and Porter's gazes as he said, "I'm not exaggerating when I say that your son is truly the luckiest young man I've ever known—even heard about. Not only will he live and possibly have no long-lasting damage"—he held up another hand in warning—"so long as he follows all my recommendations for recovery and his follow-ups, but his survival alone is truly unheard of. The entire hospital staff is shocked—and delighted, of course—to learn that he's pulled through. His body experienced extreme trauma, and he'll need to take it really slowly as his heart heals and his ribs mend."

The doctor shifted his weight with a soft squeak of a sneaker. "And though his spine reveals no damage, he's going to feel like a freight train slammed into him for a long time. But, Mr. and Mrs. Rafferty, that your son is alive at all is a true miracle. If you were busy praying, then you should probably give thanks to that higher power, because it came through. Your son will have scars, and he'll be creaky for a long while, but I'm cautiously optimistic that a year from now he won't show many signs of this incident, beyond the scarring of course. Not even a miracle can stitch together a hole that size without leaving a trace."

He shook his head, ruffling his shiny short hair. "I still can scarcely believe he made it. No one's ever come back from anything even close to this. The damage to his body is so severe as to be lethal, and yet his body's still managing to function on its own. Even his heart is pumping without assistance, and I literally just finished piecing it together." Another incredulous shake of his head before he slid the cap back on.

"Thank you, Doctor," my dad said. "We appreciate everything you did to save Brady, so very much."

The surgeon nodded again. "I'm very skilled at what I do, but not even I would have been able to bring him back from that without a hand from above. Brady's as fortunate as it gets. You might want to have him pick some lottery numbers for you." He chuckled at his own joke. "If you think of any other questions, I'll pop back out in a while."

"Thank you again, Doctor. We are so grateful to you," Celia gushed, reaching to squeeze his hands before pulling away quickly when he froze at her touch. "When will we be able to see him?"

"He's still under anesthesia as he's being closed up. It'll be a good while before he wakes up. And even then, we need to monitor him extremely closely. He's out of the woods, but I plan on watching him like a hawk just in case something surprises us. Visits will be short and for immediate family only."

"We're all his family," Griffin said right away, his determination vibrating through his chest against my back.

Porter glanced at him, then told the surgeon, "That's right. All of us here are a family unit."

"Fine," the doctor said. "But visits will be limited to one at a time, and for a max of fifteen minutes. Nothing stressful or disruptive. He needs to rest to finish pulling out of this as well as possible." Again, he met all of our waiting gazes as if to impress us with the gravity of the situation—like we could have missed it. "He *died* tonight."

At that, my chest tightened painfully again until my mom, Monica, asked, "Have you already run brain scans?"

"We have. Brain activity is normal. Like I said, luck was on your side tonight."

He offered a grim smile at odds with the totality of his news, turned, and walked away, back through the double doors.

I spun in Griffin's arms to face him. "Brady's alive." I tested out the words, unsure they'd reach past my numb shock. "He's gonna be fine." My voice rose as the news sank in. "Oh my God, Griff, Brady's gonna be fine."

His smile started in his eyes before spreading across his cheeks, until I was soon staring at his bright, straight teeth—thanks to a year of braces when we were in the fourth grade.

"He's gonna be fine," I repeated on a rushed squeal that sounded nothing like me, and then I jumped at him, wrapping my legs around his waist while he twirled me around like we were in some stupid rom-com.

But all around us, the others were celebrating too. I heard them but didn't see. All I felt at that moment was Griffin, the way he held me tightly, how his touch was so natural that my body wanted to melt into him.

He laughed, and I threw my head back, indulging in the lightness of heart that hit me as hard as the earlier devastation.

When Griffin stopped spinning me, I suddenly realized I was wrapped around him like a monkey and eyes were on us. I untangled from him to stand on my own feet but didn't waste a second overthinking.

I looked at the others, their expressions a copy of mine: ecstatic, relieved, overwhelmed, still frightened and overcome.

"Brady's fucking alive." I grinned until my cheeks ached, and my mom didn't even correct my language for once.

And when the sun burst above the buildings spread across our view, coloring the sky like an artist's canvas, I finally allowed myself to accept that the night hadn't broken us after all.

Brady was alive.

5

Miracle Kid

Pulling up in front of the hospital, I idled at the curb, not bothering to text Brady that I'd arrived. He'd exit the building the very instant he was set free, just as he'd been doing after every checkup over the last two and a half weeks since his accident. Brady and Layla shared a car, a 2014 Shelby GT500 named Bonnie that purred happily, even though it hadn't seen a certified mechanic since Celia and Porter bought it as a surprise gift a couple of years ago. Before then, none of us knew much about cars, but when Brady fell in love with the Ford Mustang, so did the rest of us.

He taught himself how to maintain her, and then how to do his own upgrades—the four of us right along with him, devouring instructional YouTube videos like it was our damn job. Not that Brady—or Layla, for that matter—needed the extra horsepower. Ridgemore was a sleepy mountain town wrapped in winding roads that cut into steep hillsides covered in dense trees. But Brady was an all-or-nothing guy. He wouldn't stop until he'd tinkered with every single part in that car.

The hospital's sliding doors opened, their telltale *whoosh* filtering in the lowered windows of Griffin's own Mustang, his 1976

Cobra II we'd fixed up together as a group project and that he'd named Clyde to pair with Bonnie.

Mine was our next project. A 1999 Mustang SVT Cobra that was left out in some junkyard to rot. My parents saw my baby, had it towed to the house, and slapped a ribbon on the rust-riddled shell as an advance graduation present. Propped up on blocks now and stripped down to her bare bones, she was rough and ugly, but she wouldn't be for long. Not once we got through with her. She was going to be a wet dream of factory-original-matched electric green or shiny cherry black. I was still deciding.

Brady's shoulders were rounded and his back hunched, as if his every step caused him pain. He walked gingerly, but the ferocity of his scowl and the cyclone brewing in his eyes gave him away. I rushed out of the car, playing my agreed-upon part, and swung open the passenger door for him.

He folded into the seat a little too easily, and I reminded him, "Not so fast, man."

He glared up at me. "Shut the damn door, Joss."

I chuckled instead of taking offense and closed the door with the respect the Mustang deserved, running a reverent hand along her deep-impact blue paint job. Brady had been a lit stick of dynamite since he was discharged from the hospital and allowed to go home. Once the shock of how close he came to dying wore off, he hadn't been his usual self. Not that Brady was ever as easygoing as he liked to think he was, but I kept waiting for this version of Brady to shoot lightning from his ass or something. It was why we rock-paper-scissored to decide who'd come pick him up. Normally, none of us would mind the drive to the hospital, a scenic stretch of road, especially in Clyde, but Brady's company lately was the kind that made a girl appreciate solitude.

I waited until I turned on to the road toward home. "If anybody's watching, they'll know you're feeling fine from how you got in the car."

He spun in his seat toward me with his usual agility. Despite the severity of his injuries, and the fact that barely two weeks had passed, he was healed up and itching to get back to his usual workout routines. All that remained was a puckered scar the size of a lemon on his chest where the rebar had pierced him.

"I hear it from my parents a hundred times a day. I don't need that crap from you too," he snapped, facing forward again and slumping into his seat with a sullen pout.

"I know." I kept my eyes on the road, peeved that I was already annoyed with him when I should just be grateful he was sitting next to me—*alive*. "But we've been hearing it too. If you didn't have your head shoved so far up your ass, you'd realize you're not the only one dealing with helicopter parents all of a sudden."

Well, so much for the patience I'd just finished promising myself I'd have with him. . .

"Your parents aren't asking you to walk around like some wimpy asshole every time you leave the house. My mom actually asked me to limp—can you believe that shit? I didn't even hurt my fucking legs." He snarled, but this time not at me.

"You did nearly break your spine in half though." The surgeon hadn't mentioned it, but I'd been the one to see Brady strewn across that pillar like a damn sacrificial offering, not the doctor. A lot worse could have happened. A lot worse *did* happen. It was just that we got a miracle out of the deal—somehow.

"Dude," I said, more softly this time as I glanced his way. "You *died*. Do you get that? Do you *really* get what that did to us? To your parents? Of course they're gonna treat you like you're made of porcelain for a while. Give 'em a break. It'll wear off."

He ran his hands roughly through his hair, short on the sides, longer on top, before allowing them to plop to his lap. "It's not that though. That part I get. I know the accident was bad."

"*So* bad, dude. You have no idea what it was like to see you dead like that."

"But I wasn't really dead."

"Oh, you were. At least for a while."

"Okay," he said shortly, probably sick of hearing it. "But I'm not now. Even so, that bit I get. Mom and Dad hovering over me like they can't believe they almost lost me. Okay. But it's not that, and you know it."

Did I? I glanced at him again.

"All their rules only apply *outside* of the house. When I'm home, they probably wouldn't care if I start doing backflips."

I snorted. "Pretty sure your mom'll handcuff you to a pipe if you start doing shit like that before she's ready."

He huffed. "Actually, she just might. I keep catching her just staring at me. It's the weirdest thing."

"Again, give her time. Both of them. Layla too, while you're at it."

He waved away my concern. "Layla's fine."

I wasn't so sure. I noticed the way her eyes grew haunted when she stared off into space for long moments, thinking no one was watching her.

"If anything, our parents are probably driving her nuts too," he continued. "They won't shut up about how no one should see me moving around so well. That I already drew too much attention to myself by surviving. Blah, blah, blah. Like, seriously? Who the hell's gonna be watching me when I'm walking around the hospital? No one's just sitting around with their thumbs up their butts, waiting for me to show up for my appointments."

I hesitated. "I've seen people watching you, actually, at the hospital. You're the miracle kid."

He rolled his eyes and scoffed. "Great nickname I get out of the deal. Do they not realize I'm about to turn eighteen?"

I shrugged. "Your birthday's still a few months away."

"Doesn't make me a 'kid.'"

No, it didn't. Brady had outgrown his boyishness years ago, a fact that the girls at school who liked to drool over him hadn't failed to notice. At Ridgemore High, Brady was considered hot stuff. So were Griffin and Hunt, for that matter. The sexy big fish in Ridgemore's puny pond.

"I'm not kidding, Brade," I said. "I've seen the nurses and doctors watching you. A lot."

"Still, nothing for our parents to be so freaked out about that they have me fucking lying to everyone. My mom actually threatened to take Bonnie away if I didn't tell the doc that I'm having heart pains and a stiff spine. Aching everywhere. My mom made me rehearse the whole convoluted story."

I downshifted into third gear, sailing around a tight curve, then eyed him. "Really?"

"I shit you not. It's like she's become another person. Both of them."

Celia may as well have threatened never to let him leave the house again. Brady loved Bonnie like she was an actual woman ready and willing to act out his every teenage fantasy.

"Well," I said, "they don't want someone to pull up in an unmarked black van and take you away."

When Celia and Porter had first shared this concern while staring down the five of us, it had shocked me. Sure, I'd seen plenty of government ops take people away to study them in secret underground facilities—*on TV*. That didn't happen in real life. Not to us, not to anyone we knew. But after a wave of awkward laughter, the rest of the parents had crowded in, glaring at us as one unit until we didn't dare so much as crack a smile. No matter how ridiculous it might be, there could be no doubt that our parents were worried someone might take too much interest in Brady's miraculous recovery and steal him away from us.

Brady sighed and crossed an ankle over a knee, his long legs pushing up against the dashboard. "It's not like people don't survive crazy situations all the time. It happens. Stories about moms thin as twigs finding the super strength to lift entire cars off their kids. Or like Truant Bell, you remember his story? The dude who fell two hundred feet off the crag leading down to Raven's Lagoon?"

I nodded.

"He broke like every bone in his fucking body. They had to slice him open and put metal all up in him just to piece him back together. Told him there was zero chance he'd ever walk again. But then what happened? He heals when no one thought he ever would, starts walking again, and then, like a motherfucking badass, asks to go under the knife again to have all that metal taken out. Everyone thought he'd lost his damn mind. But what was it, three years after that? Dude's doing actual backflips. Like a hoss." He looked at me. "See? People survive from things like I did all the time."

"Yeah, sure, but you didn't just get hurt. You *died*."

He grunted, but I cut him off, knowing full well he didn't want to hear what I was going to say next.

"And you didn't just die for a couple of minutes like those people who drown and get no oxygen for a bit and then come to, miraculously fine, no brain damage. You weren't dead for even ten minutes. It was like thirty minutes from the time you fell till the ambulances got there, and then another twenty till you got to the hospital. They didn't manage to revive you on the ride over, only when you were on the gurney—one last-ditch attempt away from being wheeled into the fucking morgue, Brady."

I threw him a quick glance. "Not even the ER, the *morgue*. If we hadn't begged them to give it one last shot, you'd be six feet under right now. The EMTs didn't even want to defibrillate you anymore, said there was no chance you could come back, *sorry*, and all the usual platitudes. You were as flatlined as flatline gets, according to them. But Layla and I stuck out our boobs, batted our lashes, and legit begged. If not, you'd've stayed dead."

He frowned. "Are you actually saying I owe my life to your rack and my sister's?"

I didn't even blink. "Yes."

Shaking his head, he stared out the passenger window at the trees flashing by in a blur, still a few minutes out from the turn that led to the cul-de-sac that opened up to all our houses. Not only were the five of us tight, our parents had been friends for decades, and when they moved to Ridgemore, they bought neighboring houses—how quaint.

"You should've seen the EMTs when you gasped and started breathing," I added. "They looked two seconds away from shitting themselves."

"So . . . what?" Brady finally asked on an exasperated jerk of his shoulders. "I'm supposed to hide out for the rest of my life, pretending I'm all fucked-up when I'm not?"

"No, of course not." Though given how panicked our parents were, it was actually possible that was what they expected. "Just until Kitty's lady-boner goes soft and your story fades away."

Kitty Blanche was a recent hire for the *Ridgemore Gazette*, with the kind of tenacious ambition for Brady's story that suggested she thought it had the potential to elevate her to star status. Her near-daily articles on Brady's accident, and then miraculous recovery, garnered national attention. So many reporters swarmed our little town that Sheriff Jones had to park cruisers at the entrance to the hospital so they wouldn't converge there, bothering patients and staff. Despite his efforts, the occasional reporter still snuck in. Kitty, usually a redhead straight from a bottle, had donned a long blond wig the last time I saw her sniffing around the recovery wing of Ridgemore Hospital.

As if Brady's thoughts also drifted to the journalists we'd eventually given up on evading, he asked, "Which house are we going to? Please say yours."

I chuckled. "Yep. Mine."

"Aw, thank God." He sighed in relief, not because my house wouldn't be swarming with reporters as much as his since they'd figured out we hopped houses constantly, but because my parents went back to work at the lab a few days after his accident. His parents didn't, choosing to set up a home office instead, all the better to monitor his every move.

"The others there too?" he asked.

"Mm-hmm."

"Did you guys draw straws again to see who'd come pick me up?"

"Nope."

He turned my way, a smile already playing at his mouth. "You wanted to come get me?"

"No, I lost at rock-paper-scissors. We didn't have straws or sticks."

A frown wiped away any hint of a smile, and he crossed his arms over his chest, not even wincing as they pressed against his scar. "Nice, guys, real nice."

"You know we love you, Brade. But no offense, man, you've just been surlier than a girl ditched on prom night lately."

"Yeah. I fucking *died*. I think I've earned the right to a little moodiness."

"Oh, so now you died. When it suits you."

"You'd think you guys would be too happy I survived to be trying to ditch me."

Damn. "We are. One hundred percent we are. So much so."

"Odd fucking way of showing it. . ."

"It's been a lot for all of us. You went through the bad stuff, but in a way we went through it right along with you. I think we all need to cut each other some slack."

He turned accusatory eyes on me until I added, "And we def need to cut you a huge break and allow for mega mood swings."

He pursed his lips, probably unsure whether I'd insulted him or not. Since I wasn't entirely certain myself, I grabbed his hand, gave it a quick squeeze, then gripped the steering wheel again in time for the tight turn into our neighborhood.

"I'll never stop being grateful you're still here with us. My heart about exploded into a million tiny, jagged pieces when I thought we'd lost you."

He must have picked up on my sincerity because he reached over to pat my thigh quickly before returning his hand to his side of the car. For Brady, that was practically a declaration of platonic love.

I swallowed thickly, but didn't give in to emotion. "Just stop being such a dick all the time, mm-kay?"

He barked a laugh. "Joss Bryson. Mistress of the words."

I smiled back, trying to catch his gaze before we reached the zoo of hungry reporters, but he didn't look my way. So I asked, "Anything else bothering you?"

When he only snorted, I qualified, "You know, other than dying, coming back, and being forced to play the role of invalid?"

"Nah. I'm fine." But his words hung suspended long enough to indicate he wasn't telling me everything.

"*Brady.*"

"Okay, fine. I've been having nightmares. A lot."

"Oh, well, I'm sure that's normal. Who wouldn't dream about dying and all that shit?"

"No, it's not that. Of us, being kids. We're locked up in some"—he shuddered—"creepy-ass place. Like mega creepy vibes."

I slowed down, preparing for the onslaught of questions and cameras I knew was coming, and flicked another glance at him. "You're for real right now?"

He nodded.

"Okay. Then hold that thought till we're with the others. We won't let you take on the nightmares alone."

Ordinarily, Brady would have shrugged me off, told me he wasn't a freaking kid and he didn't need our support with something so stupid. But he did none of those things, which told me that whatever he was seeing in his dreams was worse than he was saying.

With my lips already pressed into a tight line of concern, when the reporters swarmed the entrance to my driveway, I injected extra *fuck you* vibes into my death glare. It worked. None of them advanced on the car while I waited for the gate to slide open, none but one. Kitty.

She smiled at me like she was on camera already. Like she knew something we didn't.

Then she was gone as I gunned the engine to shoo them all the way away, waiting until the gate snapped shut behind me before I headed down the long drive to my house, where Brady and the rest of us were hidden from view by thick walls of trees.

Where Brady was free to be the miracle that he was.

6

Us Against the World

My driveway was a half mile long, cutting through the forest that surrounded the house. I eased off the accelerator, enjoying the winding drive now that we'd left the reporters and their cameras behind. Our four families were the only ones who lived off this cul-de-sac, which was already far removed from the other houses that comprised the Periwinkle Hill neighborhood. If our parents shared one thing in common, it was their love of privacy, a fact we were particularly grateful for now that Brady was a person of interest.

Before I even got Clyde into neutral, Brady shoved open the door and was hopping out with the kind of athleticism he'd always had. He was like a damn cat, always landing on his feet, no matter what—*except for that one time at Fischer House*. Away from prying eyes, he strutted toward the others, who were hanging out around my Mustang.

Griffin's head was under the hood, but when he emerged, his eyes landed on me first. Like always. They scanned me from head to toe before jumping to his car and Brady. I seized the opportunity to return the favor and check him out as well. He was in board shorts that rode low on his hips, a tank that gaped around the arms to reveal hints of the tattoo that wrapped around his side, and he was barefoot. I smiled at what I saw, careful as always to make sure it broadcast how *platonically* into him I was.

He trained his gaze on me again, smiling back with a devilish smirk.

Just friends, Joss, I reminded myself with renewed fervor. It was all any of us could ever be.

"Hey, guys," I called as Hunt slid out from under my car. He lay flat on a creeper, his long legs folding in half to push himself up to his feet while he wiped his hands on a rag.

"What's up?" he asked, then looked at Brady. "How'd it go?"

"Yeah." Layla sat leaning against a tree trunk. With a chuckle, she set down her sketchpad and pencil and stood. "Did you rock the limp Mom begged you to do?"

Brady huffed. "Fuck no, I didn't. Mom's lost her damn mind. That doesn't mean I have to be her stupid puppet."

Layla groaned, flicking her choppy bangs out of her eyes. Her hair was currently blond, though I doubted it would last for long. She changed hair colors like most people changed shoes. "Then dinner tonight's gonna be fun."

Dinner at the Rafferty house was a daily ritual Celia had been insisting on since her kids were old enough to run off with us and not want to come back for a regular dinner appointment. When we were nine, we snuck machetes and saws to cut paths through the forest to connect our houses. When we were eleven, we built a large treehouse on my property—with some help from our parents. Coming inside on a timetable always sucked. But Celia was unbending when it came to dinnertime.

"Text your mom and tell her we'll come too," I offered. "That way you won't need to deal alone."

Layla slipped her phone out of her pocket while Brady said, "It's not like she's gonna hold back with you guys there." But even so, he tipped his head at me in silent thanks.

"Mom's really been off the chain, like for real," Layla said, her fingers flying across her screen. "I get why, but still. She's out of control." She pocketed her phone again. "She actually tried to convince Brade to show up at the hospital in a wheelchair."

Hunt whistled. "Damn. That's messed up."

"Sure is. She even had one delivered to the house before Brade lost his shit on her and made her send it back."

Brady snorted. "Hell, she's probably just hidden it from me somewhere, waiting to talk me into it."

"Totally possible."

Brady poked his head under the hood of my baby. "So, what'd you guys work on while I was wasting my fucking time playing a part for Mom?"

Hunt drew to his side, bending at the waist to examine our work. "We were just hooking up the V8 now that it's finally in."

"Yeah, looking good. Joss, you're gonna have one sweet ride when we're through with her."

I grinned. "Don't I know it."

Not only was the shell of my baby an early gift, but my parents also offered to buy the parts, so long as I kept bringing home straight A's for the entirety of my senior year. If I didn't, they'd warned, I'd have to find a way to pay them back, but that last bit was hot air. School had always been easy for me—for the others too. We'd never had to work at it, but we had used "study groups" time and time again to excuse hanging out on school nights. My parents could afford the cost of the car, especially since we were putting in all the labor, so I accepted with a solemn promise to excel at my studies. It was a good thing none of the others had been there with me at the time or they might have busted out laughing, betraying how little effort I was going to have to put in to follow through.

Layla heaved a sigh that sounded wistful as she stared up at the trees. "I still can't believe school's about to start back up. I'm so not ready. I need at least another month of just this."

"Tell me about it," I said, wondering if I could get away with doing a little sanding on my car's exterior with everyone there. I wouldn't be able to hear what they were saying, and I hadn't forgotten Brady's nightmares.

"Rich'd better not start shit, or I'm gonna make him pay for what he did to Brady," Griffin warned as he folded his arms over his chest, making his biceps look bulkier than they were. Griffin, just like the rest of the guys, had lean muscles and was stronger than he looked. So were Layla and I.

After we built our treehouse, we added on a large wooden platform behind it, fancying ourselves martial artists in training. With no one to teach us, and our parents off working all day, every day, even over the summers, we fashioned our own idea of badass ninja training. It began as an insane amount of push-ups, sit-ups, jumping jacks, running the trails we'd carved out behind our houses, but it quickly evolved into something fairly sophisticated—and all our own. We never talked about it with others, not even our parents when they asked specifically about what we were getting up to.

After many years of training together several times a week, if not daily, I had no doubt Griffin could take down Rich in an instant. But then there'd be more questions, more attention leading back to the incident with Brady.

"No fighting," I said. "No more. Not after what happened at Fischer House."

"That was just a fluke," Brady started before I cut him off.

"Granted. But no more risking something like that happening."

"You mean, a random collapse of a fucking balcony—that looked perfectly sturdy, by the way, before I walked out onto it?" He raised his brows, emphasizing how unlikely the scenario was to repeat itself.

"No, I mean, we don't put our fates in the hands of others. Never again. We don't do anything that could lead to shit that bad happening. Rich is a prick. We know that. The douchebag himself probably knows it. That's what all his bluster's about while he struts around with his chest pushed out like a damn cartoon."

"I bet he's got a little dick," Layla added. "It would explain a lot. Otherwise, he's good enough looking, richer than gods, has everything he wants. It's gotta be the little dick."

"Well, the little dick'd better not get on my case about anything," Brady snarled, "or I'm joining Griff in beating the ever-loving shit out of him."

Hunt grunted, his way of saying there was no way he'd let his bros fight without him at their sides. Like any of us would stay out of it if it came to that.

Brady leaned back against the side of my car. "I swear, if a single one of those idiots calls me Miracle Kid, I'm gonna punch him in the nuts."

I nodded. "Fair enough. But at least try to give them a warning first before you make them sterile for life."

He shrugged, and I knew I was going to have to stick to him like glue once classes started.

"Just picture Kitty Blanche's face pasted over theirs," I tried.

"The fuck?"

"If Kitty susses out that you're fighting at school instead of gimping around like you're supposed to, our parents will morph into fucking fire-breathing dragons. They'll probably all start working from home to keep an eye on us twenty-four seven."

After Layla and Hunt groaned, I added, "And Kitty's got her ways, you know that. She's found out about stuff already that she shouldn't have. Like, who the fuck told her I checked Brady's pulse again right before he went in the ambulance and that he still had none?"

"Or that we used 'our feminine wiles' to get the EMTs to blast him one more time," Layla said, adding in air quotes while batting her eyelashes exaggeratedly.

"That's right." I scowled, annoyed once more at the headlining story that denounced Layla and me as hussies instead of devoted family willing to do whatever it took to save one of ours. "The woman's got eyes and ears where she shouldn't."

Hunt's grunt this time was a *we'll figure it out* reassurance. Griffin and Brady nodded their silent agreement.

"That reminds me." I pinned my attention on Brady, and he frowned at me, anticipating what I was going to say. "We've gotta talk. Or Brady does, anyway. He's got something to tell us."

"It's no big deal," he piped up, too quickly, and I stiffened, feeling the others do the same around me.

Layla picked up her sketchbook and pencil, tucking them under her arm. "Let's grab some drinks and head to the treehouse."

"Guys, I'm for real," Brady said. "It's no big deal. No need for a treehouse meeting. It's just some nightmares, that's all."

The four of us waited. We knew him too well.

"Okay, fine," he relented quickly, aware of how ridiculously slow we were to give up. "They're creepy as fuck, totally weirding me out. They're of us when we're kids, and we're locked up in some facility we can't escape. Mega dystopian vibes."

"I still think I need a drink for this." Layla headed through the garage to enter the house. "You guys coming?"

We were already behind her. Once we were sprawled out on the couches in my family room with our own chilled bottles of beer—something our parents allowed so long as we didn't drive afterward—Brady didn't wait for us to prompt him.

"All of us are there. I'd say we're like five or six, I don't know—maybe four . . . it's hard to tell. But we've all got shaved heads, buzz cuts, and we're wearing identical blue jumpsuits. Almost like mechanic's coveralls, that's what they remind me of. And there are other kids there too, but I didn't recognize any of them. But in the dream, I know who they are, and they know us."

"Shit, that is creepy," Hunt said.

"Dude, you have no idea. They stick us in these white-walled rooms that all look the same. One bed and nothing else inside it. We have to use a call button to be let out and accompanied to the bathroom, that kind of deal. Staff watching our every fucking move on cameras, or through windows in the doors to our rooms."

I leaned my elbows onto my thighs and slid forward, mostly to put more room between Griffin and me so I could focus on what Brady was telling us. "So what are we doing there?"

"Not sure, really, but I get the feeling they're experimenting on us . . . like we're lab rats, and there were, like, dozens of us kids being led around like mindless little zombies." He shuddered and took a drink of his beer.

"Weird as fuck, dude, but at least it's not real," Hunt said.

"Yeah, that's the only good thing about any of it. No way can it be real. We were already here in Ridgemore then, just a few years out from building the treehouse and all that. But. . ."

"But what?" I asked.

"But . . . damn if it doesn't feel real."

"Dreams are like that," Griffin said in his rational voice.

Brady *tsk*ed at him. "I know what dreams feel like, man, come on. I just mean . . . it feels as real as my normal memories, ya know? Like this really happened to us, but then so did us growing up here since we were really little. Our parents moved us all here when we were three, remember?"

The four of us watched him closely. Could trauma from dying affect his perception of reality? If so, would telling our already paranoid parents about this help or hinder? Maybe Brady needed a shrink.

"Great, thanks," Brady said with a huff, sinking heavily back into the couch. "You're all looking at me like I'm a brewski short of a six-pack." He took another sip. "I knew I shouldn't've told you."

Layla did her own *tsk*ing. "Don't be an ass, Brade. We tell each other everything. Just 'cause we're processing doesn't mean we think you're crazy."

I drank to cover up what I was sure was guilt scrawled across my face. The four of them could read me like a damn book.

Brady snorted, eyes on me. "Yeah, right. None of you are thinking I've lost my mind." He grunted. "They're just dreams, guys. No biggie. Just forget I said anything about it."

Trying to redeem myself, I said, "They aren't just dreams, Brade, they're fucking awful nightmares, and we're gonna figure out how to stop them, all of us together. Just like always." I took a moment to make eye contact with each of them. "It's been us against the world forever. Nothing's changed."

"Yeah, except for me fucking dying," Brady added with every ounce of sullenness he possessed.

"A big deal, admittedly, but that doesn't change the fact that we've got your back through thick and thin. No matter what. Even if that means we're gonna crawl into your motherfucking nightmares and stop them from messing with you."

"That's fucking right," Griffin whipped out, a damn promise.

Hunt's brows rose. "I don't gotta say it. You know I'm always here for you, man."

"And I can't escape you even if I tried," Layla said on a chuckle, but we knew she didn't mean it. "My room's right next to yours."

Staring at us, taking our measure over his beer bottle as he drank more, Brady finally said, "Appreciate that, but these are my *dreams*. There's nothing any of you can do to help."

"I'm not so sure—" Hunt started, but froze, staring at something over my shoulder. He placed his beer on the coffee table, then jumped to his feet, already running.

Without understanding what was happening, we followed his lead, and when he slid open the sliding glass doors that led to the backyard—too fast, too hard—we ran out after him.

A mechanical whir drew my attention to a zooming dot, doing its damnedest to fade away quickly.

"Somebody tell me that's not a motherfucking *drone*," I barked.

No one did.

7

What Dreams Are Made Of

What little bit of summer vacation was left dragged by in a battle with our parents. Whether we were all together or separate, each in our own homes, it didn't matter. Whenever there was an adult around—and there nearly always was now that they'd *all* decided to work from home—they were trying to convince us to home-school instead of finishing out our senior year at the school we'd attended since first grade.

Some, like my dad and Brady and Layla's mom, Celia, went for the bold, bulldozer approach of persuasion: *Do as I say or else.* Others, like Hunt's mom, Alexis, and Griffin's dad, Orson, tried the buddy-buddy approach, even going so far as to hang out with us for hours at a time, pounding back the brewskis, before dropping the *no school for any of you* hammer—as if we had no idea what they were up to. . .

They didn't relent, and neither did we. Ever since that drone had shown up at my house, they'd been doing their best to envelop us in bubble wrap—and these were the same parents who allowed Layla to ink us with her tattoo gun. We were the envy of our other friends because our parents used to treat us like young *adults*. So long as we were responsible with the privileges they extended us, we could do just about whatever we wanted.

Not anymore.

"That stupid fucking drone," Griffin muttered under his breath, clearly on the same wavelength as I was as he pulled into Ridgemore High's parking lot and eased Clyde into the space next to Bonnie. Brady's parents still wouldn't allow him to drive, so Layla was in the driver's seat while I rode shotgun with Griffin, Hunt in the back.

Griffin pocketed the keys and looked out the windshield for a beat, studying the school we'd fought so hard to attend.

Hunt slid forward across the back bench seat, leaning his arms on either headrest. "It really can't get much more absurd. Us, fighting to be in a school we outgrew ages ago."

I grunted. "I swear, if Mrs. Moody tries to teach us about the Civil War one more time. . ."

Griffin groaned and propped open his door but didn't get out yet. "Kill me now and spare me from listening to her drone on and on. I didn't fight my parents this fucking hard for *her*."

"No shit," Hunt said. "I'd have given my mom her class, no problem."

I shook my head, repeating, "That fucking drone, man."

We assumed we had Kitty Blanche to thank for the total invasion of our privacy. Our parents just about blew a communal gasket when they found out about it, forcing us to keep the shades down day and night, making us swear a legit oath not to discuss anything related to Brady's accident or recovery whenever we were outdoors, a privilege they might not have allowed at all if we weren't so clearly going stir crazy, and if Bobo, my two-year-old pit bull terrier, didn't need the exercise as much as we did.

Brady hopped out of Bonnie's passenger side with enough pep in his step to tell me there was no way he was going to gimp out like Celia had flat-out begged him to do. Layla waited for us between both cars, studying her brother, who was rocking the scowl that had taken up permanent residence on his face as if Layla had tattooed it there.

I rolled up my window before pitching my voice low to Griffin and Hunt. "Has he told you guys? His nightmares have been getting worse. I think they're really starting to mess with him."

Hunt dipped his head lower to better examine our friend through the front window. "Yeah, I don't think they only happen when he's sleeping anymore. He's got a constant haunted look about him." He shook his head. "It's not good."

"He'll be fine," Griffin said. "He always is. He went through shit, that's all. He'll go back to being the usual Brady in no time." He offered us a confident smile, but I wasn't buying it. For as much as he pretended he didn't, Griffin worried about Brady. We all did.

We grabbed our books and joined the others to walk the same path we did last year, since we were first allowed to park in the junior-senior lot. Around us, kids were squealing and greeting each other loudly after a summer of not seeing one another—rushing to find their classes and claim their seats before the first bell rang. But even in their haste, I felt their eyes on us, and it wasn't just because the Miracle Kid walked among us. Our tight crew had always garnered attention. Even when we were still losing our baby teeth, others were drawn to our closeness.

We made a pit stop at the lockers before heading to our first class, AP Biology. I leaned into Hunt as we approached the classroom. "Did you already read the textbook?"

He shrugged off my question, which for him was as good as saying, *Hell yeah, I did. Gobbled that shit up in a couple of days.*

I chuckled despite his silence. The guy could devour books like no one else I'd ever met. He didn't have a photographic memory, but he did have an uncanny ability to absorb information. Whatever book he got his hands on allowed him to quickly learn the material. And languages? If not for the need to hear them spoken to grasp intonation and accents, he would probably already speak a dozen of them fluently. Dude had a brain the size of a damn beach ball.

Griffin's hand landed on the small of my back, allowing me into the classroom ahead of him. I tried and failed to temper the small smile this gesture brought to my lips. Lately, Griffin's thoughtful touch had become more frequent, more noticeable. My heart sped up, but I told it to take a chill pill. None of us could ever be together like that. The five of us would always remain friends. Our bond was too important and too vital to risk messing up.

We settled into our desks, Griffin directly beside me. I spent most of the fifty-minute class reminding myself of the myriad reasons I couldn't go there, not even in my mind, as Mrs. Surman went over the syllabus for the upcoming semester. It was boring and unnecessary.

A glance at Brady told me he wasn't paying attention either. His eyes were haunted again, smudges under his eyes indicating he'd been sleeping less than he was telling us. There was no escaping his dreams when they caught up to him even in waking hours.

We bounced from bio to AP Chemistry and then to AP World History before the bell finally rang to announce lunch. We hadn't discussed what we were doing ahead of time, but we didn't need to; it was what we'd done every day the previous year. We piled into one car—Griffin's—and drove to Hughie's Hoagies, a nearby delicatessen where we knew the employees by name. While I worked my way through an eight-inch Italian sub with extra peperoncini, we waited for Brady to share. We knew he didn't want to. But then, he never did.

He huffed, tossed his beanie on the seat next to him, and took a humongous bite of a Reuben sandwich, chewing obnoxiously while glaring at each of us in turn. When Layla snorted at the show he was putting on, he rewarded her with a double dose of *Fuck you all, I don't feel like talking.*

We waited him out. Like always.

After a deeper scowl than usual, he sighed loudly. "You guys are pains in my fucking ass, you know that, don't you?" But then he nearly smiled. "You know how I told you our parents are there too?"

Chewing, I nodded.

"Well, this last time I saw Alexis actually injecting me with stuff, then drawing blood. And then I saw her talking with Orson about the results. But mostly I see us shuffling around like we're brain-dead, and our parents keeping track of everything we do on a clipboard, probably making a damn note every time we take a shit."

Griffin popped a salt and vinegar chip into his mouth. "So more of the same."

"Yes . . . and no." Brady set down his sandwich and played absently with his friendship bracelet, which had held up since we were twelve.

Now he really had our attention. Brady was not one to fidget. Or to think before he spoke, for that matter.

Even so, we knew not to push him unless we had to. Hunt took a long sip of his sparkling water, belching softly afterward. Layla ate the remaining bites of her meatball sub before Brady finally continued.

"You know how I've been telling you they're dreams? Nightmares, really, even though they've started happening in the daytime now too, which is all sorts of fucked up?"

"Yeah, man," Griffin said. "We listen when you talk."

That reminder of how we were hanging on to his every word led to a fresh round of fiddling with his bracelet, the threads hanging from its ends frayed and showing their age. Seeming to notice what he was doing, he frowned and picked up his sandwich, though he didn't take a bite.

"Well, they don't feel like dreams anymore."

"You said that last week," Hunt commented, a gentle smile softening his words.

"I guess I did. Anyway. . ." Brady paused to breathe.

All the delay tactics were putting me on edge, and I exchanged a look with Layla, then Griffin. They were both staring hard at Brady, anticipation vibrating off them.

Brady inhaled deeply again, setting his sandwich down yet again without eating. "What I'm seeing, all this stuff with us as kids in the lab or whatever the creepy place is, well, the images are starting to override my real memories of us growing up here in Ridgemore as young kids. The time in Ms. Gail's pre-K and kindergarten? Gone. First grade with Mrs. Cowan's all but gone now, too."

"Wait," I interrupted. "What do you mean, the memories are gone? If you remember our teachers' names, then it must all still be there, right?"

He shrugged. "I don't know. Now all that's more like a story someone told me, not my own memories. It doesn't feel as real, like the memories are turning into a postcard or a TV show I'm watching, like that."

"And the time in the lab?" Layla asked delicately, as if she didn't really want to know. "What's that like now?"

He met his twin's waiting gaze. "The time in the lab feels real, not Ridgemore. Even the bright lighting everywhere in that place feels familiar. Everything about it feels familiar, like I'd know it again if I saw it. And, guys, when we were there, we didn't call our parents Mom or Dad. We didn't even know their names. We were their patients, their experiments, nothing more. They were the white lab coats; we were just a handful of kids who all looked the same, walking around in identical clothes, same posture, same vacant look in our eyes, all that."

"Well, that obviously can't be right," Hunt said. "See? That's proof that whatever's going on with your dreams or memories, none of it's real."

Brady didn't even blink, just pushed his plate out of reach. Normally, the guy could eat his weight in Reubens. "Sure as shit feels real. Too real. I'm worried I'm losing my mind. Like, okay, I died, right?"

We nodded. None of us would ever forget.

"So maybe when I came back, some screws that got loosened when I was dead didn't get tightened back up. I don't feel like the same person anymore."

I dropped my sub and didn't even bother wiping my fingers before reaching across the table to grab Brady's hand. I waited until he met my eyes. "Brade, you're not crazy. You're not losing your mind. Whatever's going on, we'll figure it out. Together. Okay? Just like we always do, just like we always have. You've never been alone, and you're not alone now. We've got your back, like always."

"That's right," Hunt added gruffly, and Griffin grunted his agreement, though I sensed his attention drift across our linked fingers. I didn't dare loosen my hold on Brady though.

His gaze was lighter now, hopeful, as he looked up at us from under his lashes. "Are you guys sure? Would you tell me if I'd gone bonkers?"

"Dude," Layla said, "since when do any of us pander? You know I'd tell you if you'd gone fishing and hadn't come back."

He blinked at her, then barked a short laugh. "Yeah, you're right. You def never hold back."

"Exactly. And I'm not holding back with you now. What Joss said is right on the money. You're not crazy, and you're not going through this alone. We might not be able to dive into your dreams with you, but we would if we could."

"Fuck yeah, we would," Griffin interjected, and Hunt *uh-huh*ed.

"If your accident mixed some memories up, so what? You're motherfucking *alive*, dude. Who cares if things got jumbled a bit? It'll sort itself out in time."

"Layla's right," I chimed in. "Give yourself time. It's only been a month since the Fischer House party. That's not that long, considering everything you went through. Then the hospital, and our parents. If we should discuss whether anybody's gone nutty, we should be talking about them."

"No shit," Hunt said. "I actually caught my mom watching me while I slept the other night." He shuddered, crunching into a dill pickle. "Talk about weird. She was just leaning against the door, staring. It was hella odd."

"What'd you do?" Brady asked.

"Nothing. Pretended I was out and didn't notice. But I started locking my door at night after that."

"She let you?" I asked, brows high. Hunt's dad had died in a car crash when we were little, just before our parents moved to Ridgemore and started us in pre-K here. She'd never been the helicopter parent she was now, but she was still the most worrywart of them all. Brady's near death had been really hard on her, flushing out old traumas, evident in the frequent nibbling at her lower lip she'd been doing lately.

Hunt shrugged. "She hasn't *not* let me. She hasn't said anything about it."

"Just wait," Griffin predicted.

"Yeah, probably. Since the drone showing up at Joss's, it's like she wants to fucking hold my hand all day and night. I hope she gets over it fast. I'm trying to be supportive 'cause of Dad, but come on already."

We all nodded our understanding, even Brady. We knew each other's parents nearly as well as our own.

I released Brady's hands and picked at my sub. "You still haven't told Celia and Porter about the dreams?"

He and Layla shook their heads in unison, the fraternal twins appearing more similar than usual.

"Hell no, I haven't," Brady said.

"And he's not gonna," Layla added.

"That's right. Mom's already more intense than either of us can handle. She legit tried to bribe me today, telling me she'd give me a thousand bucks if I'd just limp around for at least the first month at school."

Griffin whistled. "That's a whole new level, bro."

"For sure. Let's hope we don't see if there are more levels after this one. I won't be able to take it."

Layla crumpled up her wrapper and rose from the table. "Time to roll, guys. We don't wanna be late on the first day back."

But truly, I doubted any of us cared. School was more of a social scene to us than anything else. We could pass all our classes with our eyes closed.

A few minutes later, we were piled back into Griffin's Mustang and nearing the school when he slowed down well ahead of the turn.

"What is it?" I asked from the back seat. When it was Griffin's car, I usually rode shotgun, but I'd left it for Brady today.

"Fucking reporters," Brady grumbled. "They're almost worse than our parents. It's like they won't be happy till they're all the way up my butt."

"That visual, Brade?" Layla said from beside me. "We're plenty good without it, mm-kay?"

Griffin glanced at us in the rearview mirror, catching my eye first. "Does anyone care if we miss French and British Lit today?"

"You already know my answer," Layla said. "Does this mean we're already playing hooky?" She beamed.

Brady stared stoically ahead, waiting, hoping, unwilling to ask for our support in this way.

"Fuck yeah. Let's do it," I said.

Griffin zoomed past the school entrance without hesitation, and Hunt whipped out his phone. "I'll text Zoe. I'm pretty sure she's in both those classes. She can cover for us."

As one, we looked at Hunt.

"Zoe Wills?" Layla asked.

Hunt nodded while he messaged.

"You have her number?" I followed up.

"Uh-huh."

"Huh," I said.

Layla bared her teeth in a wild grin. "You like her."

"No, I don't."

"Yes, you fucking do. Why else would you have her number?"

"Because it's convenient in times like this," Hunt dragged out.

The rest of us snorted, grunted, or laughed, or a combination of the three.

"Yeah. Right," Brady said, sounding lighter already now that we were heading away from Kitty Blanche and her posse and toward the busybodies we called parents.

I wasn't entirely sure it was an improvement, but whatever helped Brady, we'd do it.

"I call the punching bag first," I singsonged, knowing we'd end up at the treehouse, all but guaranteed.

"I call the dummy," Layla chirped, then rolled down the window, smiling as the trees whipped by us.

This was familiar territory. Our crew was what we'd always known. Together, we could bounce back from anything and everything. Together, we'd pull Brady through.

8

That Closet Sure as Shit Doesn't Lead to Narnia, and Other Woes

Brady and Layla were the first to get a car. Their parents were tired of carting them around, and often also the rest of us, a position they were vocal about. Even though we spent much of our time in our collective backyards and the forest that extended beyond them, our parents were all too ready to grant us our independence.

That was before Brady's accident, of course.

Since we'd been able to count on our own set of wheels, we'd been skipping school. Not often enough to draw attention to our absences, just enough to keep ourselves from dying of boredom, which was a real possibility. Challenging, Ridgemore High was not, its system for students leaving during the school day happily lax. A signed note from a guardian was all it took. I'd been a master forger of my mom's signature for years, and I'd claimed more appointments than I could count—doctors of all sorts, shrinks, even orthodontists, though I'd never had braces. So far, we'd never been caught.

We'd also never taken off without signing out at the front office the way we were supposed to.

Hunt's phone vibrated, and he checked it. "Cool. Zoe says she's got us covered."

"How?" Layla asked. I was wondering the same.

His fingers flew over the screen. "Asking."

We waited while Griffin's Clyde hugged the winding road that eventually led to our houses, whipping around bend after bend. Bonnie would just have to stay in the school parking lot overnight. No one would think too much of it, assuming we'd left together for some reason.

Hunt grimaced apologetically at Brady, who didn't notice from the passenger seat, where his focus was trained on the road ahead. "She says she used the Miracle Kid excuse, citing group trauma that came up on us all of a sudden. Says she called on our teachers' sympathy, and it worked."

Layla swiveled to study Hunt from the middle of the bench seat. "She for real said all that?"

He shrugged, still messaging back, his phone buzzing frequently in a way that told us Hunt and Zoe had more to say to each other than what he was repeating aloud. "Seems like."

Brady groaned from the front seat, but Layla ignored him, her eyes narrowing on Hunt. "You *do* fucking like her. Why won't you just admit it?"

"Of course I like her. If not, I wouldn't give her my digits." He glanced up at her. "Duh."

"No, you doofus. I mean, you *like* like her."

He smirked. "You sound like you're a third grader, Lay." And he went back to texting.

"So. . .?"

He didn't look up, eyes trained on his screen. "So what?"

"So . . . are you gonna ask her out or what?"

"Haven't decided yet. I like her well enough. She's cool for a chick."

"Hey," Layla and I protested together, and I reached across her to slap him on the thigh.

He laughed, clearly having done it on purpose. "But I'm just not that into her."

"Why not?" Layla asked, intent on getting to the bottom of Hunt's feelings.

He shrugged again. "I don't know. She comes to mind every once in a while, so it's not like I don't think about her, but I don't think about her too much. She's nice and pretty and interesting and all that—smart too, I think—but I don't need her in my life. I mean, I've got you guys."

"Yeah," I said, "but you can't bone us."

"Joss is right," Layla added. "What about getting your needs met?"

Another shrug as he slid forward to tuck his phone back in his pocket. "There are other girls far better at the casual thing. I don't get the feeling Zoe'll be into casual, and I don't want to get tangled up in anything, especially not right now." He flicked a look at Brady, who stared ahead, unusually quiet. Ordinarily, he would have been the first to be busting Hunt's balls about some girl.

Layla followed the trajectory of Hunt's gaze and nodded, letting the topic drop. We talked about mindless nonsense until Griffin pulled Clyde into the space we'd carved out of the forest past our driveways for just this purpose. Our parents never drove this far, and when we parked our cars in far enough, bushes and trees concealed them from easy view. As far as we knew, they'd never found this hiding spot.

I stepped out of the car first and waited for Layla to slide across the seat. She was getting out when she halted, her gaze going vacant for a moment.

"What's wrong?" I asked.

She groaned. "I just got my period."

"*Ewww*," Brady said. "Not where we can hear, Layla. That's gross."

Layla rolled her eyes. "Dude, it's a bodily function. Get over yourself. Do you see me freaking out when you burp and fart around me?"

"Yes, you fucking complain about it every time. You sound like Mom, getting on my case about stupid manners."

"Clearly with good reason." Layla stood and moved away so I could shut the door behind her. Shorter than me by a few inches, she glanced up at me. "You got any tampons on you? I didn't pack any. It's the first day of school and my period's fucking early. I don't have my usual stash."

"Aw, *come on*," Brady whined.

Hunt palmed him on the back. "Do we need to go over the birds and the bees again?"

"Of course not, asshole," he growled, stepping away before Hunt could drape an arm over his shoulders. "What the fuck would we need to talk about the mechanics of sex for? I've had more practice than you by a mile."

Hunt smiled easily. "And you wouldn't be getting in all that practice if the girls didn't get their periods. For that matter, Celia would've never pushed you out of her vajayjay—"

"That's enough, Hunt," Brady snapped as if Hunt were insulting his momma instead of discussing the obvious.

I shook my head, chuckling despite the fact that my friends could often be annoying morons. "We're closest to my house. I'll sneak in, grab some, and meet you guys at the treehouse."

"Sounds good. Thanks, Joss." Then Layla hooked her arm through Brady's, leading him into the forest and onto the faintly worn trail we'd carved out between the trees, whispering *vagina* as they went, just to freak him out some more. Hunt soon followed, but Griffin lingered, his eyes running the length of me.

"You okay?"

"Yeah, sure I'm okay." I smiled softly at him. "You?"

His eyes, a hazel brown, lit up as he returned my smile. "Always." He stared at me for another few beats, heating my skin everywhere his gaze traveled, then turned and trailed down the path after the others.

I waited a moment, lingering in the heat still tingling across my skin, then walked in the opposite direction before breaking into a light jog, covering the short distance to my house quickly. I emerged from the trees at the back end of our property, so I couldn't tell if my parents were home by their cars in the driveway or garage, but when I spotted Bobo loose in the backyard, I knew they were there. We never left my dog outside if we weren't home to keep an eye on him.

The black pittie was already charging my way before I popped out from among the trees. But I adopted Bobo when he was a puppy, and he was trained not to make a peep unless I wanted him to.

Crouching to greet him, I allowed him a few sloppy kisses before pulling my face away. "Such a good boy," I cooed, scratching behind his ears and then all over, concentrating on the white patch on his throat and chest. Softly, he whined, the entire back half of his body wagging along with his tail until he plopped onto his back, asking for belly rubs.

"So spoiled." But I didn't hesitate to indulge him, chuckling despite myself. "You missed me, huh? Well, I missed you too."

His whine intensified as if he understood me.

"Just don't tell Mom or Dad I'm home early, okay? I'll get in trouble. I'm supposed to be at lame-ass school." Another whine in solidarity. "Yeah, exactly. You're lucky you don't have to go to school."

My parents had insisted that if I was going to bring home a pit bull, I needed to take him to "doggy academy." I refused, figuring out how to train him myself, and Bobo took to my instruction so well that my parents never protested when I broke my agreement with them.

After an intense scratching behind his ears, the only other white tuft on his otherwise black fur, I told him, "You stay here. I'll be right back."

He leaped to his feet to follow me, a stupidly cute smile stretching his cheeks.

I pointed at him. "*Stay.*"

He complained softly but obeyed.

"Good boy," I whispered and crouched low, slinking along the bushy mountain laurel until I reached the sliding glass doors that didn't squeak.

I left my shoes outside and padded around with silent footfalls until I clutched tampons in one hand like the ready excuse they'd be if either of my parents ran into me. *Why am I home from school in the middle of the day? Oh, my period came early. What a bummer. Just grabbing some quick supplies and heading back. No, I couldn't use the school nurse's stuff. She only stocks crappy, chemical-y brands.*

When I emerged from the hallway leading from my bedroom, on the opposite end of the house from their room and office, I paused, tilting my head like Bobo did, listening.

"Reece," my mom called out from the far end of the house.

"What?" my dad shouted back, sounding like he was in the kitchen. Hearing the fridge door confirmed my guess.

"They're in the treehouse and they're talking about some nightmares Brady's been having."

"Wait, what?" A cabinet shut loudly, metal tinkling across china as Dad likely gathered his plate and utensils before crossing the kitchen, dining room, and entering the hallway that led to their shared home office.

"They're skipping school already?" he asked. Not, *What the fuck are you talking about, woman?* as he should have.

I froze, listening to his slippers as they squeaked across the bamboo floor of the hallway.

"Hurry," my mom hollered. "He's talking about a lab from when they were kids."

"Oh, *fuck*," my dad grunted, running the rest of the way. "What's the lab look like? How's he describing it?"

But then their voices faded as I registered the distinct sound of them descending stairs. Only there were no stairs in that part of the house. . .

And what the ever-loving fuck were they doing spying on us in the treehouse? How did they even know the others were there?

I hesitated, only for a few seconds, before clutching the tampons to my chest and tiptoeing after them. *Period came early. Home for supplies. Heard you guys yelling. Figured I'd come check to make sure you're all right before I head back to school like a good kid.*

Also, *what the* fuck *are you two up to?*

When I reached their office, the door was open and Dad's plated bagel sandwich was abandoned on his desk, the fork for his potato salad on the floor, a splatter of mayo and potato on the carpet.

And he didn't stop to clean it up. . .

That realization sank in my gut almost as heavily as what I'd already heard. My dad was no clean freak, but Mom was. A cleaning service came to the house a few times a week, and even so, she still did more tidying up than any one human ever should. He would never have left a spill on the floor like that, not when she was around.

Only he had. And he apparently hadn't given so much as a minor fuck about the mess.

My heart beat more quickly as my attention landed on the ajar closet door . . . and the corridor extending inside it . . . like it was leading to motherfucking Narnia or some shit.

"What the. . .?" I breathed to myself on an inhale. After shoving the tampons in my back pocket, I flicked one of my braids over my shoulder to get it out of the way and leaned forward without stepping into the carpeted closet that obviously was no such thing. Unworn winter coats were shoved far to one side, evidently part of the ruse to hide this entrance . . . from me. Their daughter.

Bitterness swelled in my chest like acid reflux, but I ignored it and focused. A single unanticipated creak of a floorboard would give me away. A spiral staircase with a black iron railing led downward, so I crouched low and perked my ears like I was Bobo listening for the sound of his food clattering against his stainless-steel bowl.

I could no longer make out what they were saying, though I could hear them talking in a blend of unintelligible excited sounds.

But what I *could* make out with ease was Brady's voice, then Layla's and Hunt's, and finally, Griffin's. He was saying, "Brade, if you wanna talk about this more, we should wait for Joss. She'll be pissed if she knows we've been talking about your dreams without her."

Despite the confusion and betrayal building inside me in equal measure like the churning lava of a volcano, I warmed at Griffin looking out for me.

"What's taking her so long, anyway?" Layla asked, her words traveling crisply up to greet me. "She should be back by now. Maybe she ran into her parents. Hmm. Should I go rescue her?"

"No," Brady said. "You'll just make things worse. Joss can handle herself."

Layla snorted. "Of course my girl can handle herself. But you know what Monica's like. She might've trapped her up in a web of motherly guilt. Not even Joss is immune to that shit."

"Wait," Dad said more loudly so I could only just make out his exclamation. "Where's Joss? She's not here, is she?" Despite the volume, I registered the panic in his questions.

When my mom followed up with a sharp, "You didn't leave the closet door open, did you?" I didn't wait to hear more.

In a squat, I sidestepped the fallen fork and rushed across their office, filled with their desks and regular, non-suspect office supplies. By the time I slid out of the room, I was running full speed, dodging furniture I could have avoided with my eyes closed. Before I heard them climbing the stairway in their secret room, I was sliding the same door I came in through shut behind me, swiping my shoes, and running in my socks full-out until I slid into the shrubs that would conceal me.

In an instant, Bobo was on me, ears alert, tongue lolling, tail perked as he waited to see if I would bring him along with me.

Normally, I would have asked him to stay in the yard so my parents wouldn't figure out I was home, but after what I'd just witnessed, there was no point to the subterfuge. Plus, I was so pissed I could feel my nostrils flaring, and Bobo was as good a friend as any of the others, sometimes better. At least he wouldn't ask questions I didn't have answers to.

"Come on, boy. You're coming with me."

We jogged all the way to the treehouse, Bobo's collar jingling as we ran. By the time we arrived, I still hadn't figured out what the hell to tell the others, so while my friends greeted Bobo and he went for a second round of pampering, I headed over to the punching bag. Without handing Layla the tampons I'd gone into my house to get in the first place, I wrapped my hands and faced the bag.

My mind was consumed with my discovery as I landed my first punch, and I tuned out their questions as I kept hitting the bag.

I'd tell them everything eventually, of course. Soon. But not quite yet.

Those were *my* parents. My *parents* were the liars. *My mom and dad.* The two people I was supposed to be able to trust more than anyone else in the world had been hiding an entire room from me in our home, like they were secret agents or some shit. They were *spying* on me and my friends!

I even ignored Griffin's rumbles of concern as I pounded my frustrations into the bag, intending to keep going until the bones in my hands ached and my knuckles bled.

9

Ass Over Teakettle in an Upside-Down World

I didn't stop punching, striking, kicking, and slamming nearly every body part into the bag until sweat dripped down my sides. Griffin stationed himself off to the side, where I couldn't help but see him, arms crossed, silently waiting for my attention. When I finally gave it to him, I noticed everyone staring at me, including Bobo. The droop of my dog's eyes told me he was trying very hard to behave when all he wanted was to beg for my assurance that everything was okay.

He, like my friends, realized something was wrong. And boy, was it ever.

I rarely went this hard or for this long anymore, and whenever I did, I eschewed my school clothes for exercise gear. The waistband of my jeans was soaked; the band of my lacy bra was so wet it felt like a bikini top; even my sleeveless shirt clung to my skin in patches. Sweat prickled at my scalp, and I had a strong urge for a shower, but no way was I going back to my house and risking an encounter with my parents. Despite the hard workout, I hadn't come close to sorting out my feelings about their secret room.

While lost to the punching bag, I absently registered Layla snagging the tampons out of my back pocket and Brady leading a discussion about whether we should ask our parents to hire private teachers for us in a variety of martial arts. They could afford it, and we could use the additional instruction. Books, video tutorials, and our own invention could only get us so far. The conversation then morphed into which discipline we might like to start with—muay Thai, aikido, jiujitsu, kung fu, or karate. That's when I blocked them out, my mind in a loop that didn't finish processing my parents' betrayal and what any of it could possibly mean.

Griffin unwrapped my hands, watching me instead of the unwinding of the protective bandages. "What's going on with you?"

Layla, Brady, Hunt—hell, even Bobo—were silent as they awaited my response. I considered leading them out onto the large platform we erected in the back, but I couldn't trust that my parents wouldn't somehow eavesdrop on us there too. They were probably waiting for my answer now along with my friends.

"I'm fine." My response was tailored for my mom and dad's benefit. "I'm just worried about Brady. Still so glad he's okay after the scare he gave us." I chuckled, the sound ringing fake to my ears. "I guess I still haven't gotten over the trauma of it all."

Griffin raised an eyebrow as if realizing that wasn't what I wanted to say, then frowned at my knuckles. Several of them had split open and were oozing blood. He released my hands and sauntered over to retrieve our well-used first aid kit.

On the couch, Brady kicked his long legs out in front of him, where they touched Layla's. Her face screwed up in disgust as she yanked away her feet, pulling them up onto the other side of the sectional couch, near Hunt, who was petting Bobo.

Brady half scowled and half laughed at his sister. "I told you, Joss, *I'm fine*." His assurance rang as false as mine. "I wish everyone would stop constantly talking about the accident. How the fuck am I supposed to get over it if everyone's constantly bringing that shit up? If it's not the reporters, it's some other asshole calling me the Miracle Kid."

Hunt leaned forward, never interrupting the love he was doling out to Bobo. "You know Zoe didn't mean it like that. She was just trying to help us out so we don't get in trouble."

Brady shrugged noncommittally. "Whatever, man. She's obviously not the problem. Everyone else is."

"Even us?" I asked. Finally, my thoughts drifted to something other than my parents.

Brady didn't meet my eyes as he scraped at an invisible stain on the knee of his shorts. "I know you're not meaning it that way."

Layla inched closer to her twin. "But, Brade, you can't blame us for worrying, not when you've been having these crazy nightmares."

"Yeah," Griffin interjected, grabbing one of my hands to disinfect the cuts. "And they keep getting more intense. How's that not supposed to affect us?" He paused when I winced at the sting of hydrogen peroxide on raw flesh. "We've got your back."

Brady huffed. "I know that, of course I do, and I appreciate that, you know that too. It's just that it's bad enough that I had to live through it once in my dreams, but then to have to relive it again and again through you guys, first when I tell you what happened, then when you remind me of it . . . you know."

I did know, and I didn't want Brady to dish out any more information about his nightmares when we had an audience only I was aware of.

"You want us to stop talking about it all so much?" I asked.

"You got it. I think I was also a bit freaked out 'cause my parents almost caught me when I popped into the house."

"Shit," Layla grunted. "Did they catch you? We def don't need any of our parents breathing down our necks any more than they already are."

"No kidding," Hunt added. "My mom's driving me totally nuts."

I hurried to divert them from saying anything more about the parents, though if mine had listened to us before, there was no telling what they'd overheard us saying. We'd been complaining about them since Brady's accident, when they started wanting to basically put us on leashes.

"I heard my dad in the kitchen and bolted out the back sliding door. I don't think he knew I was there, so we're good, but it got my heart pumping."

Again, Griffin studied me with raised brows, mutely calling me out on my shit. He'd always been perceptive and far too observant.

He tossed the cotton ball he'd been using to clean my knuckles in the trash and handed me the kit. Our fingers touched, and I lingered for a moment before smiling my thanks and sitting on the floor, cross-legged, to slap on some Band-Aids. No one wanted my sweaty ass on our couch cushions.

When I finished, I jumped to my feet and announced, "Come on. Let's go for a run."

"What? Now?" Hunt asked while Layla shook her head, appearing to be trying to climb her way inside the couch so she'd be excused.

"Hell no, girl. It's shark week. I don't wanna move till it's over. I'm thinking buttery popcorn, insane amounts of chocolate, and a cute chick flick."

Brady started groaning before she even finished speaking, but then she knew he would. I figured at least a fourth of everything she ever said was intended to irritate her brother.

"I'm never watching a chick flick. Never, ever. And you're better than that, Lay. What about a good kung fu movie? Maybe some Bruce Lee? *Enter the Dragon*?"

Layla rolled her eyes. "Like it would kill you to watch two people fall in love and get all smoochy."

"Actually, it fucking might. Who wants to watch that shit, anyhow?"

"Um, like a hundred bajillion women worldwide. Maybe even some cool dudes, too, who aren't worried their masculinity's too fragile to handle a little romance."

I'd sat through several versions of this discussion before. We always ended up watching some action flick . . . eventually. Until we landed on that group decision, Layla tortured the rest of us along with Brady as she made an argument I knew for a fact she didn't actually care about. Even on the few occasions when she and I would catch a movie alone, we never chose chick flicks.

I walked over to her and smacked her on the thigh.

"Ow," she cried, though I'd barely tapped her. "What'd you do that for?"

"Because it's time to get your lazy ass up off the couch and come for a run with me."

"Uh-uh. Do *you* enjoy going for a motherfucking run when your insides feel like they're bleeding out?"

I slapped her leg again. "Come on, drama queen. Up you get." I spun. "All of you."

"I mean, sure," Hunt said as he stood, "but . . . right now?" Hunt loved running; it was as if his long, lean muscles had been designed for distance. He could probably run for an entire day and hardly lose steam along the way. "I'm in jeans."

"So?"

"Okay, then. Let's fucking go already."

I grinned at Hunt, didn't bother convincing the rest of them, and stalked out, whistling for Bobo to follow.

It took several minutes, and lots of loud complaining from Layla, before the others joined us in front of the treehouse.

"Girl, you literally just finished murdering the bag," Layla whined. "Why do we need to go for a run right the fuck *now*? I was thinking I could draw out some new tat designs."

"Oooh, cool," Brady said. "Anything I'll like and wanna get inked on?"

I held up a hand before they could get going. "I just really feel like a run with you guys, okay? It doesn't have to be a long one, I promise, just enough to get our blood pumping."

I didn't wait for agreement since it was a stupid ruse anyway. I turned and took off, Bobo the only one to follow immediately, an excited grin on his face.

It only took a few strides for Hunt to catch up, running amiably beside me on the dirt trail we'd carved out behind our houses, Bobo happily in the lead. As soon as we wound far enough away from the treehouse and our homes that I could be reasonably certain my traitorous parents wouldn't be eavesdropping, I halted, slamming my hands onto my hips.

Hunt slid to a stop next to me. "What's going on, Joss? Thought we were going for a nice run?"

"Nope, I've got some important shit to tell you all."

"Wait, what?" Layla asked as she drew up next to us. "I don't wanna run, but you make me. Then I start getting into it and you stop when I'm not ready to yet. What the fuck, girl? Is it PMS or something?"

"Nope. Worse."

She frowned. "What could be worse than PMS?"

"Holy fuckballs, Lay," Brady snapped. "Will you knock it off with all the period talk already? I'm not an idiot, you know. I get that you're just doing it to mess with me."

This time, Griffin was the one to cut the sibling bickering short. "What's going on, Joss?" The intensity of his stare suggested he'd already been waiting for me to let them in on the truth. I never fooled him for long, if I did at all.

I could feel my eyes welling with my inner turmoil when Layla quickly closed the distance between us, pressing a hand to my back. "What's wrong? You look like you're about to puke."

"That's 'cause the shit I'm about to tell you is about as bad as it gets. You might wanna take a seat for this."

Not one of them plopped to the forest floor, their bodies tensing instead. Bobo glanced at each of us before drawing protectively to my side, waiting for me to point out the enemy he could defend me from.

"First off, I never wanted to go for a run. Or I don't know, maybe I did—I do need to blow off some mega steam—but I suggested it for all of us because I needed to get you away from the treehouse without telling you that I did or why."

"Ooooh-kay," Hunt drew out. "You're not making much sense yet."

"I know. That's 'cause it's not sensible." I paced a few feet, turned back, then forced myself to hold still.

"You're making us nervous," Brady said.

I sighed and pointed my face to the sky, getting lost in the coverage of full tree canopies for several moments. I began talking before even looking down at them. "So what I said in there was partly true. My parents were home, and my dad was in the kitchen. . ."

"Are you trying to drag this shit out to torture us?" Brady asked. "Or is it just coming out that way?"

I smiled grimly at him. "Just trying to figure out how to tell you guys that my parents are liars. Fucking *liars*."

Griffin walked to my side and placed his hand flush against the small of my back, despite the dampness in my clothing. "What do you mean?"

So I told them exactly what happened, all of it, down to the charade I put on while we were still in the treehouse. By the time I finished, my friends were as stunned as I was. Layla dropped to the ground, her legs stretched out in front of her inelegantly as she stared blankly into the distance. Griffin was pacing, and Hunt's neck and arm muscles visibly clenched, making me wonder if he was about to bolt.

Brady leaned on a tree, eyes swirling with some of that anger and betrayal I was still feeling, making my chest feel tighter than was comfortable.

"A full-on hidden room?" he asked, the question soft with his disbelief. "How's that even possible? How could we have never found out about it before? We even used to play hide-and-go-seek in all our houses, for fuck's sake."

"Why would we go looking for one?" I countered. "In my parents' office *closet*, no less. I don't think I've ever even looked in there. It's their office. I don't mess with things in there. Not even when we were kids did we really play in there."

Hunt's eyes widened. "We never go into any of our parents' home offices. You think . . . do you think it's just your parents doing the spying on us?"

I just blinked at him.

His shoulders slumped before he quickly righted them. "Yeah, that's what I thought."

Griffin whirled to face us. "Our parents are as close of friends as we are. Even if Joss's parents are the only ones doing it, no way do the rest of them not know about it."

"It's still possible they don't," Brady said, though not even he sounded like he believed it.

Layla stared up at him, leaning back into her hands. "Seriously? No way our parents don't know, dude. If Monica and Reece are doing this shit, they all know. I'd bet on it. It's all sus as fuck."

"Yeah, I think that too," I said, voice heavy with regret. "I mean, guys, for real, what the ever-loving fuck? You should've seen it. Legit an entire secret lair opens up from behind a hidden door in their motherfucking work closet!"

Griffin propped his hands on his hips, lips pursed in a tight line of determination. "We need to get in there, see it, figure out what the hell they're up to."

"Agreed," I said readily. "It took everything I had not to march down there right then and there to catch them red-handed."

"One thing I don't get though," Hunt started, and we looked at him. "Okay, so there're *lots* of things I don't get, but one in particular at the moment. Why us? Why would Monica and Reece give a crap about what we say in the treehouse? Are they just trying to catch us skipping school or what? It doesn't make sense. It sounds like they bugged our place. But why? Why the hell would they do something like that?"

"Excellent questions," I said. "And now you understand why I had to vent on the punching bag for as long as I did."

Layla gasped.

"What? What is it?" I pressed when she just proceeded to gape.

"If your parents have tapped the damn treehouse, who's to say they haven't planted bugs in our bedrooms too?"

When Brady blanched, I didn't immediately follow why until Layla cackled.

"Aw hell, Brade," she said, "you been moaning into your sheets again, giving yourself some good tugs?"

Layla's mirth dropped suddenly, disgust curling her lip instead. "Please don't answer that question. I def don't wanna know. Talk about having nightmares. . ."

Brady appeared too mortified by the potential that none of our spaces were as private as we believed them to be to get on Layla's case for any of what she said. Instead, he muttered a growly, "*Motherfucker.* What the hell are we gonna do? This shit's majorly messed up!"

"Yeah, tell me about it." I ran fingers absently across my braids. "At least it's not *your* parents doing all the shitty stuff."

He frowned. "Yet."

"Or have they already?" Layla suggested, like a harbinger of doom. "Our parents would be attached at the hips if that wouldn't be weird for people their age."

"So here's what I think we need to do," I said. "Step one, we wait till our parents, mine for sure, are sleeping, then we sneak out at night and search the treehouse for bugs. We don't want to do it now because the rustling might give away what we're doing. Besides, who knows? They might even have cameras hidden away somewhere or some shit. They can be the size of a fucking pencil tip, I think. So we wait till they're not listening, go in, find the mics, then leave them there."

"Leave them there?" Brady pushed off the tree, anger coloring his neck. "No way. That's our place. They don't get to listen to us there, or anywhere else, for that matter."

"Agreed. But right now, our only advantage till we figure out what the hell's going on is that they don't know we found out about them listening in on us. We find the bugs just so we know what we're dealing with, and then we move on to the next step from there."

"Which will be?" Griffin asked with another arch of his brow. He was probably either amused at my plan, impressed that I'd thought it out already, or both. I ignored how much I liked that.

"Once we locate the bugs, then we spring a trap for my parents. We put on a show for them, something that'll get them out of the house and out of their office so we can get in there and scope it out. Hopefully, once we get down there, we'll be able to see if only my parents are the douchebags or if it's all of them, and what on earth they could possibly want to eavesdrop for. Either way, we need to get down there and see what it's about."

Hunt nodded. "For sure. See how far the rabbit hole goes."

I frowned. "And hope we don't end up like Alice, ass over tea-kettle in an upside-down world." I laughed, a nervous giggle that sounded nothing like my usual self.

"It's gonna be okay, Joss," Griffin said.

I faced him. "Is it though? Either my parents are secret spies with an unhealthy interest in their daughter's personal life or . . . I don't even know what else it could be, but whatever it is, I don't have a good feeling about any of it."

"Neither do I," Hunt said. "This feels off. Something's wrong, for sure."

I couldn't help the sudden surge of fear that he was right, that my parents, nice enough, kind though a bit insipid, were anything but what they seemed to be.

"What the hell are my parents up to?" I muttered, mostly to myself this time.

"Let's find out," Griffin said firmly. "Tonight."

10

Ninjas R Us

While I was no stranger to sneaking out at night, there'd been little need to do it as of late. Over the last couple of years, since I'd gotten my driver's license, my parents had allowed me to more or less make my own decisions. I didn't have a curfew, and so long as I kept my grades up to the straight A's they expected, they asked few questions about my comings and goings. I'd always assumed it was because they trusted me to make good choices. Also because I was rarely out and about without my crew at my side, and they were certain of my friends, too.

Oh, how stupidly wrong I'd been. My parents hadn't had faith in me and my decision-making abilities. They'd been *spying* on me. For how long I had no idea, but for too long, of that I was certain.

Despite the fact that I'd been able to think of little else since I discovered their secret room that afternoon, their duplicity still slammed into me like a Mack truck every once in a while. I drifted through dinner at the Raffertys' and the rest of the night like I was sleepwalking, trying to make sense of a betrayal I doubted I'd ever be able to forget, much less forgive.

Unsure what to wear to *search for listening devices installed by my own parents*, I dressed for movement, slipping on leggings, a cropped sports top, and a hoodie. I pulled my long hair, currently transitioning from my natural brown at the top into orchid pink and then wild violet at the tips, up into a high ponytail, then ran a hand along Bobo's head. The moment I'd gotten up, he'd awoken from his well-worn spot on my bed and tracked my every movement with his chocolate eyes. He might not have understood what was wrong, but he damn well knew something was.

"You're such a smart boy, aren't you?" I whispered to him, though there should have been no real need. My parents slept on the opposite end of our large house—larger now that I realized there was at least one hidden room. But if my parents had no problem with bugging the treehouse, knowing full well it was my crew's sacred spot, then who was to say they didn't have bugs planted all over the damn place? Just in case, I was erring on the side of caution.

As I leaned down toward Bobo to murmur in his ear, he turned and licked my face. I chuckled. "Hey, no, not now." He kept trying to kiss me until I finally scratched behind both ears; his eyes glazed over and he grinned—and stopped trying to kiss me.

This dog had me wrapped around his paw, but it wasn't his fault he was so freaking charming.

Around a smile, I breathed, "We're gonna sneak out."

His ears perked up, and he pushed to his feet.

"We've gotta be quiet, okay?" and I pressed my index finger to my lips, grateful I'd had the foresight to teach him the signal.

Then I rose from the bed, slipped on my running sneakers, and opened the door to my bedroom. Bobo was on my heels, his claws clicking on the hardwood floor of the hallway. We passed the guest room, the bathroom, and the sizable linen closet, then cut across the open entryway to reach the same sliding glass door I'd used earlier.

Pulling it open quietly, I let Bobo out and shut it softly behind me. I waited, my ear near the glass panel of the door. I hadn't heard a sound, but now that I was aware my parents were some sort of creepy super spies, I wasn't taking any chances. After an entire minute of nothing but the chirping of insects in the night, I led Bobo to the side of the yard, where we skirted the perimeter until we slipped through the bushes.

The moment we hit the dirt trail that led to the treehouse, I increased our pace, though I didn't use a flashlight, nor did I have my phone with me. Until I understood exactly what my parents were up to, I wasn't taking any risks. They could spot a light if they were looking, and they could track my phone. There was nothing more to coordinate; my friends knew what time to meet and what we were doing.

Was paranoia driving these precautions? Surely I was overreacting. My parents were scientists, not freaking CIA agents leading a double life. I wasn't doing anything important that anyone should take any special interest in. It was all ridiculous.

Even so, I couldn't help the instincts prickling at the nape of my neck, telling me to be careful.

When Bobo and I reached the clearing in front of the treehouse, the open space illuminated by the soft light of a not-quite full moon, the others were already there. None of them were ever early to a single thing, especially not Layla, who erred on the side of late. And though I was at least ten minutes ahead of schedule, I was the last to arrive.

After scanning everyone, my gaze returned to Griffin, as it seemed prone to do lately in spite of my efforts not to reveal my shifting interest in him—I was trying to prevent the attraction entirely. He wore a pair of ripped jeans, Vans, and a dark hoodie that only exposed part of his beautiful face—his strong jawline, full lips, and dark eyes, made darker by all the shadows cast by the arching trees stretching toward each other overhead.

Hunt was in a similar outfit, though the hood of his shirt was down. The moonlight glimmered across the silver of one of his earrings and his hair, making the black strands reflect a deep, vibrant blue. His mom, Alexis, was originally from Spain, with hair as dark as a raven's feathers. But Hunt's dad had been Eastern Band Cherokee, and Hunt took after him, with a sharp nose, high cheekbones, pillowy lips, and a warm cinnamon skin tone. He was striking.

Layla had chosen cutoffs, a tank top, and her own Vans. Like her twin, in the warm months she wore clothes that revealed her arms and legs more often than not. Also like Brady, she enjoyed showing off her ink. Unlike Brady tonight, she wasn't dressed as a cartoon ninja.

Brady, however. . . I snorted a laugh.

"What?" he asked with so much bite I suspected I wasn't the first to give him grief about his appearance.

"Oh, nothing." But I was grinning.

"*What*, Joss? Just say it."

"Say what?" I asked, feigning innocence for a beat. "That I like your getup?"

"Yeah, that," he snarled.

"Where'd you find that outfit, Brade? I mean, you know, just in case I need to dress up like a badass motherfucking ninja someday and blend into the trees like smoke."

Layla chuckled.

"Did you go shopping at Ninjas-R-Us after dinner?" I added.

Another laugh from his sister. "I told him he was going overboard, but as usual he didn't listen to me, even though I was right. Obvi."

Brady was dressed in the equivalent of a deep-dive wetsuit, only in a thinner material, that enveloped his body from his ankles up to his wrists, and around his head in a hood that exposed only a small oval of his face. He topped off the costume, which hugged his junk more blatantly than was necessary, in sleek black zero-drop sneakers.

"Assholes," Brady muttered. "Are we or are we not on a stealth mission?"

Begrudgingly, I admitted that we were.

"So until we know what the hell we're dealing with here, the less anyone sees me, the better."

"No doubt about that," Layla snorted around a single burst of a laugh.

Brady scowled at her. "You're just jealous."

"Oh no, brother, I assure you, I am not that."

"Sure you are. Since we were kids, we've been training to become legit ninjas. You're seeing my awesome gear and wishing you were the one to look so kick-ass."

Hunt, who was crouched down petting Bobo, tipped his head in Brady's direction. "He's got a point there. I mean, he might look like a Halloween version of a ninja, but still, he's on point as far as how invisible he is compared to the rest of us."

Layla rolled her eyes. "Stop before he whips out the grease paint for his face. We don't need to be invisible. We're looking for listening devices installed by Joss's parents, not sneaking in for some high-stakes mission or some movie shit."

All mirth left me then. Griffin, possibly sensing the shift in me, stepped closer and arched a brow at me in question, as he so often did. Even in the semi-darkness, his concern was evident across his hooded face.

I shook my head. "It's nothing new. Just, I can't get over what they did. How long have they been listening to us? Has it only been since Brady's deal and they went all nuts on us? Or for longer?"

Hunt stood, dropping his hands to his sides, so Bobo rounded over to me again, standing by my legs. "The question that's really been irking me is *why* would they even want to listen in on us?

They already know we're drinking and partying—we don't hide that from them—so is it just to figure out if we're drugging and fucking?"

Guilty on both counts, though not in any dangerous way. We smoked some weed but didn't do any hard drugs. And the guys and Layla had sex more than I did. The couple of boyfriends I'd had over the years had paled in comparison to my guys. Eventually, I'd stopped making room for the mediocre in my life and, apparently, started fantasizing about Griffin—and the connection he and I could never share.

It was part of the unspoken crew code. None of us would ever go there with each other.

"I don't know, man," Griffin said. "No matter which way we turn it, what Monica and Reece are up to is all shades of messed up."

My scowl deepened. "No doubt. And I want to find out just how far they've gone. Like right the fuck now."

"I brought batteries," Layla piped up. "In case the flashlights in the treehouse are dead. We haven't used them in years."

"Good thinking," Hunt said, but I was already shaking my head.

"Seriously, what if they have fucking cameras in there? We'll give ourselves away."

"If they have cameras in there, they're gonna have us to worry about, not the other way around," Griffin practically snarled, Brady nodding along with his fierce tone. "I say we don't even bother with the flashlights. I googled shit, and the bugs can be really small, like under an inch. We've obviously never noticed one before, so we're gonna have to really look. We bank on them just listening, not watching, and we're quiet about it. Your parents were asleep when you left the house, right?" he asked me.

"Yeah. Everything was quiet."

"Okay, so we go in, don't say a word, and meet out here to talk about it when we're done."

"Should we maybe lay down some excuse for us being here in the middle of the night?" Layla asked. "Something like I couldn't sleep and just wanted to chill out, hit you guys up, and you had my back?"

"That's a good idea," Brady said. Layla and I stared at him for a second. That was more praise than he normally gave her.

"He says it like that's so odd," she muttered, but didn't otherwise engage.

Griffin shook his head. "No, we should skip it. When I was researching, I saw that some of them can be sound activated. Saves on whatever power the bugs are pulling on. Better to just go in there with as little noise as possible in case we trip them."

"Okay, then," I said. "We've got our plan. Now let's go. I can't stand another minute of not knowing how big of assholes my parents are."

"Look everywhere," Griffin added. "They can literally be almost anywhere. Turn over any ledge or space that could hide a fucking penny. People use radio frequency detectors to find them 'cause they can be so well hidden."

"We should get one of those," Hunt said. "I wanna check my house too."

"Already ordered," Griffin said. "It's on its way. But I didn't think we wanted to wait to get in there to tear the treehouse apart. I know I don't."

"Fuck no, I don't wanna wait," I said, then faced Bobo. "Stay. Keep guard out here, okay, boy? You hear anyone coming, you come let me know. No barking."

Bobo chuffed like he actually got all that straight. He was smart as a whip, if still a dog. Whatever of that he followed through on would be great. At the very least, he for sure knew what to do with the terms *stay*, *keep guard*, and *no barking*.

Griffin took my hand, tugging me toward the wooden steps that led up to the *treehouse*, though that was a slight misnomer. It sat under trees, not up in them, but we named it when we were too young to pay attention to the difference, and the moniker stuck.

Before he pushed open the door, Griffin met my eyes, seeming to search for something within them. Whatever it was, he found it, nodding with satisfaction before sweeping into the treehouse first, blocking the doorway for a few seconds until he verified no one else was there. Then he stepped aside and I entered, doing my best not to be irritated at his misplaced show of chivalry.

As the others streamed in behind us, Griffin flicked on the lights. I winced at the sudden brightness, pinching my eyes shut. Immediately after they adjusted, I stalked toward the folding chairs that surrounded a small table, carried one over to a juncture of wall and ceiling, and got to work searching.

An hour passed, during which I barely kept track of what the others were doing. I checked everywhere I could think of, finding nothing at all beyond evidence that we needed to dust regularly. I was in the process of sitting down on the chair I'd been mostly standing on, blowing errant strands of hair out of my face, when Layla tapped me on the shoulder. When I looked up, my attention fixed on the hella-pissed-off pinch of her face before traveling to her open palm. There, sitting atop it, was an electronic device smaller than any of her fingertips.

"What the fuck?" I mouthed, not letting the curse drop.

"I know," she responded, equally silently.

When Hunt stalked over, hand also outstretched, fury bubbled up inside me, making my pulse whoosh between my temples. Griffin squeezed my shoulders and gestured for us to head outside.

He closed up while the rest of us seethed in the middle of the clearing. The night sky was darker now that the moon had sunk beneath the surrounding hills, but not even the dim lighting could conceal the fact that my parents were POS.

Bobo pressed against my legs, surely sensing the shitstorm brewing inside me.

When Griffin joined us, he snapped out just one word: "Where?"

"Between one of the coffee table legs and the top," Layla said. "The one leg was almost flush with the top, but not quite. The fucking bug was wedged in that little, tiny gap."

We all looked at Hunt. "On the back of the weight rack, which we never move because it's heavy as shit."

Several seconds slunk by while we processed.

"Fuck!" Brady whisper-shouted.

"Yeah, no kidding," I muttered. "And to think my parents seem cookie-cutter boring."

"Bland as damn unsalted rice cakes, for fuck's sake," Layla added.

"We need to scan the place with the RF detector," Griffin said. "If these were that well hidden, who's to say we didn't miss some?"

"How many could they possibly need?" Layla asked.

"No idea," I said. "Across the board. I have no idea about anything anymore, I swear."

Hunt swung around to drape his free arm across my shoulders. "It's gonna be okay, Joss. We'll figure things out. It's us against them now."

"It's always been us against the world," Brady added.

I nodded, at a loss for words. I leaned my head against Hunt's arm in solidarity.

Griffin grabbed the device from Layla's hand, turning for Hunt's too. "I'm gonna go put them back more or less in the same area, so at least the sound will be what they're used to. Till we scour the place with the RF detector thing, we assume they're listening to every word."

"I don't know how I'm gonna pretend with them that I don't know something's wrong," I mumbled.

"Well, you're gonna have to, girl," Layla said.

"Lay's right," Griffin said. "Until we figure out how bad the situation is, we don't let on."

"At least we didn't find any cameras," Hunt added with a frown that told me he wasn't satisfied with that consolation prize either.

"Tell your parents you're sleeping over at my place tomorrow night," Layla offered. "At least then you'll get a break from them."

"Sounds good. Thanks." But it was a stupid thing to say. Having to escape my parents because they were traitorous, two-faced assholes did *not* sound good.

Griffin went back in to plant the bugs again, this time easy to find and remove, then rejoined us, eyes immediately on me and the way Bobo was basically attached to my legs.

"You okay?"

"Dandy," I said, my voice flat.

"We'd better get back before Mom notices we're gone," Brady said. "For all I know, she might have a tracker embedded somewhere on me. After this, and with how she's been acting, I swear I wouldn't be surprised."

Only he would be surprised, for sure he would. He'd be shocked to experience the kind of treachery I was feeling from the people I was supposed to be able to trust above all others.

"Yeah, let's get home," Layla said. "I'm not risking Mom going any more DEFCON on us if we don't have to." She glanced at me. "You sure you're gonna be okay?"

"Yeah, I'm sure." And I really was. I might have grown up in the quiet town of Ridgemore, but my friends and I had never been soft. We'd kept each other sharp from the beginning, as if we'd always known a moment like this would arrive to make it abundantly clear that we really were on our own. Even in Ridgemore, we were still pitted against a bunch of idiotic teenagers who were our peers, and now persistent journalists, among others. Life threw shit at you no matter how or where you lived, and your daily experience depended on how easily you wiped that shit off and moved on.

"All right. Night, guys," I said, eyes on Bobo instead of them, and walked away.

Without verbal agreement, the four of them followed until Bobo and I crossed through the mountain laurel enclosing my yard. And when I slipped through the sliding glass door back into my house, I caught glimpses of them between branches and leaves.

No matter what, we were crew, through and through. They had my back even when I didn't ask for their support, just as they knew I'd always have theirs.

11

The Biggest Ass in Ridgemore

My alarm went off long before I felt rested. I lay in bed through three snooze cycles, wondering if I could get away with skipping school again today. This time, I wouldn't even have to lie. I'd barely been able to sleep, what with my churning thoughts, which eventually manifested in my body.

After discovering the level of my parents' deceit, I suspected I'd never suffer guilt over a dishonesty again. I just couldn't get over what they'd done. Becoming overbearing and overprotective parents who were doing their damnedest to smother me? Okay, fine. After what happened with Brady, it was relatively understandable. But spying on me? I'd never be able to move past that, no matter what reason they might think they had for invading my privacy in such an egregious way. Their actions were beyond messed up.

But skipping today would make two skips in as many days of school. Plus, I wouldn't be able to guarantee the secretary in the front office wouldn't mention my absence yesterday afternoon. My parents were aware I played hooky, but there was no need to rub it in their faces and force them to address the issue. Besides, if

I stayed home, they would be here too, and the less time I spent with them, the better.

By the time I finished deliberating, I was running late and had to zip in and out of the shower, forgoing my usual funky braids for a pair of Princess Leia buns, denim cutoffs, an off-the-shoulder top, and my favorite Converse. After throwing some spare clothes and a toothbrush into my backpack, I skipped breakfast and ran out of the house calling over my shoulder, "Running late. Griffin's gonna be here to pick me up any second. See ya tomorrow—I'm spending the night at Layla's."

Just as I heard my mom begin to respond, I slammed the door behind me and jogged up our long driveway to put distance between us. For as much leeway as my parents gave me, it wasn't customary for me to announce I was going on a sleepover without at least seeming to ask their permission. It was always granted when it was Layla's house. Even so, it wasn't how things in the Bryson household were done.

I didn't give a single flying fuck.

The front door swung open behind me just as the growl of Clyde's engine rounded a bend in the drive. I picked up the pace.

When Griffin slid to a stop beside me, I jumped in, slapping the dashboard. "Go, go, go!"

Being the excellent friend he was, he looped around his Mustang Cobra II and roared back up the road before saying, "You do know Monica's chasing us, right?"

Dread curled into a pit in my stomach before I quickly remembered everything my parents had done. I kept my gaze trained forward. "She can chase all she wants. She's gonna have to do a lot more than that to get me to willingly spend time with her again."

The words registered as true, squeezing my lungs hard enough that I had to work to suck in my next breath. My parents and I had never been particularly close; I always preferred spending time with my friends. But it wasn't as if we didn't get along. We shared the occasional family board-game-and-movie night. Just the knowledge that they were there if I wanted them was sufficient. I didn't need them precisely because they were always in the background, just a call or a talk away.

That was all changing. My gut churned more ferociously, actually growling loudly.

Griffin chuckled. "I guess you skipped breakfast."

I gave a single laugh back, loving how I didn't have to be embarrassed with him. "Yeah, I didn't have time to grab anything to eat, but it's not that."

His eyes, more hazel than brown in the morning light, flicked between me and the road as he took the turn from my driveway toward Hunt's house.

"I just. . ." I sighed, letting my head drop back on the seat. "I can't get over what they did. How could they? How fucking *could they*, Griff?"

He shifted gears, then placed his hand on my thigh. Instantly my skin heated to scorching levels, making me wonder how on earth I was going to keep my recent reactions to him under wraps.

This morning, his dark hair was messy, as if he'd already been running his fingers through it, which he did whenever he became agitated. He wore shorts that hit past his knee, a t-shirt with the *Thrasher* logo emblazoned across it, and his favorite black Vans.

He was what I wanted for breakfast, lunch, and dinner—plus snacks too.

I am so screwed.

He licked his full lips, though there was no way he could be picking up on the direction of my thoughts. I had those locked down tighter than a dolphin's butthole.

Brushing his thumb across my thigh, he kept his eyes on the road. "I don't know why they did what they did. I've turned the question over in my head a million times, I swear, but I've still got no good answer. It can't be that they're just that nosy about what we're up to, I don't think. But in the end, that's all I come up with."

When he removed his hand to take the turn onto Hunt's driveway, I felt the absence of his touch as if he'd branded me.

So fucking screwed.

"Hey, guys," Hunt said as he slid onto the back seat and I claimed shotgun once more. "Any news?"

I snorted as Griffin took off toward the Raffertys'. "You mean beyond the fact that my parents are monster fuckwads?"

"Yeah, beyond that. I already knew that bit."

I chuckled despite myself. "Nope. Nothing new." I glanced at Griffin. "That RF detector still coming today?"

"Yep. I tracked it already. It'll be here by end of day."

"Good. I need answers." I stared forward, vaguely registering tree after tree whipping by.

"Not sure we're gonna get them just by finding more listening devices," Hunt warned.

"Yeah, I know." I sighed. "I ran from my house this morning so I wouldn't have to see them, and I'll spend the night with Layla tonight, but I won't be able to keep that up for long before they figure out something's up."

"Which it is," Griffin said.

"Which it very much fucking is, but when they confront me about it, I want to be armed to the teeth with information to throw back at them."

The guys nodded before we lost ourselves to our own thoughts for a couple of minutes until Griffin turned the car onto the approach to the Rafferty house.

It was as large as mine. What secrets might their home be hiding?

Hunt leaned between the front seats, draping an arm across my seat back. "I hope Brady didn't have another dream last night. They're really getting to him."

"Yeah, they are," Griffin grunted, his lips tugging downward.

"I hate that we can't do anything to help him with them." I sighed again. "It sucks."

"It totally sucks," Hunt said. "Plus, not sure if we're helping things by asking him about them anymore. You see how upset he's been getting, saying he can't get over all the shit trauma if we don't leave things be."

I swiveled in my seat, meeting Hunt's eyes, brighter than usual in the filtering sun rays, which made them as rich and smooth as dark chocolate. "But we also can't leave him to deal with this on his own."

He groaned. "I know."

"Even if we're annoying him by asking all the time, that's gotta be better than thinking we don't care." I paused. "Right?" I wasn't used to not knowing what to do when it came to my crew. Yes, there'd been some bumpy bits of road along the way, but nothing like this, nothing we couldn't handle with a few talks, and if that didn't work, some fierce sparring when words weren't enough.

"He knows we care," Griffin answered softly.

Even though he was talking about Brady and not me, something about the way he said it made a tingle sweep across my shoulders and down my spine. Griffin was rarely soft, but his words felt like a caress against my naked skin.

I shook myself free of my stupid, wishful thoughts. It wouldn't get me anywhere except into the type of trouble I could never risk. Not when the fallout could mean losing the four friends who meant everything in the world to me. That wasn't an option; it never would be.

"I guess we just let Brady lead the way?" I suggested, knowing full well not one of us was the kind of person to pussyfoot around any subject of importance.

As if reading my mind, Hunt snorted. "Yeah, right. I'm betting Layla brings it up before we get to school."

"And if not her, you." Griffin pinned his gaze on me for a few seconds before drawing Clyde to a stop in front of the Rafferty house.

I scoffed, pretending to be offended. "As if the two of you don't blurt things out too. You're worse than Layla or me."

They knew I was full of shit as much as I did. I chuckled . . . until Brady stormed out of the house, his face thunderous, pulling the front door shut hard behind him even though Layla was trailing him.

"Aw hell," Hunt muttered.

Griffin ducked to better take in the siblings through the passenger window. "Looks like it."

Brady stomped around the hood so he could squeeze into the empty seat behind Griffin. And though I knew Hunt hated the middle seat thanks to his long legs, he silently scooted to the middle, leaving the open window seat for Layla. We knew from experience, when the twins were like this, they needed a buffer until whatever it was finally blew over.

Layla sat roughly, scarcely waiting until I was back in my seat before stretching around me to slam the door.

"Yo," Griffin scolded. "Clyde ain't done nothing to you."

Layla scowled, not offering a retort, which on its own spoke volumes. The girl always had something to say, whether we were in the mood to hear it or not. When I turned to study her, I caught her caressing the door, as if she were silently apologizing to the car. Given how hard we'd all fallen for the Mustangs, it was entirely possible.

As Griffin drove, the silence was loud in the car. When no one spoke for long enough that the silence was making me want to crawl out of my skin, I said, "Okay, so what the hell's going on with the two of you now?"

"It's nothing," Layla said, and before she'd even finished spitting out the words, Brady snorted obnoxiously.

She spun on him, glaring at him across Hunt's lap. "What? You got something to say, Brady?"

When Brady just rolled his eyes and turned his back to her, suddenly intent on staring out the window, she chuckled darkly. "It *is* nothing. I didn't do it on purpose, for fuck's sake."

He whirled on her so quickly that Hunt plastered his back to the seat, not willing to get between them. "That's no excuse. You can't be careless as fuck and then say, 'Oh, oopsy motherfucking daisy.'" He went over the top in mimicking the higher pitch of her voice, likely intending to annoy her, and let out a feminine laugh that was so grating even I felt like smacking him, and I had no idea whether he deserved it or not.

"You told Mom about my nightmares," he accused.

"Oh, shit," Hunt muttered.

"Okay, yeah, I did," she snapped. "But how was I supposed to know she was lurking around the corner like that? It was sus as fuck! I was just trying to be a loving sister, *asshole*. Fuck me for caring about you and what's going on with you."

A legit growl rumbled from Brady's chest. "Mom's gonna be breathing down my neck like a damn dragon. I'll never shake her loose now." He glared at Layla. "Thanks to you."

She tossed her hands in the air, then roughly shoved her back-pack down between her feet. "Seriously, Brade, you've been a bigger pain in my ass than usual since your resurrection. I'll never stop being glad you're back and that you're okay, but you've gotta stop being such a raging dick already. I can't take much more of this."

"So it's all about you. What's new?"

Layla's nostrils flared as she gritted her jaw. She might be smaller than Brady, but she held her own in ferocity. "You know what? *Fuck you.* Fuck. You. I'm done. I'm so fucking done."

Then she turned her head and stared out the window, refusing to look at her brother.

Brady opened his mouth, seemed to reconsider, then shut it, folding his arms stiffly across his broad chest and looking out his own window again.

"Well . . . this is fun," Hunt said.

Brady grunted.

After Griffin ate up much of the distance between us and school, I finally spoke again. "I'm not gonna try to talk you two out of being pissed at each other. That's just a waste of air and I know it. You'll be mad till you don't feel like being mad anymore. But shit's gotten real lately, and the rest of us need to know what's going on."

Neither Brady nor Layla reacted. From between them, Hunt rolled his eyes at the somewhat familiar scene. Since Brady's accident, the two had been bickering even more than usual.

"She's right," Griffin said, checking out the siblings in the rearview mirror. "Until we figure out what's going on with Joss's parents, we've all gotta be playing with a full deck."

"This has got nothing to do with Joss's parents," Brady answered, anger still riding his words, though less so.

Griffin arched a brow at him in the mirror. "Even so, you're our friends. Tell us what's going on."

I waited, wondering if Griffin would add a *please* to the end of his request.

"Fine." Brady kept his arms crossed but faced us. "Layla couldn't keep her fat trap shut, as usual—"

"Hey, fucktard—" she interjected.

Brady shot eye daggers at her. "Go ahead, deny it."

She turned away from him again. "Whatever."

Satisfied, Brady harrumphed. "So Layla asks me if I've had any more nightmares, and when I tell her that yeah, I did, she asks if they were about the lab again. Mom flies around the corner, freaking out, asking about the nightmares. She made me describe everything. She even took notes. Fucking *notes*, guys. She's lost it. She's probably on the phone making me an appointment with some shrink right the hell now." His eyes drifted to his sister. "All thanks to Layla's big mouth."

Layla shook her head hard enough to dislodge some of her hair from the little clips pulling it back from her face. "Dude, all this shit's *not* on me, and you know it. Stop blaming me for our mother being crazy. We need to put a cowbell on her or something. She's legit spying on us, I swear."

I froze. "Like for real, you think she's spying on you?"

"No, not for real." Layla huffed, but she didn't sound entirely convinced. "She's just still really upset about Brady dying, that's all." I was pretty sure none of us missed the uncertainty in her statement. "She'll get over it. We've just gotta give her time." She glared at Brady again. "And it'd really help things if my brother weren't the biggest ass in Ridgemore."

He chuckled. "At least I don't *have* the biggest ass in Ridgemore."

She reached across Hunt to slap Brady, but even while the smack was still ringing, she started laughing. "Dude, you're fucking ridiculous. I have a tight, perky little ass and you know it."

For a beat, I thought Brady would grimace and insult her, but then he laughed too. And just like that, the fight was over.

Griffin, Hunt, and I sighed in relief. That is, until Griffin slowed to turn into the school entrance, passing a handful of reporters who stared into our windows, camera shutters snapping, video rolling.

I expected another tirade from Brady, but he just exhaled heavily in resignation.

"I thought they'd be over it by now," Layla commented, expressing everyone's thoughts. "How long can Kitty Blanche keep this up? There've gotta be more important stories out there than my smelly brother."

But from the bulldog determination on Kitty's brightly made-up face, that wasn't the case. She actually had the balls to grin at us and wave as we passed, as if to say, *Gotcha, motherfuckers.*

"She's creepy," I muttered.

"One hundred percent," Layla agreed. "She's probably got a collection of dudes tied up in her basement or some shit."

I shivered at the thought. "No, not creepy like that. Creepy like *I will chase you down forever.*" But I couldn't really be sure. Her interest in Brady didn't feel normal.

At least Ridgemore High's principal, Mr. Thompson, didn't allow them on school property—he'd already called the cops on them twice when they sneaked in—so we got to leave at least that part of Brady's torment behind.

Griffin pulled Clyde to a stop next to Bonnie. No one had taken the open spots on either side of the Shelby, as if out of respect for us. Or maybe they were just worried we'd beat the shit out of them if they were to so much as accidentally ding a door. We'd never actually do that, not for that reason anyway, but it was better to have our peers operating under such a misconception. Worked out better for us in the end. People tended to stay out of our way.

However, as soon as we hit the walkway toward the lockers, it became obvious that not everyone who should stay clear was smart enough to do so.

"Hey, look," Rich Connely called out, loudly enough that the football players and cheerleaders milling around him would hear. "It's the Miracle Kid."

"Brady, don't," I implored, reaching for his arm. But Brady wasn't doing a thing to dampen his usual speed, despite his mom's pleas. Layla, Griffin, and Hunt lunged for him too, but Brady beat us to the bratty prick who apparently hadn't learned his lesson.

Rich's eyes widened as he seemed to register what was about to happen, but before anyone could interfere, Brady punched him square in the jaw, knocking him out in one strike.

Pike Bills was the first to pull out of our shared shock, whistling, then laughing and clapping. "KO'd. Wow, man, you don't mess around."

But Brady was already striding down the hall, forgoing his locker entirely and heading toward class.

I exhaled loudly, blowing a few loose strands of hair out of my face. Today was going to be a long day. The four of us trailed after Brady, ignoring the cheerleaders racing off to get the school nurse, who would undoubtedly involve the principal.

Brady had to know he'd get into trouble. But the relaxed tilt of his shoulders and his smooth gait told anyone who was paying attention that he didn't care. He had bigger problems.

So did the rest of us.

12

Dinnertime Isn't Fishing Time

Celia Rafferty slammed the bowl of caramelized brussels sprouts onto the table between her and Brady hard enough to rattle the serving spoon against the glass vessel. Not for the first time since I sat down with the Raffertys for dinner, I wondered if I would have been better off dealing with my parents and their duplicity instead.

"What?" Celia asked, though nobody had uttered a word. Even Porter seemed cowed by her anger, sitting at the opposite end of the table from her, far quieter than usual.

"Jeez, Mom," Brady said, "I didn't do or say a fucking thing. Chill out."

Layla sighed from the chair beside me, anticipating their mom's reaction. I would have too, except that she'd sat me between her and Celia, and I didn't want to do a thing to draw Celia's attention.

Celia pointed at Brady, scowling. "You watch your mouth. This is a family dinner. I don't want to hear any of your crass language tonight."

"Fine," he relented. "But do you have to be so intense right now?"

Celia leaned forward in her chair, drawing closer to her son. "Yes, I do. You know why? Because my son was suspended from school today for a violent act on another student."

Brady glanced at the brussels sprouts and then back to his mom.

Again, she jabbed the air between them. "Don't even start with me today. You're a growing young man and you need your vegetables. You will eat them."

Brady huffed under his breath and frowned, but picked up the serving spoon, dishing out the smallest serving possible onto his plate.

"You're not a damn bird, Brady."

Dutifully, he scooped out another mini serving. Celia sighed in resignation while plastering a martyred look across her ordinarily pleasant face. Though all the Raffertys were good-looking, the twins didn't resemble either of their parents, who had sharper features, darker hair, and lighter eyes. Celia was petite, shorter even than Layla, with a slight frame, while Porter was tall and thin to the point of being almost gangly. Both wore glasses while their children had perfect eyesight.

"You know," Brady started, already pushing the sprouts around his plate, "it's not like I just went up to the jerk and punched him for no reason. You haven't even asked me what he said."

Celia bristled. "No, I didn't, because you already told me you *hit* a boy because of something he said. Because of *words*. How many times have I told you that fighting is only for defense? You are *not* to harm others under any circumstances. That's the only reason I agreed to that ridiculous amount of training you all do."

This time, Celia cast her gaze across me too. That was one of the downsides of being so familiar with my friends' parents: they didn't hold back on my account.

She continued, "I would have never agreed to all the equipment you made us buy."

Seriously?" Brady asked, his gray eyes flashing. "You do realize this is the same asshole who got me killed, right?"

"From what you've told us, it was an altercation that led to an accident. It was no one's fault." She paused. "Is that not true?"

Brady pressed his lips together and clenched his fork with a white-knuckled grip. "Yeah, that's right. But if he'd just back the hell off from Layla already, I wouldn't have to keep putting him in his place."

"Wait, what are you talking about?" Celia glanced at Porter, who shook his head, affirming he didn't know either.

Brady huffed. "I told you already. Rich keeps bugging Layla. I was teaching him a lesson about the meaning of the word *no*."

As one, Celia and Porter whipped their heads around to stare at their daughter. Celia brought her hand to her chest. "Oh my God, honey, you didn't tell us this. Did he. . .?"

"No, Mom," Layla said, flicking a glare at Brady. "Brade's not talking rape or anything remotely like that. Rich is just annoying, is all. He keeps asking me out. I keep saying *no*." She shrugged, though I knew for a fact Rich's interest in her wasn't as simple as that. No, he hadn't forced himself on her, but he also wasn't respectful of her boundaries. I wouldn't trust him to do the right thing if Layla were too drunk to stand up for herself around him.

Celia's eyes glistened for a few moments before she blinked away the moisture. "You two don't tell me anything anymore. I'll bet Joss talks to *her* parents."

I smiled noncommittally and served myself some glazed baby carrots. "This looks delicious. Thanks for having me over."

"You're welcome anytime, sweetie, you know that." Celia's smile seemed genuine before it dropped from her face like a ton of bricks as she glowered at both of her children.

"Look, you two need to keep the line of communication open between us. We can't properly protect you if you don't tell us what's going on."

"We don't need your protection," Layla said.

"Yeah," Brady added. "Besides, I'm watching out for Layla."

After sliding a piece of grilled lemon chicken breast onto her plate, Layla said, "I'm plenty capable of looking out for myself. If Rich forgets his place, I've got no problem kneeing him in the balls."

Celia shook her head. "Layla, you too with the language. But yes, if any man doesn't respect you and your body, you scream for help and knee him in the groin. That's good."

Layla rolled her eyes. She might be the girlier of the two of us, but she was no screamer. She was more likely to slam a cinder block over a guy's head than cry for help.

Celia visibly released the tension in her shoulders, smiling tentatively at her son. "You see what happens when you fight with that boy? You can't antagonize him. We can't. . ." She bit her lip before releasing it. "You've gotta take care of yourself. You have to stay safe."

"I *am* safe, Ma. I promise. And I didn't do anything to antagonize Rich. He called me the 'Miracle Kid.' I punched him. End of story."

Her brows arched in disbelief, exchanging a glance with her husband. "So I'm supposed to believe you punched a boy in the face so hard that you left him unconscious and got suspended from school for three days, all because he called you by one of your nicknames?"

Brady released his fork with a loud chink against his plate. "'Miracle Kid' is *not* one of my nicknames. I hate it. I don't ever want to hear it again."

"Why, Brady? Tell me why?"

"Nothing. Never mind." He snatched a bread roll and took a bite so large that he couldn't speak around it.

Celia stared at him while he made a show of chewing. At least he did so with his mouth closed, which wasn't always a guarantee with the brute.

Finally, she sat back and took a long sip of her wine, eyeing her children and me over the rim of her glass. "Have you had any more of those nightmares?"

"Come on, Mom," Brady whined. "Leave it be already. They're just dreams. I don't wanna talk about it anymore."

"If you won't willingly tell me, then I'm going to ask. You're my son. I have to know what's going on with you, especially after. . ."

"After what, huh? Why won't you just say it and be done with it already?"

"Fine. After you *died*. You died, Brady. You can't possibly expect that not to affect your parents who love you."

"She's right about that, son," Porter said, earning a sharp look from his wife across the table at the possible implication that she wasn't right about the other points too.

"I didn't mean it that way, honey," he said.

She scowled at him, then met Brady's gaze again, this time clasping his hand. "We love you. You're our baby, and don't go rolling your eyes at me. It doesn't matter how big you get, you'll always be my baby."

"Mom," Layla protested.

"You too, Layla." Celia paused. "We're just worried about you, that's all. Second day of school and you're already punching kids and getting suspended. That doesn't sound like you at all."

Layla and I exchanged a quick look. That actually didn't sound too unlike Brady. Yes, his temper was quicker to flare lately and slower to cool, but he'd always been the most explosive among us, the easiest to provoke.

"Tell me about these dreams, honey," Celia implored. "Have you had any more of them?"

He withdrew his hand from hers and crossed his arms. "You mean since this morning? I haven't even slept again since you *took notes* about my last dreams."

"Okay, fair enough. But I want to know everything that's going on with you, okay? If you have any more of those kinds of dreams, I want you to tell me right away so I can help you with them."

Brady shot Layla a look across the table that could kill. At least she had the grace to offer him an apologetic twist of her mouth.

"Fine, yeah," he finally said. "So, can we eat now? 'Cause I don't feel like talking about this stuff. So if you're gonna keep at it, I might just skip dinner."

Celia stared back at him in a standoff. Daily family dinners at the Rafferty house were inviolable, and Brady damn well knew that.

After several tense moments, his mom relented. "No, we don't need to talk about this anymore . . . for now. Let's just eat. The food's getting cold. Honey," she said, looking at Porter while she accepted the serving dish of chicken from me, "why don't you tell the kids what we were working on today?"

When Porter began speaking about cellular regeneration, I zoned out, relieved that at last the tension was leaving the dinner conversation.

Our parents were scientists. They'd met at their previous company, where they'd worked in the same research department. Whenever they were together, they often geeked out, throwing around tons of science-y terms. While my friends and I were bright enough to understand what they were talking about, at least in general terms, there was little that got us to glaze over faster. They were such nerds.

The rest of dinner passed in amiable, if superficial, conversation. By the time I licked the last remnants of chocolate mousse from my spoon, I was beyond ready to disappear into the privacy of Layla's room for a long while. But as I put my dirty dishes in the sink, as was common practice in the Rafferty home, and turned to follow Layla from the kitchen, Celia called my name.

"Yeah?" I asked.

"Help me load the dishwasher, will you?"

I glanced at Layla.

"Mom, we've got homework to do," she said.

We did, but that wasn't her priority any more than it was mine.

"Then you go get started on it and Joss'll be right along."

Layla glanced from me to her mom and back.

Celia shooed her daughter with both hands, *tsk*ing. "Go. You're being ridiculous. Joss will be right behind you."

Layla's eyes broadcast a definite *sorry* before she left me in the kitchen alone with Celia.

"You want me to load, or rinse and pass?" I asked.

She waved a hand in the air between us. "Oh, don't worry about that. I'll do it. You just keep me company."

"Oh-kay."

Celia pulled on long kitchen gloves while she waited for the water at the sink to heat. As soon as she started wiping food remains off dishes, she said, "So how've you been?"

"Uh, fine?" I leaned against the counter beside her.

"Everything going well with school?"

"Yeah, so far." We'd skipped half our first school day and Brady had gotten suspended at the start of the second.

"And how are Monica and Reece doing? I haven't had the chance to visit with them lately."

That was definitely bullshit. Yeah, they might not have hung out in person, but I knew our parents had an active group chat that chirped at all hours. She was certain to know more about them than I did, especially since it turned out they were freaking liars.

But if Celia wanted to play some kind of game, that's what I'd do. "They seem okay. Maybe a little worried about Brady still, that kind of thing. But I think they're finally getting used to working out of the house instead of going in to the office."

"Oh, good." She started rinsing and loading silverware. "It took Porter a while to get used to being home all the time too. But I love it. No more rushing around in the mornings, no more not being here for when my kids need me. It's the best."

"Uh-huh," I murmured noncommittally, wondering what she actually wanted with me. Celia and I had always been friendly. Before Brady's accident, she hadn't been quite this much of a nut, and she was usually pleasant enough to be around.

When we were younger, she always had the best snacks. On the weekends in the summertime, she sometimes made ice cream that would give Ben and Jerry a run for their money. She would add real candy bar crumbles along with gooey caramel ribbons. Of all the parents, she seemed to be the only one interested in homemaking. If my mom could get away with takeout seven days a week, she'd do it. I'd even recently overheard her talking to my dad about maybe hiring a chef to come in and prepare meals for the family a few times a week.

"Speaking of my kids needing me. . ." Celia said in the least subtle segue ever. "I'm really worried about Brady—about both of them, actually. After Brady's accident, he shut me out, and I think Layla's trying to stick up for him, keeping whatever he says private. You know how they are. They go at it like cats and dogs, but when it comes down to it, they love each other."

She scrubbed at a skillet with unnecessary vigor, swirling a pad of steel wool around like it was the solution to all of life's problems. "But what they seem to forget is that I'm on their side. I need to be able to help them, you know?" She glanced at me quickly, then returned her attention to the pan she was trying to scrub into an early demise.

"What happened to Brady, well, it was really hard on me and Porter. And I know Brady's going through so much with it, and it's just really important to me to be able to help him. He's my baby." She chuckled softly. "Even if he is already like twice my size. I can't stand to see him hurting and not be able to do something to soothe him. But he sees me as just his *mom* and forgets I'm actually well known in the professional ambits for my studies on the mind and its behavior. I don't want to be tooting my own horn here, but I'm considered foremost in the field of brain activity, including the aspects of memories and dreams."

Another glance at me before picking up the next pan and going at it just as hard, her forearm muscles clenching from her frenzied movements. "I can see that Brady's hurting. He might not admit to it, but I see it. I'm his *mother*. I can always tell when either of my babies is going through something, even if I don't always know what it is. It's not like him to lash out at that boy just for calling him some nickname, and it's definitely not like him to have nightmares."

While continuing to make her way through the dishes, Celia asked in an over-the-top nonchalant tone that set off my internal alarm, "Do you know when he started having the bad dreams? Was it only after the accident?"

When she glanced at me, I plastered a fake smile on my face. "I think so, but I'm not really sure, sorry. Brady hasn't really wanted to talk about the dreams much. He actually gets really pissed about it if we ask, so we pretty much just let him be."

"Ah-ha, ah-ha. So he only started mentioning them to you guys after the accident?"

"It seems like it, yeah." I needed to extricate myself from what was clearly an interrogation, no matter how she dressed it up.

"You're a good friend to him. I've always been so glad all of you guys are so close. I know it means the world to both Brady and Layla." Celia flicked another glance at me that worked too hard to appear relaxed. "So did he not mention anything about the dreams or that odd lab he's been seeing in them before what happened that night of the party, then?"

"Really, Celia, I don't know. Maybe you should just tell him yourself that you can help him."

She scoffed. "You see how that goes over. He immediately shuts me down. But that only lets me see just how much he actually needs my help." She grimaced, circling around a spot on a spatula that already gleamed from what I could see. "He's as stubborn as his dad, that's what. They both love to think they have everything figured out, but I know things—"

Trying to soften what I was going to say, I rested my fingers on her scrubbing arm, stilling it. "Look, Celia, you know I care about Brady and Layla. I obviously want Brady to recover fully from his ordeal, and I'll do anything I can to help him get to the other side of it. But I can't help you with the information you're trying to get."

"Oh, I'm not trying to get information from you," she let loose with a nervous trill. "I was just chatting with you, is all. I think about my kids and their wellbeing all the time, that's it."

Sure it is, Celia.

I smiled, hoping it came off as genuine, though this little conversation was making me jumpier than a damn frog. "I know. I understand. It's been tough for everyone, what happened to Brady. I'm sure it's been awful for you and Porter."

She turned to rest against the sink, dislodging my arm with a sad smile of her own, pulling off her gloves. "No parent should ever have to go through that. As long as I live, I don't think I'll ever recover from the fright of thinking I'd lost him."

This time my expression was filled with true empathy. Since Brady's resurrection, she might have turned into the kind of overbearing mother who made her kids want to run in the opposite direction, but I'd witnessed her heartbreak at the hospital before the surgeon came out to deliver the good news. She hadn't been putting on a show then.

"We'll all get through this," I offered. "We just have to be patient and give it time, with Brady especially."

She nodded, eyes unfocused, seeming far away for a few beats before she looked back at me. "You're a good egg, you know that?" Then she drew me into a hug that I returned awkwardly.

Holding me at arm's length, she added, "And if you hear anything more about my Brady's dreams and what he's dreaming about, you let me know, okay? I'll do whatever is in my power to help him."

"You got it," I said, slipping out of her hold. The moment I hit the hallway out of her sight, I practically ran for Layla's room. I rushed in, shutting the door behind me and leaning against it.

"Oh, fuck," Layla muttered. She set her phone down and sat up on her bed. "What'd she do?"

She stood and I inched close enough to whisper directly into her ear. Until we were able to check for bugs in our bedrooms, I was assuming the worst. "In a nutshell? She was fishing about Brady's dreams, trying to get me to rat on him, tell her everything, and now she wants me to report to her about anything I hear about his dreams, about the lab especially."

"You're kidding."

"Nope. You guys were right, she's lost her damn noodle."

Layla sank onto the bed, looking up at me through long, shaggy bangs, and whispered, "What the fuck are we gonna do, Joss? I can't even with all of them right now. . ."

I sat beside her. "We're gonna sneak out again tonight with Griffin's RF detector, that's what. It's time *we* start getting information of our own."

13

Bitches Beware

Layla laid down a little rubber as Bonnie rocketed up her driveway in a flash of shiny blue, shifting through several gears before we reached the turn onto the quiet residential street that served only our families.

"I can't believe he gets to sleep in. How's that punishment for punching out Rich, huh?" she asked with a pinched brow. "Suspension shouldn't be time *off* from school. He should have to go in extra days, like on weekends, or maybe over fall break. He'd love that."

She took the turn toward the larger Periwinkle Hill neighborhood that would eventually lead us out in the direction of Ridgemore High. Hunt was riding with Griffin.

"I'm thinking *I* should punch someone too," Layla went on. "I could do with some R and R."

I chuckled and stretched out my legs. "Dude, school only just started. You'd better not be tired of it already. We've still got a long haul ahead of us."

She glanced at me, driving too fast through the residential area. At least no kids were outside playing at this hour. "I can*not* wait to be done with school. I thought I'd be fine with it. Senior year's supposed to be fun and all that, right? That's what everyone says. You're still at school but you get to party and have fun for most of it. But I tell ya, Joss, I can't take school right now on top of everything else. There's too much crap going on."

"I know. Trust me, I'm feeling ya hard on this. But you're probably only saying that 'cause we got shit for sleep last night." As planned, we'd sneaked out again to check the treehouse for bugs, this time with the radio-frequency detector. The place was clear except for the two devices we'd already found. Brady was going to take advantage of his time at home to scan his room and Layla's—after he finally woke up, of course.

Layla frowned, whisked her bangs out of her eyes, and shifted through a hard turn out onto the main road. "Not gonna lie, I get cranky when I don't get my beauty sleep."

I chuckled. "As if you need beauty sleep. You're gorgeous, my friend, sleep or not."

She laughed, already sounding lighter. "Yeah, I really fucking am. And so are you."

I nodded absently, not needing the compliment. I'd only said what I had to shift her mood—not that Layla was conceited, but who didn't like to be told they were beautiful?

"Just wish Rich would back off already," she added as if half to herself.

I turned in my seat to face her. "How bad is it really? Tell me."

She shrugged, a sure sign she was about to underplay the situation. "It's nothing I can't handle."

"But you shouldn't have to handle anything—that's the whole point. He should take *no* for an answer and back away with his tail between his legs like a good boy."

Layla snorted. "Yeah, doubt that's ever gonna happen. After all the times I've shot him down, pretty sure he's not gonna get the message." After a heavy sigh, she added, "If he didn't back off after what happened with Brady, I don't think he ever will."

"You'd think that would shake him out of his delusions. . ."

"You'd think."

"So how bad is it? You haven't seen him since the Fischer House party, right? Other than yesterday, I mean, for the point three seconds before Brady punched him out."

She was quiet, eyes suddenly glued to the winding stretch of road ahead of us.

"Lay?"

Finally, she sighed, her shoulders rounding as she leaned forward, nearly wrapping herself around the steering wheel. "He's been texting me."

"What the fuck? You haven't blocked his ass?"

"Of course I've blocked his ass. But he just keeps getting new numbers and doing it again. Obvi, it doesn't take long for me to figure out who it's from, and then I block him. But then he just comes at me again that way, saying shit like, 'Hi, babe. Just want you to know I'm thinking about you.'" She shuddered. "As if *that's* fucking reassuring. . ."

"So then you need to change your number."

Another sigh. "Yeah, I know. It's just a royal pain. I'd have to let all my contacts know, and I keep thinking he's going to get over doing this stupid shit already." She flicked a glance at me. "He doesn't even get anything out of it. I don't answer after I figure out it's him."

"What else?"

"What else, what?" Her attention was back firmly on the road, and I'd bet she was already regretting getting into Rich's behavior.

"Don't give me that shit. I *know* you. Don't forget that. Just spit it out already."

She huffed, her fingers twitching around the wheel. "He sends me stuff, you know, in the mail."

A chill ran down my body despite the warm air blasting in through the open windows. "What kind of stuff?"

"Oh, you know, stupid shit. Dumbass poems that rhyme with every single line. Supposedly romantic notes where he's like, 'Will you go out with me?' He even asked me to be his 'valentine.' He sent chocolates once, which I tossed straight in the garbage. No way am I gonna put anything in my mouth he sends me. For all I know, he might roofie me even though I'm in my own house. Once he sent an envelope full of rose petals, that kind of thing. I also got a bath bomb that stank like total artificial perfume, like he actually sprayed the shit on or something. It was totally gross. Smelled like Mrs. Faulkner."

"Eww." Mrs. Faulkner was our chemistry teacher. I'd long suspected she was flammable considering how much perfume and hairspray she wore to class.

"You never respond?" I asked.

"Nope, never. He doesn't even sign the shit."

"Does he sign the texts on your phone?"

"No, not there either."

"So it might not be him. I mean, there's at least a chance it's someone else, right?"

A snort from Layla. "Yeah, right. Ridgemore's too small to have two stalker assholes after *moi*. I know I'm hot shit and all, but come on, it's gotta be him."

"And Brady doesn't know?"

"Hell no, he doesn't know. You saw what he did just 'cause Rich was trying to talk to me at some party. I think that's why I never get flowers or anything big like that. Nothing that'll draw too much attention. Small letters, and even when I got the chocolates, it was one of those mini boxes."

"What about Griffin and Hunt—do they know?"

"No, no one else does, and that's how I wanna keep it, Joss— I mean it."

"You're gonna have to tell them eventually, you do know that, right? We don't keep shit like this from each other."

"Yeah, I know. But now's not the time. There's too much going on with Brady and now your parents. We don't need to add Rich to that list. He's a raging asswad, but he's harmless. I mean, more or less. I sure as shit don't trust him enough to be alone with him. Dude's got potential entitled rapist written all over him." Her laugh was too high-pitched, nothing like her usual chuckle.

I narrowed my eyes at her, trying to get inside her head. "You think he'd do that?"

She shrugged. "No, not really, or I def would've told you and the guys sooner. Still, I ain't about to be stupid about it either. All his little 'harmless flirtations'"—she did air quotes against the steering wheel—"have put me on notice that he thinks about me *way* too much given that I've never encouraged him, not for a second. Well, maybe that one time when we were in, what was it, fifth grade? And I let him kiss my cheek. We slow danced holding each other the full length of our arms apart." She laughed, this time sounding like herself. "You remember that?"

I grinned at the memory despite the somber tone that preceded it. "We thought we were being *so* daring. I'm pretty sure I held on to Duncan Mills's shirt like it was a smelly sock."

Layla glanced at me, waggling her brows. "Hot stuff there, Joss."

I laughed, allowing my thoughts to drift to simpler times, even for a few moments. "So how long's Rich been at the gifts and texts?"

"Oh, not long, really. I def would've told you guys by now, but it's only been since Brady's accident."

"Wait," I said. My phone buzzed with an incoming text, and I reached for my bag at my feet. "That's only been a few weeks. How often are you getting these things in the mail, then?"

Her smile remained, but her fingers tightened around the steering wheel ever so slightly. "Every few days or so."

"Lay. . ."

"I know, I know. I should've told you all."

"Yeah, you should've." I brought my head back against the seat rest. "*Fuck*. What a creepoid!"

"He's too rich for his own good. He thinks he can have whatever he wants."

"Well, he can't have you."

"No shit. He can never have me." She flicked another look at me as we neared the high school. "Don't worry. It's not a big deal."

"You know it is."

"Okay, yeah, it is. It gets under my skin each time I get something from him. But given what happened to Brady, I can't complain. We're all alive. We're fine."

"Um, that does *not* become your new benchmark of okayness. What happened to Brady was awful, of course it was, but that doesn't diminish whatever's going on with you. Now I'm extra glad Brady punched Rich in the face yesterday."

Layla giggled. "Me too. Gotta admit, I was wishing I'd been the one to do it."

"There's still time." I checked my phone before tossing it back into my bag.

"What? Who is it?"

"Oh, just my mom again."

Layla looked at me. "She's *still* going on about how you left yesterday morning without saying a proper goodbye?"

I'd received ten messages from my mom yesterday. At first they were scolding. I should have waited for her to say goodbye. I should have asked for permission to spend the night instead of just assuming I could. That wasn't how our family did things, yada yada. But when my responses had been terse, she'd adjusted her tone, telling me she loved me and just wanted to spend more time with me. This was the first text of the day. I hoped it would also be the last.

"She's wishing me a wonderful day at school."

Layla rolled her eyes. "Oh em gee, she's two steps away from becoming my mom."

"Sorry to tell you this, but even though my mom's a liar and possibly a motherfucking *spy*, your mom still takes the cake. She's ready to sprout wings so she can follow Brady around wherever he goes. She'd go to the bathroom with him if he let her, I think."

Layla's face screwed up in disgust. "I think she really would. That's disgusting. Brady takes the smelliest shits. Thank God I have my own bathroom or I'd need a hazmat suit."

"Speaking of your brother. . ." I said as Layla slowed Bonnie to a crawl before turning into our school, glaring at every single reporter waiting for Brady at the entrance.

"Kitty's not here," I noted. "It's like she knows he's not at school. That's nuts."

A couple of cars piled up behind us before Layla and I gave the vultures a final death glare and she sped up. My middle fingers were itchy with the need to point at them. But after the news team got a few shots of Brady and Griffin flipping them off, which they shared in their online newsfeed, we held back.

Sitting back in her seat, Layla shook her head. "She obviously knows he got suspended. Someone's tipping her off."

I sighed. "Yup. Just like she probably has someone at the hospital giving her updates."

"What a bitch. Too bad she's not here today. Maybe I could've punched her for my R and R."

I laughed. "Bitches beware."

"That's right, girl. Bitches beware. I'm in a *mood*."

"Aren't you always?" I deadpanned, but couldn't help cracking a smile as she playfully smacked my arm. "Ow," I said on another laugh.

But then Layla scowled, and I followed her line of sight to Rich holding court around a brand-new Hummer that shone

like it was fresh off the car lot. We studied him, the girl hanging off his arm, and the crowd of groupies checking out his new
wheels, until we parked at the opposite end of the parking lot
from him.

Layla put Bonnie in neutral, yanked on the emergency brake,
and pocketed the keys. "I see Nina Waits likes his new toy."

"Looks like a lot of people like his new toy. I thought he and
Nina dated a while ago before she dumped his ass."

"Dunno. I don't keep up with the revolving door of girls he
goes through. You'd think there'd be enough of them that he
wouldn't need to bother with me." She pushed open her door,
grabbed her stuff, then gave me a wink. "Of course, none of them
compare to me."

I winked back. "Not even a little bit." After climbing out of
the car, I scanned the lot. "Where are Griff and Hunt?"

"In my dust, no doubt."

I snorted, already texting Hunt since Griffin would likely be
driving, but Clyde's signature growl alerted me to their arrival
before I could hit send. A minute later, Griffin's hand skimmed
across my lower back in greeting, sending tingles sweeping across
my skin.

"Hey, Joss," he said, pitched low enough that his words felt
intimate despite our being out in the open among our friends.

"Hey, Griff," I said, sounding like sex to my own ears before
clearing my throat and doing my damnedest to pretend his touch
and voice didn't do things to me. "Hey, Hunt," I added in my
haste to sound normal.

"Please tell me he didn't trade in his truck and get that to go
mudding in," Hunt said, eyes on Rich and his entourage.

"I wouldn't put it past the moron," Layla said as we headed
toward the buildings, all eyes on the bright yellow mini-tank Rich
didn't need.

"Hunt," a feminine voice called from behind us. We all turned.

Zoe Wills loped toward us, her fingers hooked through the straps of her backpack as it bounced behind her. When she reached us, she beamed. "Hey, guys! How's it going?"

"Hey, Zo," Hunt said, while I smiled a greeting at her. She seemed friendly enough. "We're checking out Rich's new plaything."

"Do you mean the Hummer or Nina?" Her eyes twinkled with mischief, and I decided I might like her.

"Def the car," Layla said. "Who cares who he's with now? It won't last long either way."

"True that," Zoe said, settling next to Hunt as we started walking again. "Now he's got the Hummer, still has his F-150, and apparently also a brand-spanking new Camaro, though I haven't seen it yet. What a kid our age could need three cars for, I have no idea, but he's got 'em. And Nina."

I harrumphed, glancing over my shoulder at the Hummer. It was big and fancy, no doubt, but I preferred our Mustangs any day of the week.

"Apparently he's got some billionaire uncle in town who's buttering him up with all the toys," Zoe added.

"Why?" Layla asked. "Did this billionaire uncle arrive and find him wanting for luxury?" She shook her head, flicking her hair out of her face.

Rich lived in a house three times the size of any of ours, alone with his parents. They had indoor and outdoor swimming pools, a hot tub, and an actual tennis court for his mom, who enjoyed the sport and, rumor had it, also her private instructor.

"Who knows?" Zoe said. "Maybe when you're rich as sin, the only way forward is more excess."

"Maybe," Layla said, not sounding convinced.

"Hey, guys! Hold up."

That voice had me tensing beside Griffin, already wondering which of us was going to get Layla's wish of a suspension and some R and R.

We whirled around to face Rich, who was jogging toward us, Nina and his buddies lingering behind around his new car.

"What the fuck do you want, Rich?" Griffin snarled the second Rich slid to a stop next to us. "Haven't you done enough already?"

For a brief moment, something akin to real feelings, actual remorse, flitted across Rich's face before it disappeared behind his usual haughtiness. A purple bruise cast one side of his jaw in shadow.

Rubbing at it gingerly, he cleared his throat, flicked his stare to the ground at our feet, then asked, "How's Brady doing?"

"That's none of your fucking business," Griffin said. "You leave him alone."

Griffin sounded like a bear woken from hibernation, and Hunt vibrated with tension. If anyone was going to throw a punch, my bet was on Hunt first, then Griffin right behind him.

Glancing away toward the empty sports fields that lined one side of the parking lot, Rich said, "I'm sorry for what happened, you know. I didn't mean for things to go down the way they did."

"You should be telling my brother that, not us," Layla ground out.

Rich met Layla's waiting eyes. "He doesn't want to hear it."

"Yeah, I wonder why," she snapped like a whip on bare skin.

"It's not. . ." He sighed and rubbed a hand across his neck. "Look, I only came over here to ask you guys something."

We waited.

"Well?" I barked.

He jumped, then scowled at me. I bared my teeth at him.

He frowned. "My uncle's in town and he asked me to ask you if you'd meet up with him. Not you, Zoe. Just the usual crew."

I felt my brow scrunching while Hunt asked, "What's he want with us?"

"I got no idea, but he says it's urgent."

"So?" Griffin said. "You might be his puppet, but he's not buying us toys. We don't owe him shit. We don't even know who he is."

"He won't like you saying no."

"That's his problem," I said. Then we turned as a group and walked away, leaving Rich standing there alone.

"Actually, don't wait for me. I'll catch up," I said, and before anyone could question me, I ran after Rich, who was already shuffling back toward his Hummer, as dejected as if Layla had cut him down yet another time.

I grabbed him by the arm to get his attention and he spun around, fists up. When he saw it was me, he relaxed. It would be so nice to show him the many reasons he shouldn't underestimate me. Just because I wasn't a big muscled-out dude like Brady didn't mean I didn't pack a punch. Our many years of wannabe ninja training made sure of that.

Standing halfway between my friends and his, a cocky smile transformed Rich's face. "Whazzup, foxy Joss-y? Ya want some of this after all?"

I inhaled and exhaled with a strong reminder that my deal with my parents was my car and its parts for straight A's. Possible suspensions had never entered the oral contract, but I didn't want to push my luck, not with so much work still to go on my baby, Cleo. I willed down my temper.

"No, Rich, I don't. And neither does Layla. Neither of us ever will, so leave her the hell alone already."

"She can tell me that herself then. We can all see Griffin's got the hots for you, but Hunt's not after her."

Forcing myself to move past Rich's offhanded comment about Griffin, I said, "Bullshit. She's told you a thousand times. Knock it off. No more texts, no more shit in the mail. Isn't what happened to Brady bad enough?" I pinned him with my most ferocious glare. "Drop it. Don't think about Layla again. Actually, don't ever talk to her again either. Just leave her the fuck alone, for good."

But Rich was shaking his head, a line of confusion between his brows. "What the fuck are you talking about?"

"Don't play dumb." I snorted. "Well, dumber than usual, anyhow. Back off. No more texts, no more romantic little packages. Or you'll have me to deal with, and I promise you, getting me won't be as fun for you as you think."

I turned on my heel and prepared to stalk off.

"Wait. Joss, I seriously don't know what you're talking about. I—"

"Joss?" Griffin's voice came from behind me.

Hurriedly, I whispered to Rich, "Play stupid all you want, I don't care, just *no more*. And I mean it. Leave my friends all the way alone and you and I won't have any problems."

Before he could answer, I ran the few steps to reach Griffin. Hunt, and Layla were directly behind him, concern tugging on their faces. Zoe waited for us at the hallway that led to the lockers.

"What was that about?" Griffin asked, glare pinned on Rich's retreating back as if it could do actual damage.

"Nothing big. I had some things I wanted to get off my chest. Let's get to class." And since Zoe was out of earshot, I added, "We've just gotta get through today and then we can figure out what we do next. My place after school? I'm itching to make more progress on my Cobra."

"Yeah, sounds good," Hunt said, then to Layla, "Will Celia let Brady come over?"

She sighed dramatically. "I'm sure she'll cave. All she did was take away his driving privileges over the suspension, but he didn't have those anyway since she's still going on about him being too 'infirm' to drive and all that BS. Even if she tells him *no*, he'll be able to butter her up and get away."

I grunted. "Yeah, he can just drop her a morsel about his dreams and she'll be putty in his hands."

"What do you mean?" Hunt asked.

But Zoe was moving in our direction, so I said, "We'll fill you in over lunch. Just make sure Zoe doesn't come with."

Then Layla and I plastered on smiles for Zoe's sake and aimed for our lockers. I hid behind its door while my thoughts returned to what Rich had said about Griffin.

Was Rich just messing with me?

When Griffin's hand once more swept along the strip of skin exposed between my cutoffs and my tank top, I couldn't be sure.

"Ready?" he asked, his hazel eyes more gold in the morning light that streamed in through the small windows high above the lockers.

I nodded, daring to ask myself, *Ready for what, exactly?*

14

Lies Are Best Served Fresh on a Pretty Platter

Who's up for another round?" I asked, ducking out from under the hood of my baby. She was still a rusted-out shell of the beauty she was destined to become, but her innards were coming together nicely. She was going to be a *fiiine* machine by the time we were finished with her, especially once she was ready for her shiny new paint job.

I was still debating between an electric green that would match the original factory options available for this model when it came out in 1999, and my favorite cherry black. There was a certain appeal to keeping to the original across the entire car as much as possible, but then there was the sleek temptation of sexy-as-all-get-out cherry black. I knew myself well enough to guess I'd probably end up choosing the latter, but it was a decision that shouldn't be rushed.

"Fuck yeah," Hunt answered from beneath my car a moment before he slid out from under it, beads of sweat dripping down his temples. "It's hotter than balls out here."

That it was, but I didn't bother suggesting a change in location. My driveway jutted out into an extra parking spot intended for visitors. In the double-car garage, my parents' cars were pretty much perma-parked now that they were working from home, doing whatever shady shit liar slash spy parents did in their secret lair. Since my baby was still up on blocks, she wasn't going anywhere. And the familiarity of working on our cars together soothed the unrest that had set in with the party at the Fischer House and only gotten worse with all the sketchy crap that had happened since.

Even the sight of Layla sitting on the grass, drawing in her sketchbook while leaning against a tree, was comforting. We'd spent hundreds of hours much like this, the guys and I tinkering with the cars, Layla helping occasionally but otherwise contributing to our conversations from the side. Lost in our element, content to be with each other, the outside world doing nothing to cramp our style. . .

Damn, I already missed those days. The outside world had done nothing *but* cramp our style lately.

"Beers for everybody, then?" I asked, receiving nods from the others. "Be right back."

Bobo's nails clacked across the lacquered cement of the garage floor, following me into the house. When I heard my mom's voice, I hesitated, but after a heavy sigh, continued on. It wasn't like I could avoid her forever, and the more I worked not to see her, the more she'd probably hound me to figure out what was wrong with me—a question I didn't want to answer until I understood how far their betrayal went.

I turned toward the kitchen, Bobo hot on my heels, head pointed up, alert to see what he might scavenge. My mom was on the phone, pulling a pre-prepared charcuterie tray with veggies out of the fridge. Had she already hired the chef she'd been mentioning to my dad? She must have. The only previous experience she had with a charcuterie tray was eating from one.

I snagged a carrot off the platter and tossed it to Bobo, who gave me a stupidly cute grin before snatching it from the air and chomping away.

My mom swatted at my arm, though we both knew she didn't mean it, saying into the phone, "Yeah, Celia, I know. Uh-huh. For sure." Then she pointed to the food and in the general direction of the garage, her brow arched in question.

"We'll come inside in a little bit," I replied softly so as not to be overheard on the other end of her call. I could hear Celia going on through my mom's cell, but I couldn't make out what she was saying. It was probably just as well. It didn't sound like Celia was so much as pausing for breath.

I ducked into the fridge, grabbed five bottles of some local micro-brew my dad had picked up, and stalked from the kitchen without a backward look, Bobo trailing me along with my mom's stare.

As soon as I closed the door that separated the garage from the rest of the house, I paused to lean against it, taking a deep breath of relief and hoping my mom wouldn't come out here after her call to follow up more with the offer of food. Pushing away from the door, I smiled down at Bobo, whose goofy grin was aimed up at me, and joined the others, handing out the beers that were already dripping with condensation.

Griffin lowered himself onto a patch of grass to sit against the house, and the rest of us joined him. Hunt pressed the cold bottle against his face.

"I don't know how much longer I can do this," I said, taking a long sip of my beer, enjoying its fruity undertones before stopping to examine the label. "Barrel-aged with fresh sour cherries," I muttered. "Hmm." After a second, smaller taste, I added, "Like, for real, I gotta figure this out so I can get it out in the open. You guys know how hard it is for me not to say whatever's on my mind."

Layla snorted. "I'm seriously shocked you haven't just blurted shit out already. You're being uncharacteristically restrained."

I frowned and harrumphed. "Yeah, and I don't like it. Not one bit. I need to know what they're up to and what—"

"Uh-uh," Brady interjected. "Hold up." He set his brew down on the cement and stood, jogging over to Bonnie, parked farther up the driveway next to Clyde. He returned with the RF detector, waving it at us only when he was out of range of any window my eavesdropping parents could potentially be studying us through.

"Let me do this first," he said, bending over for another quick draw on his beer. "It's super unlikely I'll find anything," he added more softly, "but no point being stupid about it now."

"Yeah, do it," I said without hesitation.

Brady had combed over his bedroom and Layla's while the rest of us had been at school, and Griffin had checked his house before meeting us last night. So far, all we'd discovered were the two bugs in the treehouse, but my house and Hunt's remained unknowns.

I relaxed into the wall behind me, sandwiched between Griffin and Hunt while we waited. Layla filled the silence.

"I can't believe how much people went on and on about Rich's stupid car today. Like, every time I start to think maybe our classmates aren't total vapid idiots, they go and remind me not to bother." She shook her head, absently studying the tattoo wrapping up her thigh, probably dreaming up what she would add to it next. "I mean, for reals, like, who gives a fuck? So he's got a Hummer. And a bunch of other toys. Who gives a shit?"

I snorted. "Nina, clearly."

"And every other skank who was breathing down his neck today, trying to drape themselves all over him. It made me sick to my stomach, like for real. Dude's a creep. Are these girls really willing to sell themselves over some cars?" She shook her head, tracing a finger along vines that erupted in prickly flower buds, already inked across her leg.

"The guys weren't much better," I said. "He had a little tribe of morons following him around like lost puppies all day long."

Layla shook her head again, finally looking up. "Sickening. I hope they all leave Ridgemore as soon as we graduate."

"Zoe's not like that," Hunt said.

"You're right. Zoe can stay. The rest can go fuck themselves far away from us."

Though our parents had attempted to pressure us about applying to universities, they'd eventually relented when we told them we were planning on taking a gap year to figure out our lives. They hadn't loved our answers but seemed to understand that pushing wouldn't help things. In fact, they'd probably make us decide never to attend university, just to spite them. All we really knew was that whatever we did, we were going to be doing it together.

"Hunt," Brady called. "Come help me."

Hunt finished the rest of his beer before heading off, and after a few whispered exchanges with Brady, deposited himself in front of the door that led into the house, in case either of my parents should come out that way to check on us.

"I swear, if that prick doesn't watch himself. . ." Griffin muttered, obviously as bothered by Rich as the rest of us. "It's like he doesn't even care what he did."

He glanced at Brady, who was running the RF detector along the walls, moving up and down each patch of wall in a deliberate pattern.

"Brady fucking died. That he's alive and well now's just fucking chance. We got so damn lucky." He blinked hard before dragging his attention back from Brady to us. "Rich could've killed him for good."

I leaned my head onto his shoulder, looking at Layla across from us. "As much as I don't want to defend the guy over anything, the balcony falling like that was random. He couldn't have known that'd happen. None of us could."

"No doubt." Griffin dropped a hand across one of my knees, cupping it, his bottle dangling from the fingers of the other. I forced myself to release my breath slowly as the heat of his palm seared my skin.

"But the fucker could at least show some real remorse," he added. "He didn't come by the hospital or call or even text any of us to find out how Brade was. He didn't even apologize until today, and not to Brady. What's Rich do when he sees Brady for the first time since he basically all but got him killed? He calls him 'Miracle Kid' when he's gotta know Brady hates the name. Even if no one told him, he knows Brady. Hell, he's known him nearly as long as we have."

"For sure," Layla said. "Rich is a lot of things, but I think he's far less stupid than he lets on."

"What do you mean?" I asked.

She shrugged, twirling the beer bottle between her hands, the gold accents on the label flashing each time the sunshine landed on them. "Just a feeling. I think a lot of his 'I'm a dumbass with shitloads of money' is an act."

"How do you know that though?" I asked, her confession of his attentions that she'd kept secret from us still too fresh.

"It's just an impression. He tries to talk to me a lot, obvi, and sometimes he's just, I dunno, different. Less teenage-boy moronic, ya know? No offense, Griff. I don't mean you. Or Hunt."

I chuckled. "What about Brady?"

She shrugged. "Depends on the day and my mood."

Griffin shook his head. "Man, am I glad I'm an only child."

Layla reached between us to slap him on the shin. "Hey! You'd be lucky to have a sister like me."

"Yeah, but there can be only one of you, which means I'd get someone else to get on my case about absolutely everything, and no thanks. I'll pass."

Layla narrowed her eyes at him, likely trying to decide whether he'd insulted her or not, and if so, by how much. Just then, a soft beep rang out within the garage.

Eyes suddenly wide, I froze for several heartbeats. Griffin leaped up, grabbing my beer bottle and setting it down next to his, before hauling me to my feet.

More beeps, now closer together, insistent, drifted out through the open garage door.

Griffin offered his other hand to Layla, helping her up. He continued to hold on to mine.

Tense with anticipation, the three of us moved to the doorway of the garage. Hunt had been sitting, his back against the door to the house. As drawn as the rest of us to news of how deep the treachery went, he stood to lean forward, his foot pressed to the door to keep it from opening.

Beep, beep, beep, beep, the radio frequency detector chirped like a too-peppy harbinger of doom.

Brady stretched, his tank top arcing to expose a toned waist as he extended the gizmo up until it nearly reached the seam of wall and ceiling.

The chirping sped up as Brady slipped his arm under the top shelf that held old tennis and racquetball rackets.

"Griff," he grunted, and Griffin raced over to help him slide the shelf far enough away from the wall that he could squeeze behind it. After a few tense moments, Brady emerged wiping cobwebs off his hair, a tiny listening device squeezed between his fingers, and a ferocious scowl tugging down his brow and lips.

It was nothing compared to the furious disappointment I could feel tightening my face, making me want to tear into the house and shake some truths from my parents. I stomped over to the bug in Brady's flat palm just to glare at it, waiting for my pulse to calm.

Layla stepped beside me and pointed at the bug, at its hiding place, then to the door leading into the house, where both my parents roamed.

Brady met my eyes. He was waiting for me to give the go-ahead. Pursing my lips and willing myself to breathe, I nodded silently.

Brady was wedged between the shelving system and the wall when Hunt startled, the door pushing against his foot and sticking. He turned and pressed both hands to the door.

Another time, the door bounced. Then, a knock.

"Joss, honey?" It was my mom. "Something seems to be jamming the door. I'm trying to come out."

"Oh, yeah?" I called out loudly enough to reach through the door. "Be right there."

Brady tossed the RF detector to his sister, then turned to replant the bug. Layla immediately shut the device off and shoved it into the kangaroo pocket of her short overalls. Griffin slid in to help Brady quietly lift the shelves back into place. Moments later, Hunt swung the door open on my mom, smiling more genuinely than I could have managed.

"Hey, Monica," he said with a calm that was still out of my reach. "Here, let me help you with that." He took the antipasto tray from her.

Mom followed with a pitcher of chilled lemonade and a stack of plastic cups.

"Thanks, Mom," I said, registering the distaste in my voice and rushing to conceal it. "That looks awesome. But how about we eat inside instead? It's hot out here."

"Oh, good idea," she said breezily, telling me that she hadn't picked up on my discomfort, or she was a far better actress than I was. "It's so much nicer in the AC. I don't know how you guys stand to be outside so much. And that treehouse of yours," she continued as she walked back through the door, "it gets stifling in there."

"You know how it is," Layla said with a troubled look at me before following her into the house. "No pain, no gain. We've gotta get our workouts in."

"Well, I wish you'd consider letting us put AC in, then." My mom's conversation faded as she moved through the house, Hunt and Bobo following her and Layla.

Griffin's hand landed on my back again. "You okay?" he whispered, likely very conscious of our total lack of privacy, perhaps even thinking of the many private conversations we'd had while tooling over my car.

Brady's gaze was pinned on me, his gray eyes as stormy as my insides.

"Yeah, I'm fine," I bit out, not bothering to soften my voice. It didn't matter that even though my mom wasn't listening to us, my dad still might be. For all I knew, they recorded everything my friends and I said to each other to listen to later, like the freakoids they were.

Griffin's hand tightened on my back, and Brady took a step closer.

I shook my head, lowering my volume. "Seriously, I'm fine. Let's just go inside and get this over with."

The only thing I felt like doing was upending my mom's fancy tray all over her head and pristine kitchen. But if it was necessary to follow through on this ruse just a little longer, then I'd do it. Because it wouldn't be long now before I confronted my parents. They were already on borrowed time.

We'd have her little snacks and lemonade—as if she were some damn innocent Betty Crocker—and then we'd scan my bedroom for bugs. After that, we'd check out Hunt's house, the only other place left to scan for listening devices.

After that, we were springing a motherfucking trap for my parents. I was getting into their secret room and figuring out what the ever-loving hell was going on. Things were definitely *not* okay in the Bryson household.

It was past time for the charade to end.

Brady jogged over to grab our beers, mostly empties, and then followed Griffin and me into the house. He tugged the door firmly shut behind us to keep in the air conditioning my mom

was always droning on about, like her mind was constantly occupied by such nonsense.

Lies.

So. Many. Lies.

Now, to find out just how many.

15

Gourmet Silver Linings
Spring the Trap

Hunt sat in the spacious butterfly chair in the corner of his bedroom, staring blindly at the electronic listening device in the palm of his hand. It seemed too small to create so much heartache. Leaning on his thighs, head hunched forward into his shoulders, he hadn't said a word since the radio frequency detector had sung its foreboding, chirpy tune in front of one of his many laden bookshelves. A special edition of J. R. R. Tolkien's *The Hobbit* had concealed the bug, wedged behind a shelving bracket immediately above the large, illustrated tome.

I patted him on the knee. I knew all too well what parental betrayal felt like, but at least a scan of my bedroom hadn't turned up anything odd beyond a single pearl earring I didn't remember ever owning and that was so not my style. The same for the rest of us. Only Hunt had had his privacy invaded in such a devastating way.

He didn't react to my touch, nor to Layla's when she slid behind him to rub his shoulders.

The longer Hunt remained silent, the tenser the rest of us grew. I rolled my neck to loosen it just as Griffin cracked his knuckles close enough to my ear that the popping made me cringe.

Brady was tightening and then loosening his arm muscles over and again. I couldn't decide if it was a newly developed coping mechanism or if he was just that ready to tear Hunt's mom and my parents a collective new one. If it was the latter, I was up for it. The need for answers roiled beneath my skin like a live wire.

"Hey." I gave Hunt a strained smile, attempting a steadiness I wasn't feeling. "Why don't we go for a nice trail run, huh? We've all been so tense lately, what with everything that's been going on. A good run'll help clear our heads. I know I could sure use the fresh air."

Alexis, if she was listening in, would likely interpret that as a reference to Brady's accident and possibly also his nightmares. I could really use normal parents who didn't shop at freaking spy stores. But the excuse to get us out of here so we could vent openly was a start.

Hunt didn't so much as blink for at least half a minute, staring at the sleek loss of trust in his hand. When he finally did lift his gaze, it wasn't to meet any of our eyes. He stalked over to his bookshelves with long, determined strides, lifted a stone dragon bookend, and smashed the device to pieces before any of us could do anything to stop him.

"Hunt!" Layla cried out, scrambling toward him, though there was no saving the bug now. "What the hell are you doing? Now they'll know we found the damn thing!"

She was right, of course. We'd left the bugs where we found them to buy us time to figure out our next moves.

Brady scooped up the pieces. "Well, it's sure as shit done now. Ain't no putting this thing back together."

"We had a plan, man," Griffin said, but while his words were scolding, his tone was resigned.

Hunt returned both the bookend and *The Hobbit* to their spots on his shelves, his jaw so tight it pulled at his skin. Then he stuffed his hands in his pockets and walked toward the large window that overlooked the forest, thick with verdant trees.

Hesitating only a moment, I followed, resting my hand on his back, which seemed to vibrate under my touch—unless that was me, my fury. It was hard to tell anymore with how wound up we were lately.

"I get it," I murmured softly, though for once we didn't have to watch what we said inside one of our houses. "I'm sorry, Hunt."

"You're not the one who should be sorry."

I waited. The others drew closer, flanking him while we stared out at the woods that were as familiar to us as our homes. We'd run wild through these trees for most of our lives.

Hunt shook his head slowly, his shiny black hair sliding. "I just can't believe it. I almost suggested we not even bother sweeping my room." He chuckled bitterly. "I thought there was absolutely no chance, no way my mom would do that to me. I've never given her a single reason to distrust me. Everything we do's out in the open. I've been acing school since always, and my going to college seems to be the only thing she's interested in lately."

"None of this makes any kind of sense," I grumbled. "It's fucking insane." I paused. "Though I guess the bug here does make me question whether my parents were the ones to plant them in the treehouse. They were def listening, but who's to say the others aren't too?"

Layla's brow bunched in confusion. "But what the fuck for? I just don't get it. I mean, yeah, sure, we're loads more interesting than any of them. Their favorite thing to do is geek out about cellular this and DNA that." She paused, tipping her head to one side like Bobo did. "What could nerds like them want with listening in on us? I mean, *what*? What the hell are they up to? Are they just trying to relive their youth through us? Getting off on listening to us . . . talk?" Her forehead scrunched further. "It can't be that. Seriously, I don't get any of this."

Hunt whipped around to face us. "It's time to confront them."

"Yeah, for sure," I replied immediately.

"We still don't know—" Griffin started, but Hunt was shaking his head again.

"I get it, bro, I really do. You like to play smart with all your cards in your hand. It's the best way to do things. Consider all the options before making your move. But I'm telling you, man, I can't live with my mom in this house, knowing what she's fucking done. It's just me and her here. I'm gonna lose my shit if I have to fake it with her. I can't do that. I'm not made that way."

"I feel ya, bro," I said. "I've about given my mom a piece of my mind at least a dozen times, and I can barely look at my dad. He pretends he's innocent and easygoing and all. What a fucking liar."

Griffin looked from me to Hunt, then back to me again. "Okay, then. So we do something about it. No more waiting."

"Good with me," Layla said, grinning maniacally. "Let's blow their shit wide open. It's gonna be awesome."

I highly doubted that, but who was I to mess with her enthusiasm? If she could be excited about any part of this shitshow, then good on her.

"So how are we gonna do it?" Brady asked, plopping into the open butterfly chair, draping a leg over one side of it. "I think we should get them all involved. They're all sus as fuck as far as I'm concerned."

I perched on the other side of the chair, which would have been big enough for two of us if not for how sprawled out Brady was. He slid over to make room for me, but just barely.

"I've been raring to go," I said. "I think we need to get down into my parents' secret room before we talk to any of them."

"Too late now," Layla said. "Alexis'll figure out that Hunt's bug isn't working anymore."

"Yeah, she will. But who knows? She might find another explanation for it, at least until she comes in to inspect and finds it missing. But until then, she might think it ran out of batteries or whatever." Hell, I was no spying specialist. "We might be busted already, but she also might excuse it away. It's not like we've done anything that would tip them off that we're on to them."

"Before now," Brady said, still holding the electronic crumbs in his hand.

I shrugged, less bothered by Hunt jumping the gun than the rest of them. We were lucky I hadn't done it before him. "Nothing we can do about that now. But we gotta get into the secret room, stat."

Layla rummaged around in her oversized purse, pulled out a bag of barbecue chips and passed them around. "So what's the play here?" she asked, crunching loudly. "How do we get Monica and Reece out of the house on our schedule and get them to stay out long enough?"

I grabbed a handful of chips and tossed the bag onto Brady's lap. "That's tricky. If it were just one of them, that'd be easy. But to get them both out at the same time? And to leave me free? Not sure. If only they did a date night or something like that."

Layla snorted. "I can't remember the last time our parents went on a date, even before . . . you know, everything went down. Mom's too uptight."

"And now she's got her head stuck up my ass," Brady added, making Layla scrunch up her nose.

"Seriously, Brade? Do you never think before you speak?"

"I do about as much as you do. Have you heard some of the shit that comes flying out of your mouth?"

Layla's nose crinkled even more. "Again, word choice is everything."

With a heavy sigh, Hunt lowered himself to the floor, leaning against his bed, stretching out his long legs in front of him. "You could pretend to be sick? Maybe have the school nurse call them?"

"I could do that, I guess, but it's likely only one of them would come get me. Or they might even ask one of you to drive me home if they're in the middle of some work thing. You know how they are."

"Yeah," Layla said, serious for once. "If they could swaddle their work and stuff it into diapers, they'd baby the shit out of it while we fended for ourselves."

"Weird analogy, but yeah," Griffin said. "Even when my dad's hanging out outside of his office, he's nearly glued to his tablet. Like it'd kill him to step away from work for a hot second."

Layla snorted. "They act like they're saving the damn world. Like a frigging gene splice is gonna make some kinda difference."

Hunt rubbed at his chin then moved on to play with his earring, today a small silver hoop with a single piece of turquoise hanging from it that used to be his dad's. "I never really stopped to think about it before, but doesn't it seem weird that they never really try to talk to us about what they're working on?"

"They do," Layla said. "Or at least our parents do, anyway."

"Do they really though?" Brady asked over the loud crinkle of the chip bag. "They talk about genetics and heredity, but only in general terms. They don't talk about their specific projects."

Layla frowned, I suspected in part because Brady was right, and she hated that. "Damn, I guess that's true. I can't think of a single project they've told me about over the years, though they're always talking to each other about the specs. But never in a way that I know what the hell they're going on about. Not that I ask either. That shit's *bo-riiing.*"

"Weird though, right?" Hunt asked. "It'd be one thing if we were all dumbasses like Pike, but we're smart, and they know it."

Work was our parents' favorite thing to focus on, but a tie for second was discussion of our future education plans—which none of us had at the moment—and how each of us consistently tested at the top of national percentiles, labeling us as gifted students.

Beyond test results, we'd been able to read and otherwise absorb material far past our grade levels for ages.

"Huh," Griffin grunted, taking a seat next to Hunt, one leg stretched long, the other bent, his hands and chin resting on his knee. "Never noticed that before. Seems like I should've, now that you bring it up."

"So it's across the board?" Hunt asked, eyeing each of us. "Do any of you know what they're working on now?"

I huffed. "Other than spying on our asses, you mean?"

His eyes hardened. "Yeah, other than that."

"Nope," I said. "And my mom'll chat on and on if you let her." I twirled one of my many small braids. "Just not about what's most important to her, supposedly. And I don't mean when they pretend it's us." I paused. "Maybe it is us, at least some. To be fair, they do give us everything we need and let us pretty much do whatever we want."

Griffin's foot stretched to tap mine. "That's not necessarily the same thing as caring about us." Layla and I opened our mouths, but he shrugged. "I guess I know they care about us. It's just . . . this shit isn't sitting right with me."

"No kidding," Hunt said. "It might be giving me indigestion, though I'm not sure what that feels like, so I can't be sure." He crunched on a couple more chips, and I laughed. Hunt could eat a rock and digest it without problems. One time the five of us had eaten some bad shrimp, and he was the only one who hadn't ended up miserable with food poisoning.

"I could be in an accident of some sort," I suggested. When Griffin's eyes widened with what might have been panic, I hastened to add, "To draw my parents out of the house together, I mean. It does seem a bit cruel though, especially after what happened. And while I'm angry enough with them to punch a hole straight through a wall, I'm not sure I'd feel good about putting them through that."

"They're *spying* on us, Joss," Hunt practically growled. "Their own motherfucking kids. Maybe they deserve whatever scare we give them."

"Yeah . . . I guess so. If only we hadn't seen them so freaked out at the hospital and, you know, after. But yeah, we could do that. Only we'd have to pretend I'm seriously hurt, or they won't both come. And how do we pull that off convincingly? Besides, then I'd have to be out of the house too, and I've *gotta* get into that room."

Griffin leaned forward, his chin fully atop his bent knee. "What if you say you want to go out to dinner, maybe to Romeo's?" The food at the mom-and-pop Italian restaurant was made from scratch and to die for. "You could sweeten the offer by saying Monica could get a night off from thinking about what's for dinner. We know she hates cooking. If it weren't for your dad, you'd all probably never eat."

"I didn't tell you guys. She was talking about hiring a chef, and now awesome food has been magically appearing in the kitchen. She must've already hired the person and they come while we're at school." I scowled. "She didn't even tell me about that, I just happened to overhear. Now I'm wondering just how much shit they skip telling me."

"Yeah," Hunt said with a purposefully fake, chipper laugh. "Like hey, forgot to tell you I installed motherfucking listening devices in your room."

"Yeah, like that." My scowl deepened.

Griffin continued, "If you tell them you want to discuss the universities you might want to attend—"

Layla groaned loudly, flopping dramatically to the floor between us all, draping an arm over her eyes. "Not the dangling university carrot. We only just got them to shut up about that already."

"But that's exactly why it'll be irresistible to them," Griffin said. "Romeo's food and a chance to convince their only daughter to make"—he hooked his fingers in air quotes—"'responsible choices with the gifts she's been given'? There's no way they'll be able to pass that up."

"True." I rose to stare out the window again. "But then I won't be there to check out their fucking secret lair."

"But it'll get them out of the house, and we can get in there and tell you what's up."

Hunt bent his knees, resting his elbows on them as he leaned his head back on the bed. "You won't be able to be there, which sucks, I know, but then we can be sure we won't be caught red-handed. You can text us a heads-up before you guys leave the restaurant."

"Yeah." I said, still unwilling to miss out on the big discovery.

"You won't need to put on any theatrics," Griffin added. "No pretending."

"Other than pretending she's interested in spending her entire dinner talking about boring universities," Layla said. "Just because they went to school for a combined century or two and have enough masters and PhDs between them to wipe all their asses, doesn't mean that's what's best for us. Like, can't they give a girl a little bit of time to figure out her life before she has to dive headfirst into a major? Fuck!"

I turned just in time to catch Layla blowing her frustration out in a flutter that sent her bangs flying. Despite the topic of discussion this afternoon, I couldn't help a chuckle. "Damn, girl, tell us how you really feel."

"She's such a fucking drama queen." Brady crumpled up the empty bag of chips and tossed it one-handed into Hunt's garbage bin, nailing the shot as usual. "Always with the fucking exaggerations."

Layla rocketed up to sitting. "You must be thinking of yourself, ya damn drama queen." She smiled mockingly. "Just 'cause I'm your twin doesn't mean you need to be confusing us all the time, jeez."

Brady rolled his eyes, huffing loudly—and dramatically. The pair of them could be crowned drama queen and king. "That's stupid, Lay. Doesn't even make sense."

Before they could get going—and they would—I interrupted. "You guys'll take pictures for me? So I can see what's down there? And tell me about it?"

"Of course," Griffin said. Then, extra gently, "We'd never leave you out."

I stared at him, for just a moment allowing myself to get lost in his eyes, in his comforting smile. "Fine. I don't like the idea of missing out on getting in there, but it's the best plan. Easy, guaranteed to work. We can set it up ahead of time, no guessing how my parents will react. Let's do it."

I whipped out my phone and started typing.

"You're gonna set it up *now*?" Layla asked. "For tonight?"

"I would, but I'm sure my mom's already figured out what we're doing for dinner. Dad's probably already done prep, or this new chef has. I'm setting it up for tomorrow."

"Good," Hunt said. "The sooner, the better."

"I couldn't agree more." My fingers flew across the screen.

> **Joss:** U guys wanna do Romeo's for din tomorrow? Got a hankering for their lasagna & breadsticks.

I sent, then sighed, really wishing I didn't have to add this last bit that would seal the deal, no matter what project they'd been planning to work on tomorrow.

> **Joss:** I was thinking we can talk about universities over dinner.

It took a total of thirty seconds for a response to arrive.

Mom: Sounds like a great idea, honey! I'll book us a table right now.

Dad's message arrived a minute later.

Dad: I'm in! Lasagna, yum. Also, proud of you, honey. You'll never regret anything you learn.

I was tempted to correct their ready assumption that I was agreeing to attend, but I didn't.

Joss: What time R U making the reservation for?

Mom: 6:30.

I sent back a thumbs-up they'd both see, then tucked away my phone in my back pocket, grimacing at my best friends.

"We're on for tomorrow at 6:30. We'll finally know what's up."

"Awesome," Layla said, but what was there to celebrate, really?

Nothing like tricking your parents to figure out how deep their deception went. At least I was getting lasagna out of the deal. Silver linings and all that.

I had to find them wherever I could.

16

When Cool Secret Lairs Aren't Cool

Every fake smile caught in my craw like a burp I was too polite to let loose. The only saving grace was that my parents were all too happy to drone on and on about the benefits of attending post-secondary schools, saving me from the awkwardness of feigning enthusiasm. I was getting away with a series of *uh-huhs*, *yeahs*, nods, and grunts. They were too swept up in their recruiting fever to notice, when ordinarily they'd surely censure me for it, emphasizing how important it is to verbalize concise arguments for my position. I'd heard that a thousand times at least over the years.

Their current favorite picks for me were the usual top Ivy League choices—Harvard, Princeton, Yale—and then other "superb choices," such as Notre Dame, Stanford, and Duke. They hardly paused to draw breath, much less to ask me which I might prefer. They had me in their web and had no plans to let me go, not until after dessert. At least the lasagna was as good as I remembered, and the breadsticks were extra salty, the marinara dipping sauce delicious. I'd have felt like a cheap sellout except for my phone burning a hole in my pocket, waiting for a buzz that would tell me my friends were sending the all clear for us to return home.

I was halfway through an awesome tiramisu, my brain on overload from too much college propaganda, when my phone finally buzzed.

My mom was two glasses of red wine deep, her smile more frequent than usual, my dad nursing a single martini.

"I know I'm not supposed to look at my phone during dinner," I said, "but can I do it this one time? Really fast? I think Layla might have a study question for me. We're working on an assignment for AP Bio together, and we didn't get a chance to go over everything before I had to jet for dinner."

The lie came so easily. Maybe my skills were hereditary.

My mom waved generously across the table. "Sure, honey." She beamed at me, probably already picturing me walking across some fancy university stage in my cap and gown. "Just make it quick, and don't get used to it."

I smiled like she was just so damn magnanimous. "Thanks, Mom. I'll be fast."

My fake smile dropped the second I glanced at my screen.

> **Griffin:** Change of plans. Shit's worse than we thought. Come home now. We'll wait for you here. There's no way we can fake our way around this. You'll get your answers tonight.

I gulped.

> **Joss:** K. C U soon.

I took longer than necessary to put away my phone, trying to give myself time to recover before having to stare either of my parents in the face.

"Everything okay, Joss?" my dad asked. "You look pale all of a sudden."

"Yeah, yeah, I'm fine," I eked out robotically. Tonight might truly bring an end to their lies. What had my friends found? What could be so bad that they'd want to show me right now?

"I'm just a bit tired, is all," I added, taking a few final bites of tiramisu, no longer savoring it as I was before. "There's been a lot going on lately."

"There really has," my mom said, not understanding the half of what I was referring to. "Let's get home, Reece."

While my dad flagged down our waiter and paid, my meal settled like a stone in my stomach.

The drive back, though only fifteen minutes long, felt like a couple of hours. By the time we pulled up to the house, my nerves were shot to hell, and I had to pee.

Waiting behind them while they unlocked the door, I searched my mind for what to say. I couldn't just let them walk in on my friends without warning. At the very least, I had to be there with them.

"Um, actually, I want to talk to you guys about something. It's really important. But I have to pee like a racehorse. Can you, ah, wait for me in the dining room while I run to the bathroom?"

My dad pushed open the door, glancing at me strangely over his shoulder. "You okay, Joss? You sound weird."

"Yeah, yeah, I'm fine," I said, squeakier than was necessary. "Just gotta pee, and what I need to talk to you about's really important, so just wait for me, 'kay? Don't go anywhere."

Before either of them really answered, I ran off to the closest bathroom, relieving myself in record time, which still left me massively unprepared for how to tell them we'd caught them with their hands deep in the damn cookie jar.

Whatever she saw in my face had my mom jumping to her feet, only to steady her tipsy self with a hand against a chair, the other over her heart. "Oh my God, Joss. You're pregnant."

My thoughts had been racing ahead of me—down the hall, through the office, into the closet, and descending the secret stairs. They rebounded like they were pinned to a rubber band. "Wait, *what?*"

"You've been looking pasty, peaked. And then you had to pee so badly that you ran to the bathroom."

My dad's face was pinched with worry as he approached me. "Is that true, Joss? Are you pregnant?"

Rolling my eyes, I smacked a hand to my forehead. "No, guys, I'm not pregnant. *Jeez.* Thanks for jumping to crazy conclusions though. Nice to know you've got confidence in me."

My dad's cheeks colored, and he *ahem*ed, running a finger around the collar of his shirt. "That's . . . that's good, honey, real good."

I would have laughed at his obvious chagrin, except *secret lair*.

My mom didn't bother looking apologetic, but kept staring at me, waiting, as if I still might admit to a surprise pregnancy after all. Like she had nothing to hide, and *I* was the one not being straight with *them*.

After meeting her stare for a moment, all too ready to hurl my own accusations at her, I said stiffly, "No, it's nothing like that. I just didn't know what to say." I tugged on a braid then tossed it over my shoulder. "I still don't, so just follow me, I guess."

"Hold on, honey," my mom said, already turned around and heading toward the kitchen. "Let me pour myself another—"

"Wine's not gonna help you with this."

She whirled to face me, halting mid-step. "What are you going on about? You're being very weird."

"I know I am, but I have good reason for it, trust me." As soon as the words were out, I chuckled bitterly. *Trust.* Definitely not the theme of the hour.

"What's going on?" my dad asked, looking between me and my mom, who was in the kitchen despite my protests, winding a corkscrew into a bottle of her favorite cabernet sauvignon.

I sighed, studying my dad really hard. He was slim and athletic, though not overly so, despite running several miles most mornings. His hair was short, shabby, and brown. His features were pleasant but not particularly remarkable. Nothing about him or his way of dress would make him stand out in a crowd. My dad was, to all appearances, an ordinary middle-aged man who happened to be a science nerd. How did someone like him have secrets as big as whatever my friends had found? How could inoffensive, easygoing Dad be okay with eavesdropping on his daughter's private conversations? None of it made any damn sense.

Again, I exhaled loudly. "I'm trying to show you guys what's going on. So will you come with me already?"

"Of course, honey," my mom said over the *glug, glug* of her pouring. "Be right there." She took a sip and sauntered toward me, kicking off her shoes and nudging them to the side as she went. "Let's see what you want to show us."

Wordlessly, I started down the hall, feeling their presence behind me as surely as if they were giants marching me to a horrible fate. My skin, much of it exposed in my tank top and denim shorts, pricked and tingled everywhere. I kept running my tongue over my teeth without reason; my muscles itched for a release of tension, urging me to go on a run. Only, no matter how long I ran or how far, there was no chance I'd outrun my problems.

"Where's Bobo?" my dad asked as we wound down the hallway and took a turn.

I didn't answer, certain he must be downstairs with my friends. If not, he would have been at the garage door to greet us.

Once their office entrance was in view, they slowed. I could feel their change of pace even with my back to them.

"Where are you taking us?" my dad asked, a new unease riding his question.

I hesitated, then peered over my shoulder. "To your office."

My mom's eyes widened to an extreme before she seemed to notice and tempered her reaction. She trilled, and she never did that. "Ah, ha ha, why to our office, silly goose? There's no need for that. Whatever you want to show us, you can do it out here. Or in the living room. Or maybe out on the deck? It's so nice out there this time of evening."

Eyes fixed ahead, I muttered, "I wish that were true and there was no need for this," then slipped into their workspace, stalked to the open closet door, and waited beside it.

As soon as they entered the room, my parents staggered.

My mom hastily set her glass on a shelf, on top of a book—ordinarily, she'd never risk a stain—then leaned on my dad's desk, breathing unevenly.

My dad seemed not to be breathing at all, his eyes unfocused as if he weren't really seeing me anymore.

I crossed my arms. "So . . . anything you want to tell me?"

No change in reaction from either of them for long moments until they eventually looked at each other, an entire silent conversation passing between them.

"What is it, Mom?" Bitterness at their blatant deception drifted like poison through my system. "You look peaked and pale. Are you pregnant?"

She looked at me, free of the anger she'd ordinarily express at my mockery. Finally, she shook her head, her shoulder-length hair as slow to move as she was. "It's . . . it's not what it looks like."

"Oh, really?" I snapped. "So it's *not* a secret space inside a closet in your office? There isn't an *entire room* hidden inside my very own home, one that I never knew about?"

"Well, it is like . . . that," my dad said gingerly. "But it's not as bad as it looks."

"Really?" My jaw was so tense it began to ache. "Because it looks pretty fucking bad. And don't comment on my language"—I flicked a warning look at Mom—"I'm not in the mood." Sass like that would usually earn me a severe talking-to, but I couldn't care any less in that moment. "It's not just the secret room, and you know it. You've been *spying* on me! On your own fucking daughter! What the hell? Seriously, *what the fuck?*"

"You. . ." My dad never finished.

"We don't know anything about that drone," my mom piped up. "That wasn't us. Just like we told you."

I flung my hands in the air before letting them land against my thighs with a loud slap. "Well, I'd fucking hope it wasn't you. That'd be the cream on the pie of all the lies you told me. Though, you didn't actually tell me it wasn't you, because of course it never occurred to me then that my own parents would be lying to me left and right. What about all those lessons growing up about the importance of honesty, huh?"

I huffed at the absurdity of those teachings when examined in this light. "How many times did you tell me that my integrity was all my own, the one thing no one but me could insist on? That my integrity would be something I'd be fucking proud of, for fuck's sake."

Despite how shocked they were to be found out, I still half expected a scolding. It didn't come.

Finally, my mom pushed off the desk and walked over to me with a drawn-out sigh. "Is this about your phone?"

I only glared harder.

She glanced at my dad. "I told you we should've left her phone alone. Kids these days are too tech savvy." Then to me, "We had to tap your phone, honey. But we did it for good reason. We had to make sure you're safe."

"Tap my phone?" My volume rose dramatically over the simple three words. "*You tapped my phone?* Holy shit, guys. What is wrong with you?"

"Oh, fuck," my mom said under her breath, seemingly upset only because she'd admitted to something I hadn't known, not because of what she'd done.

Dad was already *tsk*ing. "There's nothing *wrong* with us, so watch your tone, young lady. We've only done what we had to do, nothing more, nothing less."

I glowered at him. "Yeah, right. Because *your* parents listened to your private conversations, right?" He stiffened. "That's what I thought. Gran and Gramps would've never done that to you. They would've never betrayed your trust like that."

Yanking my phone from my pocket like it was infected with a lethal plague, I flung it across the room. I might never touch the damn thing again.

"I just really can't believe you two. Like, at all. You're nothing like I thought you were all this time. Here I am, asking you to explain how you could possibly do something like this to me, and all you're doing is saying you had no fucking choice?" I snorted loudly. "As if. We found the fucking bugs."

My parents hadn't seemed capable of growing any pastier. I was wrong. Dad paled further, sweating like he was two seconds away from upchucking all over the carpet. I almost wanted him to. It would serve him right.

"No apologies. Nothing," I went on. "I can't believe it, I really can't, but it's actually worse than I thought it'd be. You don't even care about what you did! You're just justifying it."

"Joss," Griffin called up from what sounded like the bottom of the hidden stairs. "You might wanna hold off on saying how bad it is till you see just how *bad* it fucking is. Get your ass down here. You're not gonna believe this shit."

My mom shed her sluggish shock to lunge at me, gripping my arms hard enough to make me wince.

"Let. Me. Go," I snarled.

Grimacing, she loosened her hold. "Sorry, honey, I didn't mean to hurt you. But *please*, don't go down there."

"Who's down there?" my dad barked.

I frowned at him, doing nothing to curb the disappointment written all over me. "If that's all you care about, you'll find out soon enough."

"No," my mom yelped. "Don't. Honey. We can explain."

"Don't 'honey' me. That's for people who care about each other. Who trust each other." I was going to keep spewing, but then clamped my mouth shut, snatched my arms away, and ran into the closet. Mom's fingers snagged on my shirt, trying to hold me back, but I tugged loose, racing down the stairs, nearly sliding and falling, catching myself on the metal railing just in time.

My eyes met Griffin's first. He was at the base of the stairs as I'd thought, waiting for me with Bobo at his side. His face was tight, his eyes grim, like murder warmed over.

Before I even looked beyond him, my heart sank so far it might have temporarily exited my body through my feet.

"Oh, shit," I muttered to myself under my breath, all but stumbling into his arms in my haste as he caught me.

Though *in his arms* was one of my favorite places to be, I jerked out of them, barely glancing at Bobo, the only one who was happy. His tail wagged for me, and he whined as I staggered away from him, absently reaching for him, petting the air behind me. Never once had I ignored him before. He was my good boy.

Hunt, Layla, and Brady were lined up behind him, as somber as Griffin.

I felt like I absorbed them and our surroundings one item at a time, though I understood even then that everything was blurring together in a hazy rush.

The room was large, spacious, and surprisingly elegant and sophisticated for a hidden underground lab. Because that's what this was: *a lab.*

It had no windows, illuminated solely by incandescent lights—my mom refused to use fluorescents for their artificial tint and constant buzzing. There were more workstations and counter space than two people should ever reasonably need. Microscopes, a centrifuge, test tube racks, stacks of clean specimen slides, computers, printers, file folders, and extra monitors were neatly organized and displayed. A handful of stools sat in front of counters and the one large island; comfortable-looking leather chairs rested next to each of the two desks. A small glass-walled refrigerator, the kind used for biological material, hummed quietly in one corner. Speakers sat on the opposite end from it, across the space, pointed toward the center of the room—the best practice for eavesdropping, no doubt.

And worst of all, perhaps, were several transparent glass boards with my parents' handwriting scrawled across them in crisp dry-erase marker. Eight-by-ten matte photographs were taped up between their notations.

Pictures of us.

I was there, in the center of my friends, the four of them spread out above and below my portrait.

I stared at the photos for so long that I lost track of time, blinking numbly at poses I recognized all too well. I'd taken the shots; even my own was a selfie. They were on my cell phone. I'd never uploaded them anywhere else.

Not only had my parents tapped my phone, but they'd accessed it to steal these photos. It was the only way they could have them. I hadn't even sent them to my friends.

Eventually, Bobo pressed his face to my thigh, licking my knee, dragging me out of my daze, and I plopped to the lacquered cement floor to hug him, wrapping my arms around him while he wiggled, trying to crane his neck around to land kisses.

Of my family, he was the only one I could trust, the only one who'd never betray me.

No, that wasn't quite right. Griffin, Layla, Brady, and Hunt, *they* were more my family than my parents.

My dog and my friends. That's what I had.

I wasn't sure what I had in my parents, only that I didn't think I wanted whatever it was anymore. How could I?

"Fuck," my dad growled to no one in particular. I couldn't remember the last time I'd heard him cuss. "Monica, make the call."

"Okay," she answered feebly around a resigned sigh.

I didn't glance up at either of them. I couldn't stand to look at them. Instead, I worked on showing Bobo the love *he* deserved, scratching behind his ears, under his chin, and when he rolled onto his back, across his white belly.

"Celia?" I heard my mom say into her phone. "We've got a major problem. The kids found our lab."

When she stopped to listen, Dad addressed my friends. "You guys should've tripped the alarm. Why didn't I get a notification?"

That was what he cared about? What. An. *Asshole.*

"Because Hunt and I disabled it." Griffin's voice was colder than an ice storm and just as turbulent.

"That shouldn't have been possible."

"Yeah, well, looks like we're all surprising each other tonight, doesn't it?"

"Looks like it," my dad muttered.

Mom drew to his side and announced, "The others are heading over now."

At last, I glanced up at them. My parents were no longer pale, their shock replaced by what looked like determination. I read trepidation on them, yes, but no remorse. Not a lick of it.

I shook my head and nuzzled Bobo some more, holding back tears I refused to shed. Screw them. Screw them hard.

"We should wait to talk till the others get here," my mom added. "Better to do this just once and get it over with."

"What's *this*?" Layla asked.

"Explaining ourselves."

"Hmmph," Layla grunted, saying without words that no explanation would be sufficient to make this go away.

That's right, girl. I couldn't agree more.

"Are all our parents coming?" Hunt asked, his question monotone, as if he were keeping his feelings locked up just like I was.

"Yes," my mom answered.

"So they're all involved, then?"

Neither my mom nor dad answered, telling us very loudly that every single freaking one of them was as much a traitor as the next.

Griffin was right. This was as bad as it got. All I could do was hope there was no way it could get any worse, because just then I wouldn't bet on it.

17

Yada, Yada, Lie, Lie, Lie

Despite the lack of notice, my friends' parents arrived in record time, making their way down to Mom and Dad's underground lab without needing directions, a fact I was certain my friends hadn't missed based on their squinty-eyed looks. I wasn't the only one with traitors for progenitors. There was a whole club of them.

I'd barely had enough time to take Bobo out for a quick pee break and to give him some water so he could begin the cycle anew before I found myself back in the secret room, surrounded by incontrovertible evidence that the adults had an entire hidden life we'd known nothing about.

The parents drew stools around the center island, and I couldn't help but notice how familiar they seemed with the setting.

My friends and I were wound tighter than a spool of electric wire with the current already running through us. We stood together, unable to sit still, our backs pressed against one of the long counters. Close enough to our parents to call them out on their shit, not close enough that they could touch us. The days of wanting comfort from Mom or Dad seemed so distant that

I couldn't reconcile the people who faced off with me now with those tender memories.

It was as if there were two opposing groups in the room, each a stranger to the other.

Even Bobo had chosen sides. Since we'd come back down here, he hadn't moved more than a few feet away from me, and then it was only to soothe my friends. He might not understand the nuances of what was happening, but he damn well knew something was very wrong—and that the adults were the source of the current tension.

Our parents kept sharing loaded looks, the couples murmuring under their breath to each other.

Griffin pushed off the counter, arms crossed protectively, and snapped, "So? How long are you gonna make us wait to tell us what the hell's going on here? Seems like the least you could do after all this"—he flicked an accusatory look at the board with our faces staring back at us—"is own up to it without all the suspense. I promise you, we're shocked enough already."

Orson cleared his throat and slid his glasses up the bridge of his nose. "Son, it's not as bad as it looks."

Griffin didn't soften a bit at his father's wheedling tone. "Prove it, then."

The parents stared at one another.

"Seriously, guys?" Layla whipped out, her eyes vibrating with her intensity. "Whatever's going on here, I can tell you right the hell now that it's not right. This"—like Griffin, she glanced at our portraits, the evidence none of the adults could deny—"is shady as hell. I'm literally seconds away from walking out of here and filing for emancipation, and I'm not even kidding. Someone'd better start talking, and *now*. It's the only chance I'm giving you."

"Ditto." For once, Brady backed up his sister without fuss.

Celia sighed, sliding her glasses up onto her head where they sat like a headband, a far too everyday look for the mood.

"Sweetheart, I promise you, everything we did was to protect you."

Layla slammed her hands to her hips, jutting her head forward. "Are you trying to tell me that you *spied* on me and my friends for our own good?" She barked out a bitter laugh.

"I'm not *trying* to tell you that. *I am* telling you that. It's the truth."

Brady *hmmph*ed sarcastically.

"Go ahead, tell them," my mom said to Celia.

Celia swiveled on her stool. "Me? Why me?"

"Why not you?"

"Brade," Layla said without turning to look at him, "wanna catch a lift with me? I wanna get a head start on my emancipation research. I'm filing first thing tomorrow morning before the courts close for the weekend."

"Don't be ridiculous," Celia said.

Layla pushed out her bottom lip before singsonging, "Don't be fucking *liars* and *sneaks*."

"Layla," Porter admonished sharply.

"What, *Dad*? Are you really gonna be upset about my *attitude* right now? Put yourself in our shoes for a millisecond here. How would you feel if you discovered your parents were literally *spying* on you? Like, how can you not see how beyond fucked up this is? You guys have our freaking pictures tacked up on a board like we're suspects in a police investigation or some shit. And let's not even mention what's on the computers."

"Wait." I tensed even further. "What's on the computers?" I was going to need the massage to end all massages after this, just to get my shoulders in working order again.

"Basically everything," Hunt said. "Our medical histories from birth even though we've never been to any doctors that I can remember. Our school and testing records. Transcribed logs of our 'private' conversations, with highlighted parts about Brady's dreams. His complete hospital report. Literally, every time he took a shit, it's noted."

"Fuck," Brady interjected.

Hunt continued, "A file on that bitch reporter Kitty Blanche, including her phone logs. If you can think of it, it's probably in there."

"Shit," I breathed.

"Exactly," Layla said.

"How did you access our computers?" my dad asked. "The security on them is military grade. None of you have skills of that level."

"Really, Dad?" I asked. "*That's* your one question here?"

But Griffin was already responding. "Just 'cause you've got a bunch of data on us doesn't mean you really *know* us or what we're capable of."

"That's right," Layla said. "You can't get a real gauge of us from a bunch of reports and files." She shook her head. "It's looking like you don't know us well at all."

"Of course we do," Celia snapped. "You're our children. Our babies."

Layla harrumphed. None of the rest of us rushed to affirm the parental bond either.

"Good God, just tell them already." Alexis groaned.

Celia spun to face her. "If you're so anxious, then you tell them."

"Fine, I will." Alexis stood, using both hands to flip her long black hair behind her shoulders before straightening her back. Her posture was always impeccable. "We have nothing to be ashamed of. We did what we had to do. If there'd been another way, we would have taken it."

Then to us, "You might not be ready to accept that everything you see here has always been about your safety, but it *is* the truth."

When Hunt snorted, Alexis pinned him with a sharp look. "You wanted explanations, you're going to get them. Please don't interrupt me."

Hunt frowned but held his tongue. I alternated between blindly pushing back my cuticles, petting Bobo, and wrestling with the desire to scream profanities at the adults studying us with know-it-all expressions.

"We met at our first job out of college. We were all fresh and eager, excited to save the world with our newly minted PhDs. We were the best of the best in our fields, pumped to have been recruited for jobs at a state-of-the-art facility performing cutting-edge research." She fidgeted with the wedding band she still wore. "Not on marine animals like we told you."

"What, really?" Hunt interjected. "What about Harvey the octopus, the one who was so smart he could do puzzles at the same level as a human toddler?"

Alexis hesitated but ultimately shook her head.

"So Harvey was entirely made up?"

"Yes, but only for your—"

"Don't bother wasting your breath. Let me guess. For our protection."

"Exactly. All of it's been for that."

Hunt grunted. My urge to dig into my arsenal of cuss words was growing. I'd heard about Harvey too. *He was the cutest, most amazing octopus you can imagine*, my parents would tell me. *So special. Fascinating creature. So intelligent.* Yada yada, *lie, lie, lie.*

Alexis scanned the line of us, pursing her lips when she didn't seem to like what she saw. Layla had an octopus plushy named Harvey she'd loved above all others. He was still singled out from her other stuffed animals that she'd outgrown, claiming a prominent spot on one of her shelves.

Alexis seemed to steel herself. "The marine life study was the standard story used by all our colleagues. The work we were doing was top secret. We had to sign NDAs a mile long before joining the team. No one was allowed to share with anyone, not even their families."

I stared back at her blankly, unimpressed. She was trying to sell us some non-disclosure agreement bullshit? No one had made them spin their web of lies into happy tales that made Harvey come alive for us. I'd nearly named Bobo to honor this special animal my parents spoke of so fondly.

"If you weren't studying Harvey, what were you studying?" Hunt asked, his voice too even. It was his tell that he was barely keeping his shit together.

Before answering, Alexis glanced behind her at the others. My mom, Celia, and Orson nodded. Hunt's mom appeared less confident than before, and the woman was always self-assured, like there wasn't a single thing on this planet she didn't know or hadn't done, and if she'd done it, she sure as shit did it better than anyone else. Hunt probably got his huge brains from her, though none of us were too shabby as far as intelligence levels went. Even Brady, who pulled off the immature muscled brute vibe when he wanted, was a mechanical genius.

Alexis swallowed and regained her usual composure. "We were tasked with studying genetic anomalies of the . . . paranormal variety."

I blinked and waited for the joke to land.

Layla tittered. "Uh-huh. Paranormal. Right. So now what are you gonna do? Start spinning some tale for us about unicorns and fairies? Are you gonna name a fictional unicorn and tell us he hangs out with Harvey? *Come on.*"

Alexis was usually serious. The others, not as much. But six parent faces looked back at us—dead serious.

"No way," I said. "You're messing with us."

"Oh, but we aren't," my dad said. "Doctor Alexis Fletcher never jokes about paranormal genetic experimentation. She wouldn't dream of it." Then he chuckled.

Mom scowled at him. "Reece."

"What? No one died. Why do we need to act like it?" His neck tightened, the cords popping as he reflected on his words. "Well, Brady did, obviously, and that was horrific, but he's alive and well now."

Alexis resumed as if my dad wasn't still yanking his foot out of his mouth. "Our genetic studies of paranormal activity focused, at the time, especially on a penchant for advanced healing."

"Super healing, we called it," Celia added.

My heart thumped irregularly. "Are you trying to say that Brady has super healing? That he's some kind of . . . *shit*, some type of supe or something?" I heard my question as if someone else were asking. It was absurd!

"Supe?" Celia asked.

"Supernatural," Griffin grunted.

"Oh, of course." She smiled, but tentatively. "I like that."

No one gave a hairy rat's ass what she did or didn't like.

When none of them hurried to confirm or deny the picture that was forming for us, Brady whispered, "No."

"Our employer was a private party," Alexis continued, "so we had quite a lot more flexibility than if it were a government facility."

"Which turned out to be a problem," my mom said. "Later on, we discovered things weren't done quite as legally as we'd been led to believe."

"How so?" I asked.

"We'll get there. The story's best told in order. Go ahead, Alexis."

"Our experiments began on organic matter like plants, and then we upgraded to animals."

I winced. "Really? You were straight-up torturing animals in the name of science?"

This time, Alexis didn't hesitate. "It was our job."

"Still." Hunt said with a meaningful glance at Bobo.

Alexis shrugged. "Science isn't always pretty, but no one complains when they get the life-saving cure for someone they love. Anyway, Celia, Monica, and I all got pregnant around the same time."

"And Mitzi too," Celia interjected.

"Right, of course, Mitzi too." Mitzi was Griffin's mom. She'd split when Griffin was three, leaving him alone in Orson's care. "Since we were unaffected by exposure to the experiments as adults, and our preliminary investigations suggested everything was safe, we didn't protect ourselves. We didn't safeguard you in our wombs from this same exposure. It appears you were affected while in utero."

"Affected how, exactly?" Hunt asked.

"Yeah, and by what?" Griffin followed up.

"This is where it gets tricky." Alexis began pacing slowly up and down the open corridor between our two groups. "You're probably familiar with the Aquoia indigenous tribe that populated North America before settlers arrived from Europe." She looked at us, and we nodded. "Well, the Aquoia tribe has passed down legends for many generations of a mystical place that holds supernatural powers. Whoever finds this place is said to be able to return from death and walk like a god among the living."

"What's that mean?" Brady asked.

"We're not entirely sure yet. That part has been less certain thus far in our studies." She considered Brady for a moment. "It's all shrouded in oral tradition and the specifics of Aquoian culture, much of which the tribal leaders refused to share with us, even though we've explained how vital it is that we have this information."

I grunted. "Can't blame them. Conquistadors plundered their land, murdering and devastating entire peoples as they went."

"Now's not the time for your idealism," my mom said. "Things aren't always as simple as you think they are."

"Oh, I couldn't disagree more. Cruelty wrapped in the guise of imperialism is still the same vicious, despicable, disgusting thing, no matter how you want to fluff it up."

"I'm not fluffing up anything," Mom snapped. "Can we focus on what's important here?"

"I thought a moral compass *was* important," I grumbled, but let it go. I was too intrigued by whatever was to come next.

"Anyway," Alexis resumed, "our employer found what they thought was the source of this Aquoian legendary power. A lake sacred to them. We were provided with water samples from this lake, along with parts of the ore deep beneath it."

"So what was it?" Hunt asked. "Some sort of new element?"

"That was our first hypothesis. It had to be a new element. What else could it be?"

"But. . .?"

"But we didn't find any new element. In fact, we didn't even find elements that were all that unusual. These elements are found across continents, and even their same combination is found in other places, in nearly identical proportions and quantities. Nowhere else does this combination of substances lead to anything particularly remarkable."

"So what then? It's a hoax? Nothing more than an inflated legend?" Hunt asked.

Alexis glanced at my mom, who picked up the story as Alexis took her seat again.

"We considered that, and let me tell you, our employer was very unhappy while we thought there was nothing to these legendary powers. But then. . ."

"But then," Alexis inserted, "the organic matter regularly exposed to this lake water began demonstrating extraordinarily advanced healing, far beyond what it was previously capable of."

"We cut off a plant's main stalk," my dad said, "and within that same day it grew back, stronger than before."

"That's when we knew for certain we were on to something after all," Orson said. "That's when it got really exciting."

"If it wasn't a unique element or combo of them, then what was it?" Brady asked. "What else could it be? Unless you're about to say that's the paranormal part."

My friends and I looked at our parents, anticipating their answer. Even Bobo joined us in staring.

"That's the thing, see," Celia said, sliding her glasses back onto her face. "There's no ready explanation. Science gives us no reason for the super healing. I love science because everything is so clear. It either is or it isn't. You suggest a hypothesis, and then you either prove or disprove it. There's no in-between, no nebulous areas. The logical explanation for a previously unexplained result is an unknown factor. A new element would explain it perfectly, and if not that, then a familiar element exposed to a distinct combination of events and other matter to cause this reaction."

"But we tried everything, and I do mean everything," my mom said, any tipsiness from her wine over dinner entirely absent now. "And nothing we did achieved the results we needed."

"Nothing we did brought about the super healing," Celia elaborated. "Nothing. Which could only mean. . ."

"When you've eliminated all that's impossible, then whatever remains, however improbable, must be the truth," I said.

Celia's brow arched at me. "Yes, Joss, that's right."

I shrugged. "Sherlock Holmes rocks."

Layla pushed off the counter but didn't advance toward our parents. "Let me get this straight. You're saying your 'official scientific conclusion'"—she air quoted—"is that there's some supercharged lake that gives super powers?"

"Essentially, yes," Alexis said.

"Trust me, it blew our minds too," my mom added.

Layla shook her head. "So with all the degrees and accolades you have, what you came up with was, um, magic?

Supernatural forces? I don't know, what do you even call that level of cray-cray?"

"You call it the unexplained," Dad said. "'Magic' is only the precursor to what science hasn't yet been able to explain."

"Or it could just be magic or whatever." I shrugged. "Until you prove it's not that, all you've got is another hypothesis."

My statement hung in the air without comment for a few moments.

Were we really discussing the possibility of magic and paranormal activity? With our crazy parents? Maybe Brady's dreams had infected everyone and I was deep into one. That would make more sense than this.

"Hold up, hold up," Brady finally said. "Please don't tell me you're trying to suggest I've got some sort of supernatural shit going on with me."

Celia's gaze snapped up to meet his. "Brady, my love, *you died*. There's simply no way anyone could have survived what you did—unless the super healing finally manifested in you."

"But. . ." Brady shook his head several times. "That's batshit nuts. I'm not some paranormal weirdo."

"You know on TV and in movies 'paranormal' means vamps and werewolves and shit, right?" Layla asked our parents. "Like, the really, really cuckoo, not-real shit."

Our parents exchanged looks yet again.

"Uh-uh. No fucking way," Layla said. "If you tell me you think there are vamps out there, I'll—"

"That's not what we're trying to say here," Porter interrupted. "We're just laying out the facts right now. None of you ever died and came back to life as kids, obviously, but we did see signs over the years that you healed far faster and better than was usual."

"It was enough to spur us into action," Celia said. "We left our jobs and moved across the country, covering our tracks as we went. No one knows you were exposed to whatever's in that lake.

No one can ever know. Do you all hear me? *No one.* Never. Not ever. For any reason."

"You expect us to just believe this shit?" Layla asked, her voice more high-pitched than usual. "You literally just admitted to making up Harvey, and we've been hearing you talk about him our entire lives like he was your favorite mascot in all of history. The one thing this has proven for certain is that you've lied to us."

"That's right, sis," Brady said. I couldn't remember the last time he'd called her *sis*, but it had to have been around the time when we were still in kindergarten.

"Believe what you want," Porter said. "We can't make you believe a thing you don't want to. But consider this: how else do you explain coming back from certain death nearly an hour after you were totally gone? You saw the doctors and nurses at the hospital. They said it was impossible. What else do you think defies the 'impossible' if not the *paranormal?* We have truly tried absolutely everything else in our determination to discount this possibility. But it's the one we keep coming back to in the end." He nudged up his glasses, squeezed the bridge of his nose, then let them drop into place again. "You know us—"

"We *thought* we knew you," Brady corrected.

"Yes, well, you surely don't think we *wanted* to embrace the hocus-pocus theory. You think we wanted to go to our boss and say that, despite our significant combined expertise and expensive titles, we couldn't explain something so supposedly simple as H_2O and stratum composition? We're the top experts in cellular and genetic structuring in the entire world. It was humiliating."

"And also unavoidable," Alexis said. "As scientists, we don't get to choose our results, just expose them."

"Yes, but still fucking humiliating."

I'd never heard Porter Rafferty drop an f-bomb before.

"Well, there you have it," Alexis said, crossing one leg over the other before resting a hand daintily atop them. "It's more involved than this, but I think that's enough explaining for now. You all look like you need to process."

I took in my friends. Their expressions were as dazed as I imagined my own was.

"What about all this? The spying?" Griffin asked.

Good. *Right on, Griff.* I'd already lost sight of that important bit.

"We had to monitor you," Orson said. "Keep track of how you're progressing."

"We had to protect you and keep you safe," Celia added. "We intercepted every one of your hospital labs, Brady. No one there ever saw a real sample of your blood."

"Fucking nefarious super-spy shit," I whispered to myself.

"That's still no excuse for any of this," Griffin objected. "You could have just talked to us about it all, you know. We aren't your *test subjects.* We're supposed to be your *children.*"

"You *are* our children, son," Orson said. "That's why we've done all this."

"We couldn't exactly have told you we suspected you might have paranormal abilities when you were in kindergarten, now could we?" my mom asked. "That would've been some show-and-tell. . ."

"We're far past kindergarten now," Layla said, scowling hard.

"Yes, you are," Mom continued. "But when would have been the right time for that? When you were ten? Fifteen? When your hormones were raging all over the place and we were doing our best to raise well-adjusted teenagers who'd eventually develop into hopefully responsible adults . . . with superpowers?"

"We talked about it a lot," my dad added. "We could just never find the right time for it. We didn't want to upset you."

"So you spied on us instead," Layla said. "Got it. Seems *tooootally* reasonable, guys. Great job there."

"You're going too far," Porter told her.

"Back atcha, Daddy-O."

While father and daughter argued, I tuned them out, trying to make sense of things. When I failed, I cut into their back-and-forth. "I'm not even close to finished with all the explanations you owe us, but I'm done for tonight. I need some time to process before the next stage of your confessions."

The parents blinked innocently at me.

I huffed. "I'm not buying that, so you might wanna stop selling. There's obviously more to the story we need to know, but on our terms, not yours."

"Honey. . ." Mom started, standing from her stool as if she were going to hug me.

"No," I snapped. "You guys have lied to us, spied on us, and hidden an entire secret freaking lair under the house. You keep track of more than any parent should ever know about their grown children. You've run the show this whole time. Now it's our turn. Things are gonna happen how and when we want them to."

"That's right, girl," Layla said. "Exactly fucking right."

"Meeting adjourned for tonight, right, guys?" I said with a glance at my friends. When they all obviously agreed, my attention skimmed across our many combined tattoos. "Before we go: did you let us get the ink we wanted as a way to test our healing abilities? To see if we'd, like, regenerate and erase the ink or something?"

Our parents shared a similar *you caught us* expression.

"Jeez," Layla mumbled.

I muttered, "I can't even anymore. Don't wait up for me. I have no idea when or if I'll be coming home tonight."

"Ditto," Layla said, and the guys didn't bother. It was obvious we were going to process and let off steam however the hell we wanted, free of parental involvement, aka parental manipulation.

"And don't bother trying to spy on me through my phone," I said. "I won't be bringing it with me."

"But, Joss," my mom said, "there are those who'd do anything to get a hold of your genetic material. Everything we've done has been for your protection, your safety—truly. Take your phone."

I smiled tightly at her and then Dad. "You haven't managed to convince me of that fact. Better luck next time." And with that, I stalked across the room, giving the liars a wide berth. Bobo quickly followed.

I didn't suck in a full breath until my friends and I were outside and I was settled in Clyde with Griffin at the wheel. Brady was driving Bonnie, clearly no longer obeying his mom's rules, Layla and Hunt along with him.

We'd meet at the one spot our parents *maybe* didn't know about: Raven's Lagoon.

18

Puzzle Pieces That Fit Only
with Each Other

Raven's Lagoon was a twenty-minute drive from the Periwinkle Hill neighborhood. For the first half of the drive, Griffin followed Bonnie's glowing taillights in brooding silence, which I only occasionally interrupted to tell Bobo to lie on the blanket I'd draped across the back seat for him.

Ordinarily, I would have left Bobo at home. Raven's Lagoon sat in the center of steep cliffs and jagged, unforgiving crags. To get down to the shore, we relied on ropes we'd anchored to rock outcroppings a couple of years before, when we'd begun driving, earning our independence—now obviously an illusion; thanks for nothing, parents—and first discovered the place, naming it for the ravens that circled far overhead. Since then, when we wanted to get away from absolutely everyone, this was the spot. We'd never seen another person there. The caws, croaks, and chirps, nestled between walls of rock, were all nature. It was where we could pretend the problems of the "civilized" world didn't affect us.

I'd have to leave Bobo halfway down the climb, tied up for his safety, which wasn't ideal, but I couldn't bear the thought of leaving him at home with a bunch of silver-tongued traitors. With pain squeezing my heart as a regular reminder of what they'd done to their own children, leaving him behind with them seemed a worse alternative.

"Sit, Bobo," I admonished as the pit bull stood again, sliding across the seat as Griffin took a curve too swiftly. Once the dog was settled again, I studied Griffin. His 1976 Ford Mustang Cobra II lacked the dashboard lighting of contemporary cars, but even so I could make out the tightness of his jaw, the way his fingers gripped the steering wheel too hard, how his stare ahead was too fixed, his thoughts a mile away. I could probably read him in the pitch dark with my eyes closed. Everything about him felt familiar.

I searched for something to say, instantly realized nothing would help much, then slumped down in my seat, an arm twisted behind me to comfort Bobo. He was picking up on our ill ease, which was making him extra restless.

A minute later, Griffin grumbled, his voice like gravel as it tumbled across my skin. "I can't believe it. I keep turning it over in my head, but I just can't fucking believe it."

I huffed bitterly. "What part, exactly, of the whole shitshow of deceit and betrayal are you referring to? 'Cause there's a whole hella lot to pick from."

For several moments, he didn't say a word, his breathing coming more heavily. "This whole time, pretty much our entire lives, they've known we aren't normal, and they didn't tell us?" His voice rose toward the end.

I gave Bobo a final scratch, then withdrew my arm, shifting in my seat to better study Griffin. "I didn't know that's how you felt." So much for being able to read him like a book. "I thought I was the only one who felt out of place, like I don't quite ever fully belong. Even though I've always felt like I belong with you guys." I paused before adding, "With you."

Somehow I hadn't realized that's how I felt until I spoke. "Like something's just wrong about everything. I dunno, out of place, maybe? Like life's a puzzle, and I'm a piece that doesn't really fit, but someone shoved me in to finish the puzzle even though I didn't go there. So my edges feel all cramped and my mid-section feels bent when it's not supposed to bend. Maybe that's a stupid way to put it."

I sighed, scrubbing both hands across my face. "Fuck. I'm not making any kind of sense." After some hesitation, I added hopefully, "Am I?" Had I really felt so out of sorts all this time?

Yes, I definitely had. I just hadn't wanted to admit there was a problem with my entire life. Because how exactly did one go about fixing *that*?

"Holy shit, Joss. That's how I feel too. Like I'm just going through the motions of a life that isn't really mine."

For several long seconds, the night enveloped us. Clyde's headlights illuminated swaths of thick trees and brush that lined the edges of the road before an all-encompassing darkness gobbled them up. Staring out at what I could see of the forest through the double cones of light, I experienced a sudden tightness in my chest that was in addition to everything my parents had done.

"Maybe we shouldn't be heading out to Raven's Lagoon tonight. It's super dark out."

"We'll be fine. We can always park up at the top and not head down if we want. We had to get away."

"Oh, for sure we did."

"And even with us leaving our phones behind, there was still no guarantee they wouldn't know where we went. This was our best bet to actually get away from them."

"Yeah, I know. I just. . ." I rubbed my hands across my arms as if I were cold. Only, the night was mildly muggy.

Finally, I turned my gaze back to Griffin. "So, does this mean you believe them and their whole 'paranormal' deal?"

"I think it explains what happened with Brady." Ahead of us, Brady tapped the brakes before whipping around a tight bend in the road. "You saw it. He was dead. Like, you can't get much deader."

"And then he wasn't," I whispered reverently. I'd probably never get over that miracle, not for as long as I lived.

"And then he wasn't," Griffin repeated.

Together, we stared out into the dark night. When the curves became tighter, arriving closer together, he said, "I mean, if you'd've told me yesterday we were some kind of paranormal whatevers, I would've laughed my ass off."

I chuckled. "You probably would've told me you wanted some of whatever I'd been smoking."

He laughed once, and when he didn't immediately continue, I added, "But then today happened."

"And yeah, all our parents, every single one of them, are massive liars."

"But what they told us also explains a lot."

"It really does. That feeling you were just describing? Joss, this accounts for all of that. If we really are paranormal—okay, never mind, that still feels too weird to say, especially since I don't even know how to say it. But if we really were exposed to something that gave us special healing abilities. . ."

He sighed, taking a hand from the steering wheel to run it through his hair, scratching at the short hairs at the nape of his neck before clutching the wheel again. "I'm not saying I believe it. I mean, I kind of am, I guess. But what I'm mostly trying to say is that I don't *not* believe it."

He glanced at me. "All the crazy shit we've done over the years? Hell, we should've been getting hurt left and right. But we haven't."

"Well, they just said we might have healing powers, not invincibility."

"Either way, we don't even have scars. Brady has one now, but it's small considering what he survived. You heard the surgeon at the hospital. The Miracle Kid. Because the entire hospital staff couldn't believe Brady'd come back from a piece of rebar thicker than my damn arm cutting through his chest and heart."

He downshifted, taking the turns quickly now, one after the other. "That can't've just been luck, Joss. He was dead for like an hour. No pulse, nothing. A fucking huge hole straight through his chest. And then, bam, he's back."

Still processing that, I shook my head. "So then we've got supernatural healing powers. Or at least Brade does." I licked my lips. "Sounds so weird to say it."

He chuckled darkly. "Oh, I know. I feel like I'm half out of my mind just for considering it at all, and yet, at the same time, it's like the answer I'd been waiting to learn for ages. Like so much makes sense now."

"It def explains why we've both felt so weird all our lives."

"It does. It's like we're gods walking among mortals, only, ya know, not."

Silence descended again while I processed, or rather attempted to process, the unbelievable. We were drawing close to Raven's Lagoon now. A few more curves, these the tightest of them all, and then the road would straighten for a short stretch.

Bobo whined from the back seat, and I reached for him again, scratching under his chin. His tongue lolled out of his mouth. "So what's next? What do we do now? Test the theory?"

"Yeah, something like that. We're certainly not gonna rely on our parents to tell us what's what."

"Hell no, we aren't," I said.

"But let's figure that out tomorrow. I can't think about it anymore tonight."

"Agreed. I could do with some letting loose. We probably all can."

"For sure. We—"

His gaze jerked toward the dark floorboard.

"What's wrong?" I asked right away.

"Um. . ." Griffin pumped the brake pedal repeatedly, but nothing happened.

I couldn't tear my eyes off the sharp curve at the edge of the headlights' reach.

"Grab Bobo and hold the fuck on," he barked.

I didn't bother asking follow-up questions. Griffin was still slamming on the brake, but we were barreling toward the turn.

I gripped Bobo by the collar and heaved him into the passenger seat even as I ordered him, "Bobo, come." The transfer was awkward, but a moment before we sped into the curve, I held Bobo clasped to my chest.

Griffin pressed the clutch and downshifted from fifth to third gear with a series of jerks that snapped my neck against the headrest. A piercing grind came from the gearbox that no Mustang lover ever wanted to hear.

We squealed around the bend as Griffin flashed the lights several times to warn Brady, but his taillights were already beyond the next turn, which sat at the bottom of a steep incline. I might not be able to see far enough, but I didn't need to. I knew this road. The worst part was yet to come.

"What the fuck's going on?" I snapped.

"I think we're out of brake fluid."

"But that can't be."

"I know. I checked fluids just yesterday."

"You think—fuck, did someone tamper with the car?"

"No idea why anyone would, but it's the only reasonable explanation." He kept pumping the brake with the same result, the engine straining the whole time as he drove us in the wrong gear, trying to force Clyde to slow down. The car was picking up speed on the downhill despite Griffin's efforts. "I'm guessing someone poked a hole in the brake line. We've probably been leaking fluid the whole drive."

"Fuck!"

The next turn was too sharp, coming up too fast.

Griffin's eyes didn't leave the road as he gripped the steering wheel, entirely focused on trying to regain control of the car. We had to be going at least forty miles an hour. The only things left to try were to grind us into second—but that would probably strip the gears, leaving us coasting, completely out of gear, and picking up speed quickly—or to pull on the emergency brake.

The car jerked repeatedly as it resisted the low gear, and with a furious grunt Griffin shifted up to fourth. Still too low for our speed, but it would hopefully delay our stalling.

Before I could suggest it, Griffin yanked on the emergency brake.

Nothing happened, not even the usual *crickkk* when it was drawn up into position.

Someone must have cut the cable to it.

Griffin gritted his teeth and growled. "Grab Bobo and get ready to jump when I tell you."

I whipped my head his way. "What? No. Fuck no."

"Joss, I need you to do this. We don't have time to argue."

"I'm not arguing. I'm just not leaving you."

"I'll jump after you're clear."

I stared at him, the pressure of the passing seconds—moments we didn't have to spare—clawing at my limbs. "I'll only jump when you do."

"You have to get clear first while I can steer, then I'll go."

I flicked a panicked look ahead, seeing nothing but straight down as far as the lights shone, too aware the sharpest turn yet would be popping up any minute.

"Don't think. Just do it," Griffin said. "Let go of Bobo after you jump so you don't land on each other."

My lungs seized at the thought that Bobo might get hurt. "Griff—"

"Go. Now. Before it's too late."

How was this happening? We'd been fine mere minutes ago. It was like watching Brady fall to his death all over again, the balcony breaking in slow motion. . .

"I can't let anything happen to you," I said sharply, meaning it wholeheartedly. "If anything were to happen to you—"

"I'll come back like Brady did."

"*No*. If that's all bullshit? If Brady just got lucky? I can't—"

Griffin faced me for a second, meeting my eyes. "*I'll come back*."

"Don't you dare put yourself in that position. Promise me." The words lodged in my throat, everything happening too fast. I wasn't ready!

"Promise me," I growled.

Griffin glanced up ahead of us, then leaned across me, yanked on the handle, and wrenched open the door.

"Get ready," he said.

"No, Griff. No." But I wrapped my arms around Bobo just the same.

We were going faster now.

"When I say," he barked, sounding absent, like he was already calculating the precise moment for my jump.

"Griff," I tried again, unsure what to say. We were already on borrowed time. There was so much unsaid between us. So many hopes.

The door flopped shut.

"Open it back up. Now," Griffin yelled.

Without thinking, I obeyed, pushing it wide, struggling to hold it open with the rush of air working against me. Bobo shivered in my arms.

"Just in case," Griffin said—and I tensed. "Joss, I love you. Now *go*."

My brain struggled to process what he'd said, what was supposed to be happening. But when Griffin shoved me toward the door, I got my body to do what it needed to do, letting movement and muscle take over. I aimed for the soft shoulder—though it wouldn't be soft at this speed, just slightly gentler than the asphalt—and pushed off.

A moment before landing, I released Bobo. He hit hard with a heart-wrenching yelp. I slammed into the ground half a second later, the air knocked out of me entirely as I rolled and rolled. I finally bashed to a rough halt, lodged against a tree trunk.

Gasping, disoriented, I searched for Griffin and Bobo. There were no lights anywhere, just the dense darkness cast by tall trees. I couldn't immediately tell which direction the road lay as I pulled up onto my hands and knees, crawling through prickly brush that pierced the skin of my palms.

"Griffin?" I cried out, though there was no way he'd hear me. "Griffin!"

A single breath later, the sound of an engine grinding unhappily pierced the thickness of the night . . . then tires sliding across loose rocks . . . and then nothing.

"*Griffin!*" I screamed.

Crashing metal ended my cry abruptly.

For several seconds, I couldn't think, couldn't breathe, couldn't move.

Then I forced myself out of it, snapping into swift action.

"Bobo," I cried this time.

He whined off to the right.

"Keep talking to me, boy," I said, limping over to him as quickly as I could. A branch whipped against my cheek, another against my forehead, but I found my pittie and dropped to my knees next to him, running my hands over his body, searching for injuries.

"Oh my God, Bobo. Are you okay? Can you walk?"

He tried to stand but crumpled when his front leg buckled under his weight.

"Fuck," I breathed, studying his body the best I could in the near darkness. From what I could make out, he had an injured leg and probably some cuts, but nothing life threatening.

I slid my arms around him and pushed to standing with him in my hold, wincing at the pain in one of my own legs but not stopping to examine myself. None of that mattered right now.

Getting to Griffin was the only thing that did.

It took me longer to find the road than I would have liked. When I'd jumped, with all the rolling, I'd ended up farther away than seemed reasonable, and the forest's impenetrable shadows distorted direction.

When I finally reached the road, I was numb. Forcing one foot in front of the other, I struggled with Bobo's weight but just kept moving. I headed toward Griffin, the man I thought I might love in a way I didn't love the others.

Who had said he *loved me*. Maybe it was a declaration of platonic love—it was possible—but then again, maybe it wasn't.

Another hundred steps, then another. I made my legs keep going until I finally got lucky, the sparse light of the moon brushing across crushed and broken foliage the width of a speeding car.

This was where Griffin's Mustang had gone over. It had to be.

Gingerly, I lowered Bobo to the ground. "Stay here, boy. I've gotta check on Griff. *Stay here.* I'll be right back for you."

Bobo whined, but he wasn't going anywhere, not on that leg.

Once he was settled, I picked up speed, absently registering the strain I was placing on my own injuries. Things didn't feel entirely right, but Griffin was down there somewhere, past the flattened brush.

Limping, I made it to the edge, where my breath rushed out of me yet again. It was nearly straight down over the side.

"Griffin," I yelled, waiting for the slim sliver of a moon to appear from behind a cloud.

When the moon eventually cast its faint light, it caught on Clyde.

Lodged between a tree and a boulder.

Upside down, tires still.

No movement.

"Griffin!"

No answer.

No response of any kind.

Nothing at all beyond the whine of settling metal.

My heart squeezed in my chest like it was calling it quits.

I didn't let it do any such thing. I forced it to keep working. I made all of me keep functioning as I scrambled toward the edge of the ravine, scouring the mountainside, searching for the best way down.

The hum of an engine reached me over the insistent whooshing of my pulse.

It was far away, but there were no other roads snaking off this one at this point. Too many curves to make turnoffs safe.

"Please, please, please," I muttered to myself as I limped back toward the road. Without a phone, and without an easy way down to Griffin, the approaching car was my best hope.

I reached the asphalt just as the car's headlights sped past.

"Stop!" I yelled with everything I had, flinging myself into the road behind the vehicle. With every wish that Griffin had survived, that Bobo was okay, I put it all in my one plea.

"Help," I screamed one last time.

And the brake lights lit up.

Even from where I stood, a hundred feet away now, I recognized their shape.

"Bonnie," I whispered, then sank to the ground right where I stood, in the middle of the road.

Bonnie, with Brady at the wheel, performed a quick U-turn. Never had I been so grateful to be pinned down in glaring headlights.

Without rising, I waved my arms to make sure I caught their attention. I didn't stop until the roar of Bonnie's engine quieted, and the car slowed, drawing to a stop at my side.

Doors wrenched open quickly as I allowed my eyes to shut with relief.

"Joss?" Layla said. "Oh my God, what's wrong? Where's Griffin?"

I lifted my arm and pointed toward the broken branches and foliage, over the edge, to the unforgiving ravine beyond it, where the guy I loved had landed, without me ever getting to say that I loved him back.

19

The Bonds of Family Run Thicker than Blood

Layla stood over me, squeezing my back repetitively in a way that suggested she didn't even notice she was doing it. I sat on the shoulder of the road, an injured Bobo cradled in my lap, my body numb everywhere—especially my heart. I was afraid to let it loose from the temporary prison I'd hastily constructed for it. I feared what I might feel. Griffin had told me he loved me for the first time in all the many years we'd shared together as friends, and I hadn't said it back. I'd let him go over the edge of the mountain without those final words.

Now, there was no guarantee I'd ever get the chance to tell him how I felt. I didn't know if I'd ever see the guy I was now wholly convinced I actually did love. When I wasn't worried about ruining the friendships that meant everything to me in the world, it all became so simple. *I fucking loved the shit out of Griffin Conway.*

He lay close to the bottom of a crazy steep ravine, his car upside down, not a peep coming from the scene beyond the occasional creak or groan of the vehicle shifting.

"Are you sure he's down there?" Hunt asked from where he stood at the edge of the shoulder, peering down into the dark.

All that was visible of Clyde was whatever the slice of moon illuminated here and there. It occasionally glinted across the Mustang's undercarriage, a weaving of pipes and chrome that was too reminiscent of guts spilling from a body. I couldn't look anymore.

When I didn't answer Hunt, he turned to study me. "It's possible he jumped before the car went off the road."

As soon as I flagged them down, Brady, Hunt, and Layla had swarmed out of Bonnie. I'd kept my shit together long enough to run down the most pertinent information as quickly as I could. Griffin's life hung in the balance of whatever choices we made.

"Is it possible he managed to jump before the car went over?" I repeated aloud, thinking it through some more, even though it was all I'd been able to think about. "Yeah, sure. I wasn't aware of anything beyond trying to keep Bobo safe and my bones from breaking till I stopped rolling. But then I called for him right away." I gulped. "He didn't answer."

He hadn't answered any of us. It was the first thing the three of them had done after my machine-gun-fire fast update. We'd shouted for him until our voices cracked.

"I'm gonna walk back up the road," Hunt said. "See if he's in the brush off to the side."

"No point," Layla said, her voice somber as a deflated party balloon. "Brady went back that way. He for sure would've been keeping his eyes peeled. If he'd spotted Griff, he would've honked to let us know."

The five of us rarely went anywhere without our iPhones. When we weren't together, we kept in constant contact with each other. If our parents weren't assholes who tracked our every move, and we'd had our phones on us like usual, we would have been able to call for help. Instead, my insides were tied into knots so tight I could hardly pull in a full breath.

Brady had driven off to the closest sign of civilization to call emergency services. We could hardly remain within the town limits of Ridgemore and be any farther removed from people. Of course, that had been the whole point of coming out to Raven's Lagoon, which was just a few more turns away.

"I'm still gonna go," Hunt said. "I can't just stand here and do nothing. I'm losing my fucking mind."

I stared up at him, wanting to offer him comfort, but found none to give.

"Brady'll be back soon," Layla said, though she didn't sound convinced it would be soon enough. "How long's he been gone, anyway?"

None of us knew. We didn't wear watches; we usually had our phones.

Hunt wove both hands into his hair and tugged hard, grunting like a feral animal, something I'd never seen him do. "It's been too fucking long. It feels like he's been gone for hours."

It had probably only been a few minutes.

"You know Brade'll be driving like fucking hellhounds are on his bumper," Layla said. "He'll get help out here as fast as humanly possible."

"That's the thing," Hunt said, staring once more into the darkness of the ravine below. Desperation pinched every one of his features. "Humans aren't fast enough."

"We might not even be human," Layla whispered.

"I'm counting on that now," I said, running a soothing hand along Bobo's back. He'd finally stopped whimpering. I was so relieved he'd survived the jump that I didn't want to let him go. He wasn't asking to go anywhere, heavy and limp across my lap.

I clenched my jaw with resolve. "If Brady could come back from what happened to him, then Griffin can come back from this." A shiver ran through me, making my body jolt, and Bobo complained. I kissed him on the top of the head, then whispered, "He has to. Griff *has to* survive this. He fucking has to. He just fucking has to."

For several moments, none of us said anything. The chirping of insects from the heavy foliage increased in volume, setting me further on edge.

I covered Bobo's ears, then yelled with all I had. "*Griffin!*"

Though we'd called and called for him already, Layla didn't hesitate to follow my lead. We shouted until the night around us quieted, until Hunt again said, "I'm gonna climb down."

"No, Hunt, no," Layla said, not for the first time. "It's too steep and too dark. And Clyde's like a hundred feet down. We've got no equipment, no rope, nothing."

"I gotta try something. What if he needs us right now?"

He didn't complete his thought, but I registered what he didn't say just the same. *What if Griff is down there* dying *and we're playing it safe?*

"Hunt," Layla said firmly. "We can't risk you too. You could slip and fall too easily."

When Hunt's mouth only settled into determined lines, she added, "Griff wouldn't want you to risk your own life to save his."

"Maybe not. But isn't that what we do for each other? We're fucking *family*, Lay, and I'm not gonna stand here for another second scratching my damn ass while my brother's down there alone, needing me."

"He's right," I said.

Layla circled around me just to better frown down at me. I'd been the first to suggest it was too dangerous to climb down to Griffin's aid. The only safe way down was to rappel, and we needed harnesses and a rope for that.

I no longer gave a single, lonely fuck.

With Bobo in my arms, I slowly stood, doing what I could to hide my wince as sharp pain shot through my left leg and into my hip. A smattering of twinkling stars danced in my vision before I blinked them away. Breathing deeply, I waited for the pain to pass as I steadied myself.

"You'd better not be thinking what I think you're thinking," Layla growled.

"I'm going down with Hunt."

"Like hell you are. Woman, you can barely stand!"

"Maybe, but I'll live, and we need to get down to Griff, like right the fuck now."

"No, girl, not like this. If you can't fucking stand, you can't fucking climb. Don't be stupid."

Ordinarily, I'd want to bitch-slap the crap out of her for using the word *stupid* anywhere near me. But she was right, and I knew it. It was just that I didn't care anymore.

"Take care of Bobo till I get back."

Layla dodged Bobo to flatten a hand against my chest. Her fingers were light across my breastbone, but her wide-legged stance told me she wasn't going to let me climb anywhere.

"We all want Griff well and safe. But what happens when we get him back and then you've gone and fallen to your fucking death 'cause you're hurt now? He'll fucking murder us for not having stopped you."

I scowled and readjusted Bobo's weight, trying to find a position that put less pressure on my leg. Every which way hurt, and I could tell my sweet boy was in pain too.

"Griffin knows as well as you that no one tells me what to do," I said, trying to figure how I'd actually manage the climb when my body wasn't working right. "I do what I want."

"True," Layla conceded. "But you're not an idiot, Joss. Don't start acting like one now."

"Lay," Hunt interjected. "You help me as I go down. Joss can walk up the road with Bobo, searching in the brush on Griff's driver's side."

Quickly, he glanced from her to me. Layla and I nodded.

"Good," he grunted. "Let's go." He stared down the ravine as if memorizing what he could make out in the dark. Next, he got down onto all fours, then his stomach, and started inching back into the void behind him.

My heart shot into my throat, lodging there, making it hard to swallow. I croaked out, "Hunt, don't you fucking dare fall. I'll kick your ass if you do."

I might love Griffin in a way that transcended friendship, but I loved Hunt too. I loved them all. I couldn't lose a single one of them. *I wouldn't.*

Ordinarily, Hunt would have chuckled or ribbed me back. Instead, his handsome face, drawn into somber lines, its planes more severe than usual in the long dark shadows, settled into determination.

"I'm serious, Hunt," I said. "I need you to come back from this."

"I know, Joss. Trust me, I know. We'll all be back together soon."

"You won't keep going down if it doesn't feel safe?" I pressed.

Layla snorted, but it wasn't her usual sarcastic sound. She was pissed, more at the situation than at Hunt, I'd guess. "Safe? Nothing about this is fucking safe. A nearly straight-down climb on rock that's probably slick as fuck? And when it's not straight up-and-down rock, then it's covered in fallen leaves that are probably slick as fuck. And in the dark, no less? Yeah, not safe, not at all."

"I'll be fine," Hunt said, already inching backward over the edge's lip. "You know me, I can climb anything."

That much was true. Dude was like a monkey. But that was the whole point—he was only *like* a monkey. He was in zero-drop sneakers, not feet with opposable thumbs.

I stared at him, willing myself to find the right thing to say or do. To make the right decisions. I wasn't sure this was the correct one, but the alternative definitely felt wrong. We couldn't just wait when we might be able to do something to help Griffin. Anything was better than nothing, wasn't it?

"Joss, go," Hunt said, snapping me into action. Usually I'd be the first to do whatever was needed.

Limping away a few steps, I stopped and whirled back around before Hunt dipped entirely out of view. "Hey, Hunt."

"Yeah?"

"I love you, you know?"

"Yeah, I do. I love you too, Joss."

Before this night, none of us had ever exchanged *I love yous*. I didn't think even Layla and Brady had, and they were actual siblings. But I'd made the mistake of not telling Griffin, and if I did anything, I learned from my mistakes.

"You too, Lay," I said. "I love your snarky ass."

She smiled at me, but it was a ghost of her usual jovial expression. "Ditto, girl. Now go find Griffin."

Numbly, I nodded, pointing myself back up the winding mountain road, hugging Bobo tightly to my chest, limping as I studied the brush for any sign that Griffin could have jumped into it. I searched for bent branches, flattened grass, anything at all that would tell me he wasn't in Clyde, upside down near the bottom of the ravine.

Though it was dark, I was certain I wasn't missing anything of importance. I found nothing that helped. Nothing to make me hopeful.

When sirens finally cut through the night, tears stung the back of my eyeballs.

"Help's coming, boy," I told Bobo, kissing him on the ear and turning to head back to where I'd left Hunt and Layla. I needed to be there when emergency services arrived, and I was moving much slower than usual.

Pain and relief merged to create a heady mixture. Every step I took required every bit of my attention, lest I crumple before I could get there. Bobo whined a bit, but I had no more soothing to offer him.

I focused only on moving one foot after the other, keeping the dog and myself upright.

The sirens wailed louder, closer, and when I turned to look, blue and red flashing lights colored the night. Another shudder raced through me as I walked on.

When the sirens were nearly upon me, Brady slammed on the brakes in Bonnie, sliding to a stop beside me. He didn't say a word, nor did I, before I hobbled to the passenger's side and got in. Within seconds, he floored it again, still ahead of the parade of emergency vehicles. He must have indeed driven like a bat out of hell to get a response here so quickly. To us it had felt like a small eternity, but I had no doubt he'd broken every speed limit and most laws on his way to get help.

I sat gingerly on the leather seat, not bothering with a seat belt, and readied myself to jump out the second Brady pulled to a stop.

"Any update?" he eventually asked.

"No." Disappointment made the one word heavy. "None. Hunt's climbing down to try to help. Layla's got his back."

I hoped. Brady must have thought the same as he tensed beside me, his fingers like vises around the steering wheel.

"I was looking in the brush, just in case. But nothing. I think he went over in Clyde."

Tersely, he nodded.

When Bonnie's headlights shone over the shoulder with the trampled foliage, Layla was standing at the edge, waving her arms to signal this was the spot. Brady slowed, then parked far enough away to leave room for the ambulance.

I couldn't fully hide my grimace as I rose from my seat, exiting the car, and before I'd managed to steady myself on my feet, Brady was there, arms extended.

"Here, let me take Bobo."

Blankly I nodded, handing over my pittie who was groggy from pain and exhaustion. Brady hugged him close, then stalked over to his twin sister while I staggered behind him.

"How's Hunt doing?" he asked before I could.

"Fine," Layla answered, resuming her position at the cliff's edge. "He's about given me a heart attack a few times, but he's almost at the car."

Brady looked into the ravine. "I can't see him."

"I know. But keep watching. When the moon hits just right, you'll see him."

The rhythmic whirring of a helicopter sliced through the looping sirens. My relief was so intense I stumbled to the ground beside my friends and plopped onto my butt.

"Hold on, Griff," I breathed to no one but myself. "Help is here. Just hold on a little longer."

I prayed it wasn't too late—and if it was, that our traitorous parents were telling the truth for once, and we weren't ordinary humans.

Right about then, I'd kiss every one of the lying bastards smack on the mouth if only they'd be right about us.

Come on, Griff, be something paranormal. Live for me.

The first of the emergency vehicles crunched to a halt beside me.

20

My Heart Smashed to Smithereens at the Bottom of a Ravine

The sirens were too loud for my already shot nerves, but when they were shut off, the silence somehow felt more oppressive. The EMTs shouted to be heard over the approaching helicopter, the radios attached to their belts or shoulders crackling with updates and orders that made it too real. Too horrifically devastating.

Griffin was still near the bottom of a dark ravine. EMTs were rushing around us to get down to him, their movements surreal in the flashing lights of their hastily parked vehicles along the side of the road.

A woman in a dark uniform walked over to Layla, me, and Brady, who still held Bobo in his arms. When she crouched next to me, I read her badge, which declared her to be Hayden from Emergency Services.

"Hey, guys. Are you the victim's friends?"

"No," Brady retorted right away. "We're his *family*."

"And he's not a victim," Layla added.

Hayden nodded, unconcerned by our bristly reactions, as if she'd heard a version of our responses before.

"Tell me what you think I need to know," she said, having to almost yell. "As fast as you can."

The helicopter was drawing lower, scattering fallen and decaying leaves in all directions. Layla's chin-length hair circled her head, and my small braids whipped against my face amid a swirl of loose strands.

Brady said, "We're pretty sure our friend Griffin went over the mountain. His car's upside down close to the bottom of the ravine. We haven't heard anything from him or seen any movement."

I swallowed thickly as Hayden nodded again, likely thinking Griffin's chances of survival were slim.

"Our other friend, Hunt, went down to try to help him," Layla said. "He's still down there."

"'Went down?'" Hayden asked.

"Climbed down," I answered. "We didn't know how long you guys would be, so he went down to try to help."

"I see." But Hayden's lips pursed in disapproval before she leaned toward the radio on her shoulder, pressed a button, and said, "We've got a situation. Someone's climbing down the ravine to try to help the vic."

"Please don't do anything that would startle him," I said. "Hunt, our friend who's climbing down, he's free-climbing."

Hayden took a second to frown at me before adding into her radio, "The climber's going down without safety gear. Proceed with extreme caution."

She looked at the three of us. "Anything else I need to know before the team descends into the ravine?"

I shook my head. "I don't think so. Griffin thought someone had tampered with his car, cut the brake line. All of a sudden, the brakes gave out. The emergency brake didn't work either."

"And Griffin knows his car inside and out," Layla said. "He keeps everything running perfectly."

"Yeah," I added. "He told me he checked the car's fluids just yesterday."

Hayden eyed me and my extended leg. "You were in the car with him?"

"Yeah, me and my dog."

She turned to check out Bobo too.

"Griffin made me jump with my dog. By the time I rolled to a stop, I heard what sounded like him going over."

A couple of EMTs in the same uniform Hayden wore ran over to the edge of the mountain, carrying rope and what looked like maybe a harness, though I didn't get a great view before they started yelling down the mountainside. One of them shouldered a large spotlight and pointed it down into the ravine.

Hayden glanced from them to us. "They'll get your friend Hunt out too. Better to get him up and out before the chopper starts churning everything right above him."

As far as I could tell, that ship had already sailed. Even Bobo's short fur was whipping around under the downwash from the helicopter's blades.

"It'll get worse," Hayden said, as if responding to my thoughts. "We've gotta secure everything first so then we can focus on getting our team to the wreck and getting your friend out."

"What can we do to help?" I asked.

"Stay out of the way. Let us do our jobs. I'll be right back to check you out."

Brady scowled, but none of us complained. The sooner Griffin and Hunt were out of that ravine, the better.

Hayden stood and seemed ready to walk away when she faced us again. "Are you guys high schoolers? You go to Ridgemore High?"

"Yeah," Layla said.

"*Shit.* So the Hunt who's down the ravine is Hunt Fletcher?"

"Yep," Brady said. "You know Hunt?"

"I don't, but I'm Hayden *Wills*, Zoe's big sister." She paused for a quick second, likely considering her little sister's crush on the guy currently down a dark, sketchy, dangerous ravine, now beneath the whipping winds of a helicopter.

"I've gotta go make sure they're being careful with him. Stay put." She bounded away two steps before glancing back at me. "You're okay to wait a minute?"

"Of course. Go help them. *Please*. That's what I really need."

She smiled tightly. "I appreciate that, but my job's to check you out too. I'll be right back."

More people in uniform ran around us, setting up spotlights and aiming them into the precipice, making it even harder to see anything beyond their bright beams. But as the chopper flew lower, hovering directly above the ravine, I spotted the outlines of at least two people being lowered into the chasm with what looked like a stretcher in their hold, the taut line of ropes trailing behind them.

Brady knelt beside me. "Can you take Bobo? I've gotta go see. Make sure they're doing things right."

Anybody else might think it a ludicrous statement. Here we were, high schoolers, feeling the need to supervise the professionals with all the gear and experience. But the tightness in my chest loosened some, knowing Brady would be there to keep an eye out for Griffin and Hunt, and I readily extended my arms to receive the dog.

My pittie's weight settled heavily on my lap, sending a sharp wave of pain from my hip to the tips of the toes of my left leg, but I didn't utter a peep about it, telling Layla instead, "You go too. I'm not going anywhere."

She hesitated for a second, but then took off after her brother, who stood off to the side and out of the way, but perched so that he had an unobstructed view down the incline.

Bobo was sluggish, but I took the fact that he was no longer whimpering as a good sign. His leg was obviously hurt, but I hoped that was as far as the damage went. If he had internal damage too, well, I didn't want to think about it.

Forcefully keeping my thoughts from heading in that direction, I waited, each inhale feeling incomplete, ragged even, like I wouldn't be able to take a full breath until I knew my crew was safe.

An hour later, which was probably more like five minutes, Hayden squatted next to me, then opened a large bag and drew out a blood pressure cuff.

"I'm going to need you to move your dog."

I sighed, guilt rolling through me though I understood it wasn't my fault. I couldn't have known what would happen, that I should have left Bobo at home after all.

"He's hurt too."

She quickly glanced at him before pinning her attention on me again. I prepared to defend Bobo, to explain how worthy he was of her attention. But then she said, "He jumped out of the car with you. I assume it was moving?"

"Yes. The brakes had already gone out then. Griffin was trying to force the car to slow down through downshifting, but he also didn't want to strip the gears. Then we'd be speeding down the hill without anything to slow us down."

"Sounds like your friend handled the situation as best he could."

"He did. And he didn't. He didn't jump out before going over. And he should have."

"Hmmm," Hayden said noncommittally. "Can you slide your dog beside you so I can check on you?"

I hesitated. "His front right leg's hurt."

"I'm sorry to hear that, but my priority is checking on you."

I started to glare at her, realized she was almost certainly just following official procedure, and gently slid Bobo to lie on the ground beside me. The moment he was off my lap, Hayden snapped a blood pressure cuff around my arm. I kept my other hand resting on Bobo. Though his eyes were closed, I didn't want him to worry for a second that I was going to leave him.

"Does it hurt here?" Hayden asked a millisecond before she put pressure on my shinbone.

I almost blacked out from the sudden onslaught of pain.

"I'll take that as a big yes," she said, though I was unaware of how exactly I was signaling my discomfort. I was doing everything I could just to stay conscious.

"I'm gonna need a couple of stretchers over here," she said into her shoulder radio. I had no idea how anyone would hear her over the helicopter and the throbbing of my heartbeat through every part of my body.

Next I knew, Hayden was leaning over me, her face close to mine, which made me realize I was flat on my back and didn't remember getting that way.

"Stay with me, Joss. You're gonna be okay."

Had I told her my name? I must have. "I'm not worried about me," I slurred. "Griffin. Hunt."

"Hunt's fine. He's already coming up."

"Griffin," I said.

"Hold still. You're going to feel a pinch as I insert your drip line."

"Griffin," I repeated, more urgently this time. But her attention was on my arm. A quick, biting sting told me the needle was in, and then cold swam through my veins as she adjusted the IV bag above my head.

I tried to turn to look but discovered myself strapped in, my neck in some sort of brace preventing movement.

"What . . . what's going on?"

"You're okay." But Hayden was distracted by something behind me that I couldn't see.

"I know I'm okay," I snapped, pulling on my awareness, forcing it to comply. "I was just walking around, looking for Griff."

"Well, I don't know how on earth you managed to do that. Your leg's badly fractured."

"Okay. What about Griffin?"

No answer as she riffled through the large bag at her feet.

"Why am I so groggy?"

"It's the pain meds in the IV."

"No, before that."

Finally, Hayden's face appeared above mine. "Probably the pain. You held it together until you didn't need to anymore. I've seen it a million times."

Only Hayden didn't seem old enough to have seen anything like this a million times in our small town, where things like this didn't happen often.

"What about Bobo?" I was no longer able to focus on her face.

"Bobo's the dog?" Hayden asked.

"Yeah," Layla answered for me, "and he's important to her, to us."

Damn right he is.

"Lay?" I called out and immediately felt her hand in mine, the arm that didn't have a tube sticking out of it.

"I'm here."

"Tell her to back off the meds. I can barely think." I blinked up at my friend. Her face was blurry, her hair falling around it in a yellow cascade.

"Too late, woman. From the looks of you, you're gettin' the good stuff."

"I don't want the good stuff." Panic suddenly squeezed my throat. "I want Griff and Hunt and Bobo."

"Hunt's already up, and Hayden's got Bobo strapped into a stretcher, even though I don't think she's supposed to treat animals the same way she does people."

"And Griff?"

Layla paused.

I squeezed her hand so hard she squeaked, then pulled hers away, shaking it out.

"They couldn't get any of the doors open. They just finished cutting a hole in Clyde's undercarriage. They're pulling him out now."

"So he's def in there?"

"Yeah." The way Layla said it didn't make it seem like a good thing. "Brady and Hunt are talking with Wade's and Reed's dads."

Xander Jones was the sheriff and Kyle Carter one of his deputies.

Despite my fervent attempts to keep track of what was going on around me, I faded in and out of awareness. I wasn't passing out, I just wasn't able to focus, no matter how hard I tried. I registered shouted voices around me and crackling through radios, but I couldn't tell what they were saying. The whirring of the helicopter and what might have been a saw that cut through metal. More cars arriving, doors opening and closing.

"Layla?" I called, but no one answered. Again, I tried to turn my head to find my friends and Bobo. I managed only to press against the foam padding of a neck brace I didn't think I needed.

"Brady? Hunt?" I attempted, but still nothing. "Anyone?"

Hayden filled my vision.

"Are you okay, Joss? Do you need anything?" This time, her brow was low with concern. Or was that sadness?

"Yeah," I said, unsure how clear my words were. Whatever was in the IV was working overtime to knock me out. "Where's Griffin?"

Her eyes clouded before she opened her mouth to answer. In that brief moment, my heart wanted to shatter. "Is he okay? Is he. . .?" I swallowed with difficulty. "Is he alive?"

Before she could respond, a wail cut through the racket, suffocating me.

That was Layla's voice.

Hayden pressed her lips together before saying, "I'm really sorry, Joss. He didn't make it."

"No. Nope. Uh-uh. That's not possible."

My heart said it was, careening toward a lethal crash of its own. I pushed through the anguish, refusing to accept Hayden's news, though it seemed confirmed by Layla somewhere beyond my line of sight.

"Joss," Hayden began, her voice filled with compassion. "There's nothing we can do. He's gone. He's been gone."

"No."

"His neck's broken, probably on impact. There's nothing we can do now to revive him."

"Get me the sheriff," I barked as my faculties returned through sheer force of will.

"Joss, that won't do anything—"

"Hayden," I said, encouraged that I remembered her name since I couldn't get my eyes to sharpen enough to read her nametag anymore. "Please. It's important. I need to speak with the sheriff."

She wavered. "Your friends have already talked to him."

"But I don't think they've told him what he most needs to hear. *Please.* Take me to him."

She looked behind me. "You're not going anywhere."

"Then ask him to come to me. I'm literally begging you."

She sighed heavily.

"I promise you, I'm not crazy. I need to speak with him. He doesn't know everything."

"You can tell me whatever it is and I'll pass it on. He's busy coordinating—"

"Hayden. You've gotta do this. Right now. It's urgent."

She stared at me hard while I tried to make myself appear lucid. I didn't think I succeeded, because when she rose, it was with a heavy sigh, like she'd just been talked into doing something incredibly stupid.

I exhaled in relief and waited, hoping she'd actually gone to get Xander Jones instead of simply walking away from me. Since I couldn't get out of this contraption on my own, it'd be an effective escape from my pleas.

Enough time passed that my awareness slipped in spite of my ferocious grip on it. When the sheriff finally crouched down beside me, I had to fight to regain lucidity.

"Hey, Joss," he said. "Just take it easy, okay? We've got everything handled. Just rest and get better. Your parents will meet us at the hospital."

And he pivoted to walk away.

"Wait, no!" I felt as if I screamed it; I don't know how it actually came out. Either way, the sheriff turned back toward me.

Furiously, I blinked away the fog until my focus landed on his furrowed brow.

It was more important than ever that I say the right thing. I'd only get one chance at it, and I felt as if I were drunk, high, and massively sleep-deprived all at once. Not good.

But it didn't matter. It was what I had.

"Listen, Sheriff. I know this is gonna sound crazy and that you might think it's 'cause of whatever pain meds I'm on right now, but please listen to me."

"I'm listening," he said, but his gaze was elsewhere, as if he were only going through the motions.

I wasn't sure if what I was about to do was the right thing. But giving up on Griffin surely was the wrong thing.

"You know how Brady came back from the dead?"

He chuffed. "Well, it was a miracle of medicine."

"No, it wasn't. He's not like everyone else."

Finally, Xander Jones's attention was fully on me.

"This is top secret, Sheriff. Promise me first you won't tell a soul what I'm about to tell you."

"I can't do that. If it's police business, then—"

"Oh, for fuck's sake, *please*. This is my friend's life I'm talking about here."

"Griffin or Brady? I'm so sorry, Joss, but Griffin's gone."

"No, he's not. That's what I'm trying to tell you. Please promise me. Please, please, please."

"Okay, fine. I promise I won't repeat what you say unless I'm legally obligated to."

As far as promises went, even through the pain-med fog, I knew this one sucked. But it seemed to be as good as I was going to get.

"We're not normal. Brady, Griffin, the rest of us. We can't die the same way others can."

My stare might not have been sharp, but the sheriff's was like a damn razor blade as it narrowed in on me then.

"How do you mean?"

"I'm not really sure about the science of it all, but it wasn't just chance that Brady survived his accident. I mean, Sheriff, he had a hole the size of an arm going right through his chest. When have you ever heard of anyone surviving rebar through the heart?"

"Never."

"Exactly. We were experimented on when we were kids. We have super healing, or something like that." It sounded completely insane, but what the hell did I have to lose? If I lost Griffin, nothing much would matter after that. It was now or never. Time for the Hail Mary pass.

"You have super healing?" the sheriff repeated, his voice thick with disbelief.

I tamped down my own disbelief and made myself keep going, even though an insistent part of me was urging my mind to let me pass out. But fuck no.

This was for Griffin.

"Yes." I imbued the affirmation with a confidence I hardly felt. "Please, Sheriff, you've gotta believe me. You have to shock Griffin to make him come back."

This time, the sheriff sighed, sinking back onto his haunches while silencing his radio as it came to life with words I didn't attempt to decipher, my entire focus on this one mission.

"Defi . . . brate him." I heard myself mispronounce the word but didn't have the energy to correct it. "Like what happened with Brady. He only came back to life after the shock."

The sheriff did nothing more than stare at me for several beats.

"Please," I repeated. Never one to beg for anything, I was making up for a lifetime of reticence in this one night.

Eventually, he shook his head, muttering, "I must be out of my damn mind even talking about this. Your friends asked me to do the same thing. But Griffin's neck's snapped. No amount of shocking will help him now."

I inched my fingers forward, attempting to reach him through the restraints keeping me in place. It was futile, but he seemed to notice the effort.

"Nothing to lose here. Just give him a chance," I pressed.

The sheriff shook his head again. *Fuck*. I hadn't convinced him.

Tears stung my eyes, making everything even blurrier. To a smudge of tan uniform and hair, I murmured so that he had to strain to hear me over the chaos surrounding us, but it was all I had.

"If you try it and it doesn't work, no harm done. If you don't try it, and Griffin dies, I'll never recover. My friends will never recover. Please, Sheriff, for all of us. Just *try*. That's all I'm asking for. One shot. One chance."

My tears receded. I blinked them away to find him staring at me hard, until his jaw finally tightened.

"Fine. Okay. We'll do it. But you and your friends keep this between us. No one else knows."

"Yes, yes, I promise. Thank you, thank you." But before my last words left my lips, he'd stalked out of my frame of vision.

Afterward, too much time passed without any sign of what was happening. My friends didn't come check on me or Bobo. Neither did Hayden. Nothing stuck out from the din.

Then, finally, voices shouted, radios crackled with renewed urgency, and the helicopter flew so low I had to squinch my eyes shut, wishing someone would come to reassure Bobo. Several strands of my stray hair whipped against my eyes, but there was nothing I could do to stop it.

It took everything I had to hang on and not lose my everloving mind, cinched in place on this gurney, ready for transport, when I *needed* to find out what was happening. I thought of nothing but Griffin.

He's fine. He's alive. He's gonna be okay.

I realized full well I might be lying to myself, but it was the best I had.

When the whirring of the chopper finally receded, Layla slid to a halt beside me. Her hips jolted the side of the gurney, catapulting a fresh wave of pain through my leg and making my vision swim.

"Oh my God, Joss. They did it. He's alive. They got a pulse. He's fucking alive. Griff's alive!"

I tried to smile, probably failed, then allowed myself to check out. I didn't pass out, I didn't fall asleep, but I was no longer focused on anything as my stretcher jostled. I was picked up and set down. Doors shut and people talked to me.

I didn't talk back.

Griffin's okay. He's alive.

That was what I held on to.

It was enough.

21

Smash It All to Smithereens, Then Set It on Fire

The scene of my friends and our parents stuffed into the hospital in the middle of the night, desperately waiting for updates, was unsettlingly familiar. This time, I'd had my own room, though I hadn't occupied it for long. I did indeed have a bad compound fracture of my left shin that hurt like hell, but that was it beyond some superficial cuts, scrapes, and bruises.

When the attending doctor had insisted I remain overnight for observation due to the severity of the break and concern that I might develop an infection despite their heavy-handed administration of preventative antibiotics, I'd been too exhausted to fight her, especially since daylight hadn't been that far off, and Griffin was in the hospital too. Even though I wasn't able to see him from my room in an entirely different part of the hospital from the ICU, just knowing he was close—*and alive*—had been sufficient.

I was there, along with everyone else, when he was finally discharged five days later. The doctors argued to keep him longer, insisting no one should recover that well or that seamlessly from a broken neck. Our parents fought harder, spewing that it was scientifically proven that patients recovered better in the

comfort of their own homes. They leaned into their PhDs, rat-
tling off facts and quoting medical and scientific journals until
the head of the department relented, probably to get them to
shut up already. Since Griffin was in fact fully recovered and
hadn't even required surgery of any sort, his spine fusing back
together all on its own, there was really no recovery to be concerned about.

Of course that was the only thing the parents and hospital staff
talked about. Brady's surgeon even stopped by to check out the new
Miracle Kid, commenting that now there'd be a tie for the most
miraculous case the hospital had seen that year. Though the man
had laughed at his own lame joke, his eyes had been troubled. The
same was true of the other doctors. It was obvious they considered
Griffin's and Brady's returns from death impossible, despite having seen it more or less with their own eyes.

No way did our parents miss the lingering looks examining
Griffin like he was some specimen they itched to study, and since
Brady was there too, the doctors and nurses also ogled him.

By the end of the five days, our parents were as desperate to get
out of there as we were. Plus, Bobo needed me, and the hospital
wouldn't allow him inside. Though I'd pleaded my case, even going
so far as to call him a service dog, which he wasn't, once Bobo was
released from the vet, he was alone at home most of the time.

That simply wouldn't do.

Since he had been discharged, Bobo had barely left my side.
His surgery had gone extremely well. The break in his front
right leg had been much less severe than mine. Once the vet got
in there to set the bone, Bobo was getting better every day at a
nice clip. He was still on mild pain meds, but the vet promised
he wouldn't need them for long.

In the meantime, he and I wore matching casts. Thankfully, I
didn't have to wear a cone of shame around my neck like he did,
to keep him from messing with his leg. But so long as I was able

to watch him, I took it off.

Like today ,while we hung out on the couch in the treehouse. Bobo lay on his back, pressed against me, his legs—cast and all— hanging loosely in the air as he snored softly. My own bum leg was stretched out onto the coffee table. Layla bent over it, an array of permanent markers clutched in one hand while she drew on my cast with the other.

"That one's cool as fuck," Brady said, standing over us from behind the couch and pointing at a long, undulating design Layla was putting the final touches on. It reminded me of vines creep- ing up my leg, if they'd taken a healthy dose of shrooms. Nothing Layla designed was entirely ordinary. Even the small flowers bud- ding at the end of some of the vines suggested gateways to other worlds at their centers, like little open portals wrapped in petals.

"I'd tell ya I want that as a tat, minus the flowers of course," Brady said, "except now that I know our parents let us get 'em as part of their grand science experiment, I'm not sure I want any more."

There'd been a lot of that kind of reassessing of our lives over the last week, since we'd finally been able to disappear to the tree- house to have some time to ourselves. If our parents had been breathing down our necks before, they were like dragons now, always hovering, up in our business if we let them.

"It's like I can't stop thinking about everything they did and everything they told us," Layla said, marker tracing winding lines, "but I still can't finish wrapping my mind around it all."

Hunt harrumphed from the table, where he sat with a text- book and notes laid out in front of him. Knowing him, he'd prob- ably already mastered all there was to know for AP Chemistry.

"Try being the one who had the fucking bug up in their bed- room," he said while twirling a bottle of microbrew in one hand. "I've asked my ,mom how long it'd been there, and she's dodged the question every time."

RIDE AND DIE   211

"So it was there longer than she's willing to admit to," Griffin said from the other side of Bobo. Though nearly two weeks had passed since Clyde went over the side of the road, a rush of tingles still swept through me at hearing his voice. I'd almost lost him. Though I still hadn't decided what, if anything, to say to him about his *I love you* and my lack of response.

"Yeah, my thought too," Hunt said with a mock shiver—or maybe it was real, I couldn't tell. The violation of his privacy was definitely real. "Good thing I don't do pervy stuff in my room like Brady does."

"Hey," Brady protested right away, making Layla chuff with a hearty chuckle. "I don't do pervy shit."

Layla snorted, glancing up at me. I smiled back.

"Maybe you don't do *much* pervy shit," she said, "now that you know Mom and Dad are sniffing your undershorts." She grimaced. "Damn. Why didn't I think that all the way through before I said it? Yuck."

"I don't do pervy shit," he insisted. "And you never think before you speak, like, ever. But the point is I should be able to do whatever I want in the privacy of my own room, for fuck's sake. Hunt too."

"No doubt," I said, pointing an accusatory glare at the table leg next to Hunt, where one of the two bugs our parents had planted in the treehouse used to hide. We'd taken every listening device we could find and smashed it to smithereens before setting the pieces on fire. Brady carried around the RF detector in a visible holster everywhere we went, and he wasn't shy to use it. It was unlikely our parents would try to eavesdrop on our conversations again, what with the way Brady brandished the detector right in their faces, but we erred on the side of caution, checking our rooms and hangouts on the daily. We'd never trust their lying asses again.

Bobo snorted awake, suddenly alert, eyes pinned on the closed door at the front of the large room.

"What is it, boy?" Griffin asked, drawing Brady's attention to the rigid pittie.

Still wiping a towel over his neck from his sweaty workout, Brady stalked toward the door, pulling it open—revealing Celia about to walk up onto our porch, the rest of our parents trailing behind her.

"Mom," Brady said stiffly. "What are you guys doing here?"

Griffin slid to the edge of the couch, ready for action, while Celia stopped a foot away from her son. Hunt drank from his beer, eyes pinned on our uninvited guests. Layla capped her markers and set them on the table.

I sat up straight, watching closely, but couldn't do much more. I needed crutches to get around. I was already dreading the rehab I'd need to get back in shape after this long lack of mobility. Beside me, Bobo awkwardly shifted onto his side, injured leg sticking straight out, ears perked.

Celia stared at her son for several beats as if debating what to say. Eventually, she frowned. "Last I checked, none of us need permission to go wherever we want on our own property."

"Well, if that's what this is about, then we're all happy to move out and leave you to do your spying in peace."

We hadn't actually talked about moving out. Despite our distrust of our parents, I didn't think we wanted to deal with figuring out jobs along with exactly *what* we might be. Priorities and all. We needed to get a handle on what was going on with us before we considered any other major moves.

As I was certain Brady had anticipated, Celia huffed, cocking out a hip while scowling at him. "Don't be ridiculous. We don't want any of you to move out."

"Besides, none of you are eighteen yet," Porter chimed in.

Layla's smile was cold. "But we will be very soon. All of us will."

Celia turned to glare at her husband before considering us again. "Ignore him. This is your home for as long as you want it, which I personally hope will be a very, very long time. I'm not particularly eager to send any of you out into the big, wide world when someone's figured out who you are and what you're capable of."

My mom waltzed past Porter, Celia, and finally Brady, who reluctantly stepped out of the way for her to enter. Once she did, she crossed her arms over her chest and leaned against an empty patch of wall between a poster of Bruce Lee mid-flying kick and one of a Shaolin monk balanced on the edge of a staff in a monkey-going-up-the-tree move .

"That's why we're here. Your little act of ignoring us is over. There's too much serious shit on our plates right now to be dealing with your games. It's been almost two weeks since the accident—and let me amend that to say the *most recent* accident—and you've barely spoken a single word to us."

My spine was rigid while I stared at my mom. She'd never been overly maternal or soft, so her attitude wasn't entirely new. But accusing us of playing games when they'd lied to us over and over again? Oh, hell no. My jaw clenched.

"We've tried to be patient and understanding and give you guys the space you needed," she went on. "Two of you have actually *died* over the last couple of months, and we realize that kind of trauma takes a toll. And not just on you, on us too. But it seems like you've forgotten how to think of anyone but yourselves."

Did I think I didn't want to move out? Scratch that. I wanted to get the hell away from all of the parents, stat. From the way Layla was chewing on the inside of her lip like it was bubblegum, I guessed I wasn't alone in my thoughts.

The other adults filed in, standing here and there around my mom. Brady frowned, still hanging on to the open door as if to say, *No one invited you in.*

"We get that the news we shared with you came as a shock."

"You didn't *share* news with us," I said. "Who knows how long you would've kept your secrets if we hadn't found you out? You only told us because we caught you red-handed."

My mom looked at me for a moment before saying, "We've already explained ourselves. We did things the way we thought was best for you. That's our job as parents. You might not always agree with our decisions, but you don't have to. Everything we do is to protect you. That was the best way we knew how to until you were ready to find out."

"And what exactly were you waiting for to decide we were ready?" Hunt asked, his tone more biting than I'd ever heard it. "Layla's right. We're almost eighteen."

"Was it going to be our big birthday party reveal?" Layla added with a sneer. "Hey, happy motherfucking birthday. Oh, by the way, you might not be fully human, or whatever."

The *or whatever* part hadn't stopped tormenting any of us since we first found out.

"We hadn't figured that part out yet," Alexis said with a regretful glance at Hunt. "But believe us when we tell you we were doing our best. It's not like there's a handbook for how to deal with your kids having paranormal healing abilities."

Hunt met his mom's waiting eyes. "We're never going to trust you again."

Alexis flinched as if slapped, and I almost felt sorry for her. Then I recalled the listening devices and how they'd suspected we weren't fully human our entire lives without telling us. The temptation to feel sorry for her vanished.

Orson stepped into the middle of the room, pushing his glasses up his nose. "Look, we obviously disagree about how we handled things, so let's move on from that and deal with the urgent problems. Just remember that we were suspicious of your abilities when you were young children, and in our eyes, you're still our kids. It's hard for parents to see their children as adults capable of handling the same things we can."

"I thought you said we were moving on," Griffin said tightly. "Agree to disagree and all."

"Right, yes. Well, we do have to."

"We definitely have to," my dad said as he slid down the wall to rest against it, kicking his legs out in front of him, apparently settling in for the long haul.

I barely restrained a groan, sharing a loaded look with Griffin.

"Brady's situation sounds like it was actually an accident," Dad went on. "But what happened with Griffin and Joss definitely wasn't. I know as much about cars as I do about how to put on makeup for prom"—he was the only one to laugh at his joke—"but I do know you guys have those cars figured out, front to back. Someone poked a hole in the brake line and cut the cable to the emergency brake. That's not something that just happens on its own."

Dad glanced at Griffin, who nodded subtly. Clyde was finally back home, parked in Griffin's driveway, undriveable until we got around to fixing the brakes and all the damage from the roll down the ravine and then the cutting open to get him out. As soon as the local police had released the car from the investigation, Griffin had been there at the impound lot, supervising the tow out of there.

"We pulled some strings and got the case closed," my dad said.

"What?" Brady barked. "But we still have no idea who cut Clyde's brakes! That's like attempted murder or something."

"No doubt it is." I'd never seen my dad look so serious. "But we can't have the police poking around any more than they already have. Our contacts only reach so far, and we've already had to run crazy interference to keep your lab tests under wraps at the hospital."

"Exactly," Alexis said. "We can only do so much at once."

"And we can't have anything distracting us from the most pressing issue," Mom said, "which is to keep you safe. We need to find out who the hell knows about you, what they know, and how to shut them down."

"And by shut them down, you mean. . .?" Hunt asked.

"I mean, we'll do whatever we have to do to keep you safe. Whatever it takes."

No wonder my mom didn't enjoy being a domestic Suzy Homemaker. She was a ferocious—possibly murderous—scientist awash in secrets.

A foreboding shiver rolled through me.

22

The Death Event

My friends and our parents sat around the fancy fire pit my mom had installed on one side of the backyard years ago, which we'd hardly used since. She'd promised we'd spend most evenings out here, enjoying nights as a family. Now that I realized how busy she and my dad had kept spying on us, I wasn't surprised family time had fallen through so spectacularly.

There was no fire burning now, though twilight was rapidly settling around us, and all it would have taken was a click of a couple of buttons to bring the gas fire to life. But this wasn't some fun social gathering. It had been a feeble power play on the part of my crew, but the only one we'd had to make.

Once we'd realized our parents still had lots more to say and had no intention of vacating our treehouse, our priority had been to get them out. The treehouse was supposed to be sacred, our one retreat where the adults wouldn't bother us. That ceased the moment we realized they listened to everything we said within its apparent privacy. Even so, it was still ours—not theirs to encroach on.

We suggested we resume our chat over pizza, and here we were. The adults sat stiffly on one side of the long bench seat that surrounded the fire pit and we occupied the other, as if we were opposing sports teams. We each even had our own box of pizza.

My dad and Orson had handed out chilled beers and wine for my mom and Alexis. Regardless, I doubted alcohol was going to dull the edge for any of us. That would probably take an entire keg, considering the tension we were doing nothing to hide.

I sat on the far end of the bench so I could stretch out my leg. Bobo once more lay beside me, alert now that pizza scraps were a real possibility. I sipped from my beer, eyeing the six people we were supposed to be able to trust without question. When I bit into my slice, which I should have enjoyed since it was topped with some of my favorites—olive, red onion, and jalapeños—I barely tasted it.

Mom cleared her throat and leaned forward, tossing her napkin on the full plate balanced across her lap. "Are you all finished with this ridiculous standoff?"

I didn't have to so much as glance at my friends to feel them bristle along with me.

"No? Well, too freaking bad. No, you know what? I'm over censoring myself for you kids. You want us to treat you like adults, I'm not holding back the f-bombs."

"By all means, go ahead," I said. "Like I ever needed you to hold back around me."

My mom scowled, the expression gouging deep in the shadows. The only lighting was dim, lining the base of the empty pit. "Of course you needed me to censor myself. I'm your mother. We don't get to just do what we want once we have kids. You become our priorities. It's our responsibility as parents to mold you into the people you're becoming."

Alexis studied us over the rim of her wineglass. "Of course, that becomes a little trickier than usual when you have paranormal qualities."

"Exactly," my mom said. "Cut us a break here. We did things the best way we knew how."

"We'll cut you a break," I said, "when we think you've earned it."

My mom's scowl deepened further. I smiled tightly back at her. *Take it or leave it,* my smile said. It wasn't negotiable.

She sighed loudly, handing her plate to my dad, but not her wineglass, which he'd already refilled for her once. "At some point, you're going to realize that you need us. So let's cut the shit and take the shortcut. We're your only hope at understanding what's going on and staying safe."

I wished for a handy retort to that but didn't have one. She was right. We might as well be swimming out to sea with no stronger stroke than a doggy paddle.

"Tell us everything you know, then," Griffin said. "If you want us to trust you, give us reasons to."

Griffin, like the rest of us, was slow to trust, and even slower to extend it once it'd been broken.

"You know we're playing catch-up here," he added. "Get us up to speed, and for real this time. You're still holding back."

Beside my mom, my dad fidgeted before rising to bus the plates to a side table, a sign, I thought, that Griffin was right. They were majorly holding back on us.

My mom glanced at Alexis, Celia and Porter, then Orson, before nodding. "Since you and Brady were in the hospital, and we needed to keep the blood they drew away from their techs, we finally got some more recent samples to work with." My mom glanced at me. "You too, Joss. Though at least they only drew blood from you the once. That made it easier on Alexis here, who was running herself ragged intercepting."

"How would you even do that?" Hunt asked his mom. "Didn't the staff find it suspicious when you kept showing up where you didn't belong?"

Alexis shrugged. "Yes, of course. But I have my ways." When she coyly flicked her hair over her shoulder, I only then realized she meant ways of seduction. *Holy Batman and Robin.* "You know what they say: use it or lose it. Hunt is everything to me. All of you are. I'll do what I have to."

"Um, Mom," Hunt started. "Please don't tell me you had sex with some techs."

Alexis arched her brow at him. "Seduction is an art, my son. There are many ways to seduce a man, or woman, that don't end in a tangle in the sheets."

As one, my friends and I studied Alexis Fletcher in a new light. She wasn't stereotypically beautiful, but she was striking with an indefinable appeal. Add in her stalwart confidence, and I could see her seduction being effective, especially on perhaps harried, overworked, or bored lab techs.

"Damn, Mom," Hunt said. "That's some Mata Hari shit right there."

Again, she shrugged. "We aren't kidding when we tell you we'll do anything for you. We already have."

"We most certainly have," Celia said, eyeing both her children wistfully. "Anything at all for them."

After another sip of her Malbec, my mom said, "Since we haven't wanted to draw attention to your differences, not until we thought you were ready to know—"

"Which was apparently once we hit forty," Layla muttered under her breath.

"We haven't wanted to take too many blood samples over the years."

From beside me, Griffin sucked in a sharp inhale. "Which is why we never went to doctors."

"Yes."

"So our checkups were really about us being guinea pigs," Layla said.

Celia *tsk*ed. "No, Layla. We couldn't take you to regular doctors. It was too dangerous. Besides, we're all qualified to perform the examinations. We might not have MDs, but we know the body's functioning inside and out, especially where you're concerned. We can study you on a level no MD out there would even think to."

"So how exactly weren't we your guinea pigs?" Layla followed up. "You took our blood and studied it."

Celia frowned. "To monitor your progress. To make sure you were okay."

Eyes hard, Layla stared at her mother. "Potato, poe-tah-toh."

Celia threw her hands into the air, then knocked into her plate when they came back down. "And how else were we supposed to take care of you, huh? We already knew you weren't normal. What were we supposed to do, just go through life blindly without knowing what was going on with you? Lay, we're experts in this area. Top of our fields. You can't reasonably expect us not to make sure our own kids are well and healthy along the way, knowing you might have paranormal abilities. For fuck's sake, be reasonable here."

I gasped, mostly because I'd never imagined Celia Porter cussing under any circumstances. I'd figured her for using her pleases and thank yous even in an apocalyptic emergency.

Stunned, Layla blinked at her mom, who finally sighed.

"Look, whether you want to or not, you're going to have to eventually cut us a break. We did the best we could under extreme circumstances, and you're just gonna have to live with how we handled things. We really don't have time to waste here, and all we've been doing lately is waiting for you kids to wrap your heads around the situation. But that's over. No more waiting. There is at least one person out there who knows what's going on with you, and that's one too many."

Porter slid forward on his seat, locking eyes with each of us across the quiet pit. "So, are you ready to get your heads in the game or not? Because time's up."

I tensed with my annoyance. At least in this, they were right, though I refused to concede the point to them aloud. "What did you find from our recent blood tests?"

Orson answered. "Proof of your paranormal abilities."

His statement hung in the darkening night for several moments, before he added, "For the first time ever, we have real proof." Another pause. "Too bad we can't publish in any scientific journals."

"Such a loss," Alexis added. "We'd win the Nobel, guaranteed."

"Yeah, such a pity your experiments on *your children* haven't panned out," Layla said with all the snark I was feeling.

My mom rolled her eyes just a bit, and I had to keep myself from lashing out at her.

"Which is why we aren't sharing our life's work with anyone," she said. "Because you're more important to us. Like we keep telling you."

"Define these paranormal abilities," Griffin steered.

As a group, the parents shared excited looks.

Orson actually bounced in his seat. "Your blood has changed on a cellular level."

"How so?" Hunt asked.

"You—as in Brady and Griffin—have an extra chromosome, one we've never seen before, that no one's ever seen before. It's a massive scientific breakthrough. It's what we've been searching for in our research for years."

"We think Brady and Griffin dying and then reviving somehow activated the chromosomal expansion," my dad said. "It's the only thing that makes sense. It's the one thing we'd never been able to try with any of you before."

Though I didn't think my dad meant to sound so calculating when discussing my friends' deaths, it still stung. Almost losing Brady and then Griffin had been paralyzing for me and my friends in a manner we still hadn't completely recovered from. Reminders of just how close we'd come to losing each other snuck up on us several times a day.

Oblivious to our reactions, my dad kept going. "It was the missing piece that eluded us for years. With all our patients, and by that, I mean you guys," he added hurriedly, "there were no signs of healing significantly more advanced than that which could possibly be attributed to youth and a strong immune system, something we've also focused on maintaining with you all. But death . . . it was the catalyst for the mutation."

"Once this process has taken place," my mom cautioned, "no one can *ever* get a hold of your blood."

"Not everyone will be doing a DNA analysis when they draw our blood," Hunt said, reasonable in a way I definitely wasn't feeling right then.

"'Once this process has taken place?'" I repeated. "You say it like it's no big deal, but you're talking about us *dying*."

"No, not dying," my dad interjected quickly. "Coming back to life."

"And if you should be wrong about any one of us? If any of us should have an 'accident' and die, what if you're wrong and we don't come back?"

"We're not wrong," my dad said. "All six of us agree with this conclusion."

"Well then. I feel completely at ease now." In case they missed my sarcasm, I scowled at them too.

"Wait." Layla jumped to her feet, plate in hand. "Did you . . . did you guys set us up? Did *you* cut Griff's brakes?"

Celia's hand flew to her chest. "You can't be serious right now."

"Oh, I am. Deathly serious, pun fucking intended."

Porter shook his head, sadness tugging on his face. "Layla, honey, in your heart you must know that can't be true."

Layla glared at both her parents for several seconds. "I don't know what's true anymore. Other than you've been hiding shit from us our entire lives, and major shit too. The biggest ever."

Celia took in her daughter. "We've already been over this."

"Yeah, we have. But excuse the fuck out of me if I don't feel good about it. About any of it."

In solidarity, I rubbed her arm.

"So what's Joss's blood like, then?" Hunt asked. "Normal?"

"No, not normal," Orson responded.

"I thought you said death was the event that triggered the extra chromosome?"

"Yes, but none of you had normal blood to begin with. Your levels are way off the standard. Your iron is off the charts."

"As in you should be dead from the iron alone," my dad added.

"And that's before we consider the levels of radiation in your blood. They're"—Orson paused to shake his head in disbelief—"insane."

"Picture this," Dad said, "the five of you in the Chernobyl nuclear power plant when it exploded. Or you guys in Hiroshima or Nagasaki when the atomic bombs were dropped. Your radiation levels are that high. The kind no one survives. It's why we had to sub out Joss's x-ray at the hospital for a phony. Even using a CT scan, we were barely able to see what was going on with her leg."

"What kind of radioactive substance is it showing we were exposed to?" Brady asked as his sister plopped back down in her seat, seemingly in shock.

"That's a little less exact," Porter said. "You're showing some exposure to radium."

I sucked in a breath and opened my mouth, but Griffin beat me to the question.

"Like the radium used to make nuclear bombs?"

"Yes," my mom said. "But that's not all."

Layla chuckled bitterly. "'That's not all,' she says. What the hell more could there be?"

"That's where we aren't entirely certain. And we should be."

"We're the experts who'd be consulted when confronted with a human cellular anomaly like this one," Celia said.

"Your radiation levels indicate you've been exposed to something more than polonium, but we can't tell what. There's no sign of this exposure remaining in your blood. Just the reactions to radiation exposure."

"Only they aren't the regular reactions," Celia inserted.

"Of course." My mom smiled tightly before letting it drop abruptly. "Or you all would've been dead ages ago."

"Yippee," I said. "More death talk."

"If we're this radioactive, can we infect others?" Hunt asked. "I assume not, given that you've socialized us."

"It was one of the first things we tested before bringing you home," Orson said, earning a reprimanding glare from my mom. He caught her eye, then added, "No, your radiation levels don't seem to affect anyone or anything around you. The radiation within you seems to be innocuous."

"Well, that's something to wrap our minds around," Griffin said.

Hunt brought his fingertips to either side of his temples. "For sure. That's fucking nuts."

"That about sums it up," Dad said. "So now you see why we've had to keep you in the dark about this."

But neither my friends nor I conceded the point. We were nearly eighteen and only just learning about the most important parts of ourselves.

"So my leg," I said. "I'm healing at normal levels, then? You know, since I didn't *die*."

My mom smirked at me, but that was the only acknowledgment I received for my barb. "Your healing is fast, but not paranormally fast," she said. "Nothing to draw unwanted attention, at least not unless someone decides to look more closely."

"Which they might," Celia said. "That damn Kitty Blanche is a nightmare."

Griffin and Brady stiffened. The redhead-from-a-bottle reporter had called the two of them "Miracle Besties." I wasn't sure who hated the term more, Griffin or Brady.

"She knows too much," Porter said. "Sniffing around all over the place. And that drone, that was crossing the line."

They'd gotten a restraining order against her after that, but she was still allowed to investigate—just not within five hundred feet of us.

"Kitty might be working for our mystery person," Alexis said.

"Mystery person?" Brady asked.

"Someone still tampered with Griffin's car."

Porter cracked his knuckles. "We'll find out who and deal with them."

Layla chuckled darkly. "Oh, okay there, mob boss."

Porter snapped his stare to her. "We'll do whatever it takes to protect you."

Now it was Porter's turn to look murderous. A fresh surge of shock welled inside me. Had everything about our seemingly docile parents been a charade?

"You all need to stay away from Kitty Blanche," my mom told us.

"Yeah, we know," Brady said. "You think we like being accosted every freaking place we go?"

"Okay, good. Then you guys just focus on acting like everything's normal while we figure things out. It's time for Joss and Griffin to get back to school. Two weeks is enough time."

In truth, Griffin could have gone back to school a day after the accident—that was how well he'd recovered. He remained home mostly because his dad insisted he keep up appearances, and who didn't want a ready excuse to skip school? He'd kept me and Bobo company, though nearly always under the watchful eye of one of our parents, who pretended to just coincidentally be around. I'd wanted to talk to him about the big *I love you*, but there was never a chance that felt right, or a mood that didn't get interrupted at precisely the wrong moment.

Brady grabbed another slice of pizza. "First you don't want us to go to school. You practically beg us to homeschool." He took a bite of pepperoni and cheese. "Now, you want us to go. You guys've gotta make up your damn minds."

"We want you to go now," Porter said. "We'd hoped to shield you from discovery. But that ship has sailed. Whoever tampered with your car did it to test you, to figure out the range of your powers. To see if you can come back from death."

I swallowed thickly. "This person knows all that?"

Dad shrugged. "We hope not." *But we think so*, was left unspoken. "We're being cautious. Now it's even more important not to draw suspicion to any of you. It's bad enough this Kitty bitch"—I gasped, but he kept going; I'd never heard him talk this way—"is going around calling you miracle kids. We can't do anything to cause anyone to take a closer look at you."

"Which means you go to school," my mom said, "and act like everything is normal."

"Yeah, fat chance of that," I said on a huff, but then added, "Why would anyone even be looking our way, anyway? It's like Kitty was just waiting for the story to hit."

"And how would this mystery person know where to find us?" Layla asked.

My dad said, "We'd hoped no one realized you'd been exposed to the course of our experiments during our previous employment. We covered our tracks well, but it's possible someone found out."

"Were we exposed to radiation in your previous lab?" Hunt asked.

"Something like that," Alexis replied.

"'Something like that' or 'that'?" Hunt pressed.

"There's a lot we're still unsure of, but we're the best suited to the task of figuring it out."

"That's right," Celia said. "Now that we know the death event triggers your paranormal super healing abilities, we have a lot more to go on. We're on the precipice of amazing conclusions, I have no doubt." Her eyes glittered at the promise of scientific advancement. Meanwhile, I couldn't stop thinking about how her son died without her knowing for sure he'd come back.

"You may even be immortal," Celia whispered, words clunky with awe.

Immortal. The one word ricocheted off the walls of my mind without proper absorption.

There was no way. Life wasn't actually this bananas. That was just books and TV, wasn't it?

"You all just hang tight," my mom said. "Enjoy being teenagers. Be good, excel at your studies, just in case—"

"Just in case what?" I asked.

"Well, in case you can still go to university. Things have obviously changed since the new chromosome situation, but it might still be possible, once we get things under control of course."

"Of course," I mimicked. Mom was straight-up batty. Like any of us were considering college after the news they dropped on us like an atomic bomb—you know, the one we were kind of a little bit like.

"We'll handle everything," she went on. "We're experts and we've got the tech we need to back us up."

"Yeah, don't remind us," Layla grumped.

Brady pointed a finger at his parents. "There will be no more spying on us. Absolutely none."

"Sure, of course, honey," Celia said in the flippant manner of one giving lip service to what the other party wanted to hear.

"I mean it." Brady palmed the radio frequency detector at his hip. "I *will* make sure you guys are keeping in line."

"We wouldn't have it any other way." But Celia's smile was fake.

"Another important thing," Orson said, looking at Griffin. "When kids at school ask you about the accident, just say it was a miracle. That everyone was praying for a miracle, and then we got one."

Griffin's brow rose. "Twice in a row?"

"Hey, crazier things have happened. Just play it down."

"We know what to do," Griffin assured them, which I was glad for, because I wasn't sure I did. Tonight's revelation elevated teenage angst to a whole new level.

Orson slid to the edge of the bench seat to better stare at Griffin. "I mean it, son. Don't tell anyone anything. Play dumb, and I say play because we know none of you are."

"In fact," Alexis added, "we're testing a hypothesis that this latent additional chromosome might be responsible for your advanced intelligence."

Celia nodded. "You're all far smarter than your peers. It could also be wrapped up in your paranormal abilities, but we'll know more soon."

"So just go to school, stay out of trouble, and keep your heads down," Mom said. "I'd also tell you to stick together, but there doesn't seem to be a need. It's like you're joined at the hip."

I imagined my friends didn't appreciate being referred to that way any more than I did, but none of us responded, probably as ready to be finished with this talk as I was. I'd reached my information overload point.

"At least that makes it easier for us," my mom continued. "We'll take care of everything. But if you experience or see anything odd, you let us know right away. I want your phones on you at all times."

After what happened with Griffin and how helpful it would have been to have our phones then, I gritted my teeth at her. "We only didn't have our phones that night because *you* were spying on us. I still don't think you get how serious of a violation that was."

"I don't care. We need to keep you safe and off the radar. Phones on, at all times."

I didn't answer, and neither did the others.

"Now, anything else before we adjourn for the night?"

Thoughts of how I'd confided in Sheriff Jones, how that had gotten him to defibrillate Griffin, bubbled up. I'd been right, and Brady and Hunt had done the same. We hadn't told our parents. It was possible we should have, but I wasn't going to say a word until we got a better handle on the situation. They said they had the police situation dealt with anyhow.

"No, nothing else," Brady said.

"Then hurry up and get to bed. Tomorrow's a school day."

Never fond of taking orders, my friends and I stayed until every last one of them had either disappeared into the house or left for their own.

When silence finally settled around us, we stared off into the night, each lost to our own heavy thoughts.

After a good ten minutes, Hunt spoke. "What if we really are immortal?"

He didn't get an answer to his question. I, for one, had no fucking idea.

23

Life, Death, and Option C

For my first day back since our disastrous outing to Raven's Lagoon, my parents volunteered to drive me to school. When I was fast to turn them down, they even offered one of their cars. Now that they both worked from home, they could manage with one. But I passed, opting instead for Brady to pick me up. We all squeezed into Bonnie, something we'd be doing until we had a chance to repair Griffin's car and finish mine. In other words, it was going to be a while.

Thanks to the unwieldy cast that wrapped my leg from my foot up to mid-thigh, I got to ride shotgun, which left Layla, who was the shortest of us all, sitting between Griffin and Hunt in the back.

"You sure we can't skip school?" Layla asked a second time, after we'd already shut down her suggestion. "This is like the only break we get from our parents anymore, and I don't wanna waste it on school."

"Trust me," Hunt said, "I've got no desire to sit through boring lectures today with everything running through my mind. But you heard them. We need to pretend everything's normal. Which means going to school."

Brady, who usually had a lead foot in the car, was driving like we were out for a scenic Sunday drive. I suspected it was to draw out this same private time Layla mentioned.

"They assume we're as good at lying and shit as they are," Brady said.

I snorted a dark laugh. "Yeah, I noticed that. They just assume subterfuge is no biggie." I shook my head. "I seriously can't believe it took us this long to figure out what they were up to."

Griffin laughed, and the sound lifted my spirits. I glanced at him over my seat.

"How the hell were we supposed to figure out what they were up to?" he asked. "Like, we were supposed to guess that we're. . ." The lighthearted ribbing slid off his beautiful face, the brightness in his eyes fading for a moment. ". . .whatever the hell we are. I feel like I'm crazy half the time I consider everything they've told us."

"I feel like I'm crazy *all* the time I think about it," Layla said.

"But then," Griffin went on, "I can't deny it either. I went over that cliff. Clyde was flying, rolling, and then, that was it. Darkness. Until they shocked me back to life."

His gaze unfocused, as if he were reliving the memories, until he shook his head, seeming to clear the images.

Hunt stretched his legs, bumping the back of my seat until he got comfortable. "Zoe says Hayden keeps talking about it. Apparently she can't believe they were able to revive Griff. Says she never saw anything like it."

I chuffed. "Yeah, I'll bet she hasn't."

Brady chuckled.

"She wasn't on call the day of your accident, Brade," Hunt said, "but she still heard about it. Seems like EMTs are a bunch of gossips. Hayden gets the scoop and then she dishes to Zoe."

"And what's Zoe think about it?" I faced forward as we neared the school, anticipating the horde of reporters that had been a constant since Brady became the Miracle Kid.

"I'm not really sure. I like Zoe and all, I think she's cool, but I get the feeling she tiptoes around me. Like she sometimes tells me what she thinks I want to hear instead of what she's actually thinking."

"That's 'cause she wants your fine ass to bone her," Layla said. "We already told you that."

"Whatever the reason, it's weird."

"No 'whatever the reason.' That's the reason, Hunt. You're a fine motherfucker and Zoe wants to jump your bones while she's got a chance." Layla *hmm*ed. "And does she have a chance?"

"Seriously, Lay? I'm pretty sure we've got way bigger problems than whether or not I decide to sleep with Zoe Wills."

"Oh, I don't care whether you catch some Z's with her or not, I'm just talking about you dipping your wick."

"Which is obviously what I was referring to, only with a little subtlety."

Brady barked a laugh. "Which my sister doesn't have and couldn't find even if you offered to pay her a cool mil for her efforts."

"Bro, for a mil, I'd make subtlety my bitch."

Another snort. "Of course you would."

Layla leaned forward in her seat. "You don't think I could? I could. I can. I'd nail that. I'd be getting down with subtlety like Hunt wants to get down with Zoe."

Hunt groaned. "Promise me you won't go getting involved. I haven't decided yet."

"Well then, seems like you need my help deciding."

"No, I def don't. I mean it, Lay. Back off."

From experience, I understood that Layla interpreted "back off" as an invitation to stick her nose even further into whatever business was in question.

"Fine, I'll back off," she said, sounding about as sincere as our parents.

"Layla. . ." Hunt warned.

I told him, "Zoe seems nice, and not like all the kids who just want to look, sound, and be like everyone else. Like she might actually have a few brain cells to rub together. She's cute too. Why aren't you sure you want to go there?"

"Because I could maybe really like her. Assuming I get to see the real her and she stops telling me what she thinks I want to hear."

"That's good though, bro," Griffin said.

"Could be, yeah. But it's not like I can tell her, 'Hey, so it looks like we're not quite all the way human. Or maybe we are, still haven't gotten our asshole parents to give it all to us straight, but looks like if we die, we can pop right back up, assuming we convince someone to shock the hell out of us first. So yeah, might even be immortal, who knows?'"

"Okay, point taken," Layla said, the chipper eagerness to get Hunt's wick dipped gone. "Unless it's gonna be a super casual fuck, we can't involve anyone else right now."

"Exactly," Hunt said. "Finally."

"So go get your casual hookups, but nothing else," Layla elaborated, as if we hadn't gotten the picture yet. "Not until we figure this out."

When none of us responded, she pressed, "You guys hear me?"

"Of course we hear you," I said on another chuff. "Can't help but."

"Then why didn't you promise we're only going to get some in a casual manner?"

"'Cause I don't need to promise that. You know me, I don't do casual. I don't like sharing myself with someone I couldn't give a fuck about."

"It's definitely worth waiting for the right fit," Griffin said, and I had to force myself to keep my gaze glued up ahead, to the looming sign that announced Ridgemore High School. I had no doubt Griffin and I would fit together just right.

"You two can wait all you want for your hearts to sing the glory of lovemaking," Layla said. "I plan on making the most of my time till the right dude shows up. What about you, Hunt? Are you gonna join Joss and Griff in being born-again virgins?"

I shook my head. "You're a fucking nut, you know that? No one said anything about us being celibate."

"Then who ya gonna bang?"

Silence.

"That's what I thought."

Brady slowed to a crawl before taking the turn into school, but there wasn't a single reporter there. Not one redheaded bulldog. *Nada.*

"Wow, that's different," I commented with a whistle.

"And nice," Brady said.

"No doubt. Wonder if our parents got restraining orders on all of them."

"Wouldn't put it past them," Hunt said. "They're all sus as fuck."

"Hunt," Layla insisted. "You joining the casual team or the love-only team?"

"I'm not joining any team—"

"You gotta."

"Why?"

"'Cause I said so."

"Bossy princess," Brady commented.

"Hey, I am what I am," Layla said. "At least you got the princess part right. I deserve to get whatever nice treatment I want. Shit, I could even go for one of them reverse harems, ya know? Have a different flavor for every night of the month."

"All you need is the one right flavor," Griffin said, and I thought I could feel his gaze heating the side of my face. I desperately wanted to turn to check but didn't dare.

"Everyone knows ice cream's better when you can choose the flavor you want to suit your mood. Same with dick."

"After that colorful description, I'm gonna stick with the hold-out team," Hunt said.

"Suit yourself. I don't mind having enough fun for the lot of you. What about you, Brade?"

"You know me."

"Yup. The Rafferty twins'll be making up for the hold-out team. Too bad you can't tell any of the girls you're a fucking paranormal beast. You'd have them lining up to take turns with you."

"I already have them lining up," Brady said.

"That's true, homie. It's nice that we're all hot. Makes life so much easier."

"See? Bratty princess," he said, glancing at the others in the rearview mirror before slowing as he drove through the large student parking lot.

"Not bratty, just determined," she said. "I know what I want and I go get it. Nothing wrong with that."

"Maybe not," Griffin said. "But if I didn't know you, I might be tempted to take offense at all the stupid shit you say."

"Hey!"

"No, Lay," I said over a laugh that sounded too much like a giggle for my liking. "He's right. That was some stupid shit you just laid out for us. Here we are, with literal life and death matters on our hands, and you're dissecting our pen dipping and inkpots like it's your business."

"You got me there. But tell me you don't feel lighter after a while of not talking about all the life and death and *not*—aka option C—bullshit?"

No one responded. But she was right—laughing felt good.

"Exactly," she said. "You guys need me."

"No doubt about that," I affirmed right away. "I need every one of you assholes."

"We're a crew," Griffin added. "We stick together and we'll get through this, whatever the hell this turns out to be."

Brady parked in one of our usual spots off to the side of the lot and I pushed open my door, turning to reach for my crutches. When I straightened, Griffin was there, taking my bag from me and handing it to Hunt, who also waited to help. Griffin readied my crutches then guided me out. Ordinarily, I'd probably shrug them off, protesting that I could do it on my own. But since Griffin had told me he loved me, I didn't want to turn down any opportunity to be near him, even if I still didn't know he meant it in anything more than a platonic way.

"What's going on over there?" Layla asked.

A crowd was gathered closer to the school building.

"Don't know," Brady said, "but I see Rich's ugly-ass Hummer. Can't help but. Could he've chosen a louder color? Fuck. You can probably see the beast from outer space."

Rich Connely's Hummer was not, in fact, ugly. It was an expensive machine that was undoubtedly all shiny chrome and beautiful accents inside. But Brady was right. It was obnoxiously bright—though not quite as obnoxious as its owner.

With me injured, it took us longer to arrive at the group. Though I was now comfortable with my crutches, it was still slower going than I would have liked. But not even Layla or Brady pulled ahead of me, and they were the least observant of our crew.

"Holy shit," Griffin breathed. "No wonder everyone's standing around drooling. That's an Aston Martin Valkyrie."

"Damn." Brady whistled. "Who's got one of those? And don't tell me Rich or I'll puke in my mouth and maybe have to punch him again, and I don't wanna miss out on your first day back. I'd rather wait at least another week before my next suspension."

Now that we had dirt on our parents—truckloads of it— none of us concerned ourselves with thoughts of future reprimands. They'd done so much to break our trust, and so little to remedy that break, that a potential suspension seemed slight in comparison. What freedoms our parents hadn't given us before, we were now taking whether they liked it or not.

When we reached the circle of gawking students, our view of the Aston Martin still partially impeded, the crowd parted to reveal a man I'd never seen before walking toward us. His gaze was pinned on us. We were his target.

"Weird," Layla muttered under her breath before he reached us.

The man was tall, with impeccable posture and dark hair threaded through with silver. He wore a pressed linen shirt and slacks that didn't dare have a crease, despite the morning already growing hot. His shoes were unreasonably shiny, and though I had no idea what you'd label the style in the charcoal leather, I guessed they cost more than my car, possibly more than Bonnie and Clyde combined. The man, whoever he was, reeked of opulence.

"Why's he looking at us like that?" Hunt asked under his breath, but none of us could answer before the stranger reached hearing range. Also, I had no idea.

"Richard," he called behind him. Even his voice sounded expensive.

"Rich," Brady mumbled accusingly while our classmate appeared from behind a wall of our peers.

Rich jogged to catch up to the man who probably had a yacht and jet on standby. I'd never met anyone with a yacht or a private jet, but I'd bet good money this is what that lifestyle looked like.

"Aren't you going to introduce me to your friends?" the man asked before Rich reached him.

"We aren't friends," Brady said.

The man didn't visibly react beyond a winning smile. "I know my nephew can be annoying. But he grows on you if you give him a chance."

Rich, now standing beside his uncle, grimaced as if undecided how to feel about that statement. After the uncle turned to stare at him, he eventually said, "Hey, guys, this is my uncle I was telling you about before."

The man extended his hand to Brady first. "I'm Magnum Chase. My sister is this boy's mother. She chose to take her husband's name." From the way his eyes took on a sudden, predatory glint, I got the impression he thought his sister was an idiot for dropping the surname that associated her with him.

Brady hesitated for a moment, but then shook the man's hand. Magnum greeted us each in the same way, even me, and I had to shake around a cumbersome crutch.

"I've been very much looking forward to meeting you," Magnum said. "It's not every day that I get to meet not one, but two, miracle kids."

Brady and Griffin tensed. The rest of us did too.

"Yeah, well," Griffin said, "we prefer not to be referred to that way."

"Of course you do. The nickname is a crude simplification of something wondrous."

"Yeah, okay, whatever," Brady said. "Nice to meet you and all, but we've gotta be getting to class."

"Of course, of course." Magnum smiled broadly, revealing straight white teeth behind equally perfect lips, exfoliated and moisturized. "Get to class. We'll have the chance to speak more later."

Brady grunted noncommittally while I studied the man, wondering what the hell his game was.

"You'll be hearing from me soon." Then, with a curt nod, Magnum Chase turned and sauntered back to what had to be his Aston Martin.

I waited until we were out of earshot before asking, "Did that sound like a fucking threat to any of you?"

"Definitely," Hunt said. "Man's a snake behind all that luxury."

"I'd expect you've gotta be to have that much money," Griffin commented.

"So the question of the hour is: What the hell does he want with us?" Layla asked.

We exchanged a loaded look before resuming our walk into the school. There *was* one thing not even money could buy, and there was a very good chance the five of us had it.

"Let's stay as far away from the guy as possible," Griffin said.

"Now that's a plan I can get behind." I leaned my shoulder on the locker beside mine and reached for my combination lock.

"You don't think. . ." I started, drawing my friends' attention back to me when they'd already been walking toward their lockers. Griffin hadn't left my side, holding one of my crutches for me while I got my locker open. "You think he's the one who's figured us out? The one who messed with Clyde?"

"Yes, I totally do," Brady answered right away.

"I don't," Hunt said. "Only because I think he's too smart for that. A dude doesn't get to be where he obviously is without some major brains on him."

Griffin's mouth tightened. "I don't trust him."

"None of us do," Layla said. "Let's watch each other's backs. At all times."

Griffin frowned, his eyes troubled. "And check under Bonnie's hood before we go anywhere."

"Fuck," I exclaimed, loudly enough to draw the attention of others. I lowered my voice. "What the hell? This shit's messed up."

"Maybe we should tell our parents," Hunt suggested.

"Maybe," Layla said, though clearly none of us were in a hurry to loop them in when all they'd done was leave us out.

"For now," I said, "British Lit. We can figure out the rest later." Only I already had a feeling my thoughts wouldn't stick to today's lesson, no matter how interesting Ms. Tott tried to make it.

Already I was haunted by Chase Magnum's easy confidence, the kind that suggested he always got what he wanted. Without

understanding all the specifics, I suspected our already compli-
cated life had just gotten more so.

My friends and I made our way to class in silence, each of us
no doubt wrapped up in our own burdened thoughts. It wasn't
even 8:30 a.m. yet. I sighed and focused on landing my crutches.

24

Taking the Pep out of Pep Rally

Our first day back culminated in a pep rally to bolster school spirit before the first football game of the year. I didn't much care whether Ridgemore High beat its longtime rival from across the river, Mountain Laurel High School, but I did appreciate that our final class was canceled for the event.

I'd rapidly grown tired of the stares and whispers that trailed us wherever we went. There was no doubt about it—nobody at school had missed how Brady and Griffin had both survived "accidents" no one else would have. Even idiot jocks like Pike Bills and staff who didn't ordinarily involve themselves in student affairs watched our crew. Their attention crawled along my skin, making me want to whirl on every one of them and bark at them to mind their own fucking business. Had Ms. Tott not been stationed in the student parking lot to make sure none of us skipped out of the pep rally, that's precisely what we would have done.

After stashing my bookbag, I slammed my locker unnecessarily hard before sagging into my crutches and the row of dented, faded-blue metal. I scowled at Griffin, who was already studying me, the hazel of his eyes brighter than usual with their storminess.

He chuckled darkly, the roll of it making me shudder. "I want to get out of here just as much as you do."

I breathed a few times, feeling my nostrils flare, trying to calm myself. "Not sure that's possible, Griff. I don't know what it is, but every part of me's urging me to get the fuck out of here right the hell now."

"No kidding," Brady called ahead before closing the distance that separated us. Hunt and Layla were right behind him. Then Priscilla Elsop, Nina Waits, and a couple of other girls, all Rich Connely's exes, sauntered past us, ogling our group. We gave them such seething glares that Nina actually squeaked as the lot of them hurried to point their attention forward.

"That's right," Layla growled under her breath, loudly enough that they might still hear. "You don't get to stare at us."

I considered my friends. Even Hunt, who was ordinarily slower to get riled up, was tense. His jaw was clenched so hard that when he waggled it, his dad's dangling turquoise earring swung. Brady was clenching and unclenching his fists, and Layla was scouring the hallway between the rows of lockers for any lingering students who might dare to glance our way.

Intensity rolling off him in waves, Griffin's stare was only on me. I met his eyes, wondering what he was thinking when he looked at me that way.

"What?" I eventually asked when he didn't look away.

But before he could answer, if he even would have, Mrs. Moody walked up, clicking her tongue at us as if we were horses. "Come on, kids. You're late. Pep rally's already starting."

When none of us moved to obey, she extended her arms to either side and herded us toward the gymnasium—again, as if we were fucking horses.

When the gym's double doors loomed ahead, open and ominous, and we still hadn't shaken our history teacher, I halted.

"Go on ahead, Mrs. Moody. I'm really slow on these crutches. We'll be right behind you."

In truth, I was thinking there had to be some way to evade Ms. Tott. The student parking lot was big, and she probably couldn't watch all of it at once. Considering how jumpy I was, it was worth the risk of being caught.

But Mrs. Moody only narrowed unamused eyes on us, silently expressing a phrase she was overly fond of using in her classes: *I wasn't born yesterday.*

The skin around her eyes creased as she smiled tightly at me. "If your friends want to go ahead, I'll be happy to help you along, Joss."

I frowned. "Thanks, but that won't be necessary."

She waved her hands, herding us some more. I sighed loudly and hobbled through the entrance.

At once, the attention of hundreds of students and teachers landed on us. It didn't matter that music was already thumping through the loudspeakers, or that cheerleaders were dancing along, kicking their legs in skirts so short they may as well have been wearing bikini bottoms. Trained smiles plastered across their faces, they were the only ones not to look our way.

"Assholes," Brady groused.

Mrs. Moody frowned. "Language, Brady." But now that her job was done, and we were well and truly stuck at the pep rally, she walked ahead, leaving us behind.

My friends glared at the myriad sets of eyes on us, but I no longer bothered, focused on maneuvering my crutches and getting it all over with.

From beside me, Griffin said, "Let's sit in the front row so Joss doesn't have to climb up."

Across the entire length of the gymnasium, the front row was packed. Even so, people would move for us. They always did, presumably to gain our favor, and that was when we didn't look like we were ready to dismember each and every one of them.

I shook my head, my hair loose along my back for once. "No. They'll just ogle us more. The very back row, that's where I wanna go."

They didn't bother trying to talk me out of it.

Uncaring that the cheerleaders were gyrating, high-kicking, and flipping behind us, I took the slow lead up to the very back. I slumped onto the hard bench seat with a groan of relief, sliding over to make room for the rest of them. I was lifting my cast onto the empty seat in front of me when Zoe Wills spun around in her seat midway up the bleachers, her face eager, looking like she was considering joining us. Our hard expressions had her smile freezing in place; she turned around.

"Good," Layla grunted from the other side of Hunt. He sat next to Griffin, who was beside me. Brady was on the outside end. "She's nice enough and all, but if she'd come up here, a girl woulda had to murder a bitch. They need to find someone else's business to stick their noses all up in."

It didn't take long for my mind to glaze over. The football team's captain spoke, followed by the captain of the cheerleading squad. Next came Mr. Lauderbeck, who was both the PE teacher and the football coach. Finally, the school principal, Mr. Thompson, took his place at the podium at the front of the open floor and cheered into the microphone, "Goooooooo, Panthers!" while holding up the trophy the team won last year.

I rolled my eyes and rested my head on Griffin's shoulder. My leg was itching inside my cast, and I wouldn't be able to scratch it for another four weeks at least.

Griffin moved his hand to my thigh and suddenly I forgot all about my itchy skin. His fingers felt as if they were branding me down to my bones.

Despite my intentions, I'd fallen head over heels for him.

It sucked. If I could have chosen otherwise, I would have. The friendship between the five of us was the foundation of my existence, and the thought of doing anything that might endanger it squeezed the breath from my lungs, sent anxiety snaking into my bloodstream.

But my feelings were what they were, and there was no point denying them any further. I knew what I felt.

I was in love with Griffin Conway.

I'd never allowed myself to be chickenshit about anything in my entire life. If doing something scared me, I did it all the faster to make sure I'd do it regardless.

But admitting my feelings to Griffin sent nervous tingles sweeping across my body. There was always the chance that when he'd told me he loved me, he'd meant that he loved me as a friend.

If I told him I loved him as more than a friend, it might mess up everything great between us.

Sucking in a fueling breath and calling on my courage, I placed my hand atop his. I pretended the move was casual, but the whole time, my heart was thundering.

When he didn't hesitate to interlace his fingers with mine, I froze, unable to move lest I betray my elation.

I was only vaguely aware of what was happening beyond where his flesh met mine. My heartbeat settled into my fingers and palm.

The cheerleaders were waving their pompoms and chanting, "Be aggressive, be-e aggressive," when Hunt leaned his head in our direction to whisper, "The cameras are down."

His sharp gaze skirted across our linked hands before he leaned to the other side to share the same message with Layla and Brady.

Griffin and I looked at the cameras in each corner of the large space, but they appeared no different than usual.

"What do you mean?" Griffin asked Hunt without concern for our handholding.

"They usually have little glowing green lights beneath them that indicate they're on."

"They do?" I asked, sitting up straighter.

"Yup," Hunt said. "The lights've been on every other time I've been in here."

"I never paid attention," Layla said.

"Well," Hunt said. "They haven't been on once since we got here."

Ordinarily I might have been relieved we got a break from the constant monitoring. But after everything we'd experienced the last several weeks, I didn't like it.

"Who knows?" Layla said. "It's probably nothing. Maybe they're updating them or someone fell asleep at the controls." But she remained alert, sitting tall.

A minute later the fire alarm blared, cutting off yet another chorus of "be-e aggressive." The five of us exchanged wary looks.

Students below us groaned, and even the teachers didn't make a move to evacuate.

"Can we just keep going?" asked the captain of the cheerleaders, a senior by the name of Gwyneth Stradbrook.

Mr. Lauderbeck sighed, running a hand through his short hair. "No. We have to evacuate. It's the rule." But he appeared to be searching the stands for our principal.

I hadn't seen him leave, but I didn't spot him either.

"It's just another fire drill," Gwyneth whined. Her blue and silver pompoms drooped at her sides. "Come on, Mr. Lauderbeck, we worked so hard to prepare, and we're almost finished with our routine."

A dozen girls and two guys in matching blue and silver lined up behind her, identical pleading looks on their faces as if those, too, were part of their uniforms.

Mr. Lauderbeck glanced at the other teachers peppered throughout the first row while muttering, "I dunno."

But then a student screamed, and another yelled, "Smoke!" and the matter was settled.

With Queen's "We Are the Champions" playing in the background in premature celebration, half the people scrambled to get out, pushing toward one of two exits that led outside. The other half rose from their seats but didn't particularly hurry. We waited as our peers grew noisier, more boisterous.

When another person yelled out, "Fire!" over the soundtrack, even those who'd been moving slowly started hurrying.

"I don't like this," Layla said. "Seems like a bit too much to be coincidence. On your first day back?" She glanced down the row at Griffin and me. When her gaze skirted across our joined hands, I moved to pull away, but Griffin held on.

"I don't like it," she added, and I couldn't decide if she meant the fire alarm or our touch. She looked at Brady, who was frowning.

"Yeah, shit's sus." He stood. "Let's get out of here. At least we can leave a few minutes early now. Ms. Tott won't be paying attention anymore."

Brady led the way, and when it became obvious I had to be really cautious descending the bleachers on my crutches, he looked back up at me and offered, "I'll give you a piggyback ride."

"Thanks, but I'm good."

"Then Hunt or Griff will."

"I've got it, Brade," I assured. "Besides, it's just a little bit of smoke."

It was barely a trickle, escaping from the stairwell that led to the second-floor classrooms lining one side of the high-ceilinged gym. The fire must be up there.

Brady grunted at me but nodded and waited. The music finally faded and ended, though the alarm continued wailing obnoxiously.

When I made it down, most of the students had already evacuated. Teachers stood at either exit, ushering out stragglers.

Mrs. Moody whistled at us, apparently still under the impression we were livestock. "Come on, kids! Let's go, let's go! Pick up the pace. Don't you hear the alarm?"

"Joss is on crutches," Layla said with a *duh* inflection.

Mrs. Moody smirked. "I can see that, Layla. I'm not blind. But when there's an emergency, excuses won't work on me."

An incredulous "Excuses?" slipped out of me without forethought, and I had to fight the urge to slow down to a crawl just to spite the woman. It's not like I was dawdling. I was fucking *spritely* on my crutches. I was looking freaking *lively*, dammit. I would have liked to see her go even half my speed with the same bulky cast.

"Why don't you go ahead, Mrs. Moody?" I suggested with a smile that was half wheedling, half *shut the hell up*.

"I can't go till the space is clear."

"All good here," Mr. Lauderbeck shouted from the other door, loudly enough to be heard over the alarm. "I'm heading out myself."

"Yep," Mrs. Moody called to him before yelling at us again. "Move it, Joss, or—"

"We'll make sure she gets out," Brady said, cutting her off. "Just go ahead."

Mrs. Moody examined the mere forty feet that still separated us, the trail of smoke that had gotten no thicker and no more alarming, and nodded. She stepped most of her body out the door before popping back in to jab at us with an accusing finger.

"Make sure you do what you're told."

Then she was gone. As one, my crew and I tensed. We were passing the end of the bleachers, the door just ten feet away, when it closed, clicking shut.

"For fuck's sake," Brady muttered. "Woman could've shut the hell up or waited thirty more seconds for us. It's not like we're all the way out in Timbuktu. Jeez."

"Damn, what is wrong with people?" Layla huffed.

Without pause, Brady pressed the bar on the inside of the door and slammed his shoulder and knee into it. It didn't budge. His chin jerked back in surprise as he pushed harder on the bar that was supposed to open the door. He pushed, rattled the lever, and even slammed his shoulder into the door—this time on purpose—but it remained closed.

Still fiddling with the door, he looked at us over his shoulder. "I think it's locked."

"Let me try," Hunt said.

Brady moved out of the way for him, grumbling, "You think I don't know how to open a door now, dude? For real?"

Hunt did everything Brady had—with the same results. "It was worth checking, just in case." Eyes wide, Hunt looked around the space that was sizable enough to accommodate two basketball or volleyball courts at the same time, plus additional space for wrestling and gymnastics mats.

Already in motion, Hunt called over his shoulder, "I'll check Mr. Lauderbeck's door. Lay, you get the one that leads to the cafeteria. Brade, you try the one going up the stairs."

"Not sure we're gonna wanna go up that way," Brady said, but he jogged toward it nonetheless. Though slim, a steady trail of smoke continued to slip into the gym from beneath it.

While we waited, Griffin repeated everything Brady and Hunt had already tried with this door. He even took a running start before slamming into the door so hard it shook in its frame. It still didn't open. He was kicking at it as the banging of the others using similar techniques at the other doorways reached us. Too close to the smoke, Brady coughed repeatedly.

"Griff, the ball bin," I said.

Immediately, he ran over to it, sliding it on its wheels and lining it up with the door. Though the cage for sports equipment had openings reminiscent of chicken wire on the top part, it was made of steel, and its bottom and frame were solid.

"Good idea," Hunt commented, jogging up. "My door's locked shut."

"Mine too," Brady said as he and Layla returned to my side.

"It's like they're braced from the outside or something," she said. "With what we did, we should've been able to get at least one of them open."

Hunt and Griffin lined up on either corner of the ball cage and ran, achieving speed before ramming it into the door, which shuddered but held, as if it were indeed braced from the outside.

"What the fuck?" Brady growled viciously.

"I'm gonna murder someone," Layla snarled. "No way this shit's not on purpose."

Eyes big, the five of us looked at each other.

I said, "If it's on purpose, which I agree it looks like it is, then there's only one reason for it I can think of."

A rumble that sounded as much beast as man ripped from Griffin's throat. Startled, I jerked my stare to him.

He was already looking at me, his eyes nearly glowing with their fury. "Someone's trying to kill us to see if we come back to life. I will *not* let that happen."

"No fucking way," Brady rumbled with an uncommonly panicked look that dragged first across his twin before settling on Hunt and me. Next, it traveled toward the smoke. All of a sudden, the slim trickle multiplied, becoming a billowing torrent. A real threat. With the size of the gym, we still had time, but not much.

"Our parents," Hunt said, scrambling to get his phone out of his pocket.

"Oh my God, yes," Layla said on a relieved laugh. "They'll race right over here and do their crazy spy shit all over the sick sonofabitch trying to kill us."

Having to coordinate around my crutches, I was last to study my phone. Brady was cursing up a storm before I realized why.

"What the hell?" I said. "Even when there's no signal, you can still call emergency services. Why won't it let us?" Uselessly, I jabbed at my phone's screen.

Layla's eyes blazed. "Because someone with connections is trying to kill us."

I breathed heavily through my nostrils, a heat building inside me I recognized as righteous anger. "Magnum Chase," I gritted out between clenched teeth.

Layla nodded grimly, her bangs bouncing as her determination grew. "We gotta get the fuck outta here 'cause I have a gazillionaire to string up by his balls."

"Nope," Brady said. "I'm gonna lop them off first. Then, I'm gonna feed 'em to him."

I hopped around in place on my good leg, studying our surroundings. The gym was constructed of cinder blocks and had no windows. Sturdy, but not the Great Wall of China by any means.

"We break through a wall," I said. "Or through a door."

None of them laughed at my suggestion. Instead, they began scanning the gym for tools.

Griffin scrambled to a squat beside the bleachers. "These bars here look strong enough. We just need to figure out how to pry a few of them off."

I let them do that while I inspected every little part of that gymnasium. We had to be missing something. There had to be a way out.

And I was going to motherfucking find it.

25

Courtesy of Magnum Chase

Griffin and Brady pried a metal bar from the bleachers' frame, and Hunt and Layla were close to breaking off another, when the door farthest from us, the one Mr. Lauderbeck had been supervising, swung open.

I sucked in a startled inhale as thirteen armed soldiers swarmed in before the door clicked rapidly closed behind them. They wore gas masks, hardly glancing at the smoke billowing into the gym.

Layla and Hunt wrenched off the bar with a loud snap, then popped up to standing while I glanced quickly at the cameras. Green lights were back to blinking below them. It was how they knew to come in that door, the one we couldn't possibly reach in time, and not the one nearest us.

The twins gripped the metal bars, holding them in front of their bodies like the wooden staffs we practiced with on the back deck of the treehouse. Hunt snapped open a pocketknife he wasn't supposed to bring to school. And Griffin clutched a metal-barrel pen, readying to pull a John Wick move, I imagined. It wasn't much as far as weapons went, for sure, and Griff was no John Wick. But the hard clench of his jaw and even harder eyes told me that if he was going down, he was taking as many of them as possible with him first. That pen could indeed be mightier than a sword.

I prepared to lean my weight into my good leg while wielding my crutches. No doubt, it would hurt like hell. But barely bearable pain was better than dead, even if there was a chance I'd resurrect. That was the kind of result I needed absolutely guaranteed before I dared count on it.

My friends circled me as the soldiers jogged our way. In their identical black gear, they all looked the same. They all moved the same. Perfectly in sync, their feet hit the floor at the same time. They were lean, muscled, and strapped with weapons: sidearms extended with silencers, hunting knives, and what looked like hand grenades, if Hollywood Weapons 101 had taught me anything. *What the fuck?* I spotted no handcuffs, straps, or tactical batons. Their objective didn't seem to be to incapacitate, but to *murder*.

Their gear lacked any kind of insignia. The kind of killers someone as rich and connected as Magnum Chase would probably be able to hire.

That motherfucker. I was going to survive this—*we* were going to survive this—just so we could hunt the bastard down and make him pay for being such an entitled, evil twat.

With a rhythmic jostling of gear and a steady pounding of boots across the gym's floor, the soldiers crossed the distance between us too fast for me to overcome my shock. We were supposed to be groaning through the end of a cheesy, stupid pep rally, not fighting for our lives. How did shit go south so freaking fast? Just a couple of months ago, before the party at the Fischer House, my biggest worry had been how to resist my growing feelings for Griffin. How to keep our parents from trying to force us to go to university. How to figure myself out in a world that didn't understand me. If only those were my primary problems now.

My heartbeat sped up, and I started to sweat as the mercenaries came to a halt in a practiced, staggered formation, six up front, seven lined up behind them. The six in front had their sidearms drawn at their sides, not yet pointing at us. The seven in back had them aimed at our chests. They could probably put a bullet in each of our hearts and not even blink.

Their eyes on us were as steady as their trigger fingers. No emotion tightened their faces. There was nothing to indicate any kind of moral dilemma with invading a freaking high school gymnasium to hunt down unarmed teenagers.

The fire alarm finally fell silent.

"Guys. . ." Hunt murmured from my right. But what was there to say? *This* was what being royally fucked looked like.

"What the fuck do you think you're doing?" Layla barked savagely at the line of sleek, lethal badasses, as if we weren't woefully outmatched. "You need to turn the fuck around and head back out that door you came in through."

I would have jumped in to amend that they should also leave the door unlocked for us so we could get out after, but what would be the point?

The soldiers didn't respond, just kept those seven handguns trained on us. They were mostly men, but two women stood in the back row. Their hair was cut short, just like the guys.

"Go! Now," Layla snarled. "I mean it. You don't want to mess with us. We'll come back from the dead just to haunt your asses. And I've got a real mean, vengeful streak. You don't want to make an enemy out of me."

Nothing, not even a grunt or a cleared throat. Smoke eased out from beneath the door to the stairwell, thickening the air around it and inching in our direction.

"You heard her," Brady said before growling like Bobo did when he spotted a possum in the forest. "Get the fuck out of here."

The two guys on either end of the front row raised their free arms and reached over their backs. They slid something boxy from sleeves attached to their combat vests.

As one, the four of them stalked forward with their boxes. Layla and Brady raised their metal staffs, and Hunt and Griffin leaned into the balls of their feet, clutching their weapons. Even I pushed as much of my weight as I could into my good leg before settling some into my injured leg, gripping a crutch tightly enough to overcome the wince of pain that rolled through me.

"Don't take another step," Brady snarled at them, as if they couldn't have already taken us out several times over with well-placed bullets.

The mercenaries ignored him, depositing their boxes in an orderly row halfway between our two groups. The containers were about a foot long, half that wide, and an inch deep.

"Courtesy of Magnum Chase," one of the men announced as, in unison, they lifted the lids on their boxes, revealing their contents.

My breathing stuttered until I forced myself to inhale.

"That motherfucking dick-breath weasel," Layla hissed.

We were staring at defibrillators. Nestled in slim black cases, they were sleeker and more compact than the ones the EMTs had used on Brady, but there was no denying that's what they were.

Or what it meant that we were being presented them in this scenario.

"We attack," Griffin whispered under his breath. "Move fast. Protect Joss."

It wasn't much. In fact, it was far from enough. They had guns. We didn't. They probably killed adorable puppies as a warm-up before breakfast. We'd never killed a damn thing. Plus, I was hurt. The very definition of a sitting target. Even if I were to run through the pain, this bulky cast would prevent any agility.

But what else were we to do? Stand there while they picked us off one by one?

Hell no.

The soldiers retreated from the row of defibrillators to reclaim their spots in the front row.

Staff held high, Layla charged. Brady was a second behind her as Hunt lunged for the opposite side of the line. Griffin crouched in front of me, pen gripped in his dominant hand. I raised a crutch, blinking rapidly as my vision instantly swam when I settled too much weight into the compound fracture in my shinbone.

Multiple shots rang out in quick succession.

The quiet that followed the guns' silenced bangs was deafening as Layla and Hunt kept running for an instant, their momentum carrying them forward. Then they crumpled like rag dolls. Layla slammed to her knees before slumping onto her chest. Hunt simply pitched forward.

The staff clattered as it rolled from Layla's hands, one arm pinned awkwardly beneath her.

Hunt lay unmoving, his penknife still gripped in his fingers. As I watched, his hold around the blade loosened; his fingers didn't move again.

I screamed, only absently registering that Griffin and Brady were bellowing too.

Blood blossomed across Layla's and Hunt's backs around different exit wounds. The crimson spots swelled and spread, their shirts canvases of their draining blood.

Clutching his staff in both hands, Brady slashed the air in front of him before charging with a roar so feral that, had I not been watching him, I would have believed it came from a bear, not a man.

"Stop!" commanded one of the soldiers in the center of the front line, pulling down his gas mask.

I was eyeing Layla's staff when Brady swung his at the front line. The soldiers ducked and jumped out of his way before two tackled Brady to the floor. He smacked his knees and head against the floor hard enough to make me wince. One soldier settled a knee against Brady's back while the other leaned his weight onto Brady's pinned arms.

Griffin scrambled forward to snatch Hunt's knife before rushing back to me. He shoved me behind him so roughly that I stumbled on unstable footing. His chest heaved with his anger as he reached an arm back to hold me steady.

"Stop. Stop!" ordered the same man in a tone that implied he was used to instant obedience.

"Don't you fucking hurt our friend," Griffin snarled.

"Don't touch him," I echoed.

But our threats were obviously empty. We were severely outmatched. If I lived through this, I vowed to never find myself in this situation again. Having to watch my friends suffer and die, knowing there was nothing I could do to prevent it.

If I survived this—if we came back from this—I'd never fucking be a victim again. I'd be the one with the power to end someone's life. And if they pushed me, I'd do it without a second thought. Without hesitation. Just like these assholes did.

"You don't need to die," the commanding soldier told Brady, who thrashed and bucked to break free. Another pair of soldiers ran over to help hold him in place, also shoving off their gas masks.

His back pressed to my chest, Griffin tensed even more. The veins bulged in both sides of his neck while he looked at Brady, unwilling to leave my side.

"Our orders are to kill only these two and the other girl," the commander continued.

The other girl.

Me.

"No one else. We'll kill you if you leave us no choice, but you can walk out of here without going through that. It's up to you."

"'Those two' are our family." Brady's voice hitched before he shouted again. "Our fucking family, you sonsofbitches! *My sister!*"

"We were told they'd come back. All you need to do is use the defibrillators once they're gone. There are special ambulances waiting for you right outside. A whole private team of EMTs aware of your unique circumstances. They'll remove any bullet fragments from your friends, patch them up, and they'll be fine."

"Fuck you," Brady growled, straining backward with enough fury to rise nearly a foot off the floor with the weight of four men on him, before slamming back down hard enough to make him wheeze.

"You don't need to die," the commander repeated. "Just calm down. Let us do our jobs and you can live. If you don't want to defibrillate them back to life, the EMT team outside can do it. Our boss has arranged everything."

"I'll just bet he fucking has," I snarled. "I'm gonna kill him." It was a solemn vow. A promise I'd keep no matter what it took to fulfill it.

The commander turned, peering at me over Griffin, who scrambled to better tuck me behind him. "No one touches Magnum Chase. No one, you hear me?"

"You're not touching *her*," Griffin said with enough determination that, for a stuttering heartbeat, I almost believed him. "You don't dare touch her. Don't even fucking look at her."

The commander sauntered casually in our direction, causing my body to clench as much as Griffin's. There was nothing casual about this man with eyes of such a startling blue I knew already I'd never forget their exact hue—like a perfect summer sky. *Fuck him and his pretty eyes. Fuck him hard.*

"You're all a bunch of murderers," I snapped at him, at each of them. "There's no justification for this. You're killing innocent kids."

Normally, I didn't appreciate anyone referring to us as *kids*. We were *young adults*, thank you very much, emphasis on the *adult* part. But maybe there was a shred of decency in one of them. . .

Then I'd hobble over to Layla and Hunt and defibrillate them till their eyes opened. God, I needed to see them moving again. Now, now, *now*.

My breathing was too fast, my nerves twitching. I needed every single one of my crew to be alive right the hell now. Right. Now.

The commander's face remained smooth. His eyes didn't flinch. He was maybe in his late twenties, not that much older than us. Without looking, he tossed his gas mask to the floor.

"You'll all come back to life. I don't think you realize how special that is. How important you'll be to the world. What kind of life-altering work Mr. Chase can do with that."

"'Mr. Chase' can shove his pandering bullshit up his ass," I said. "You've already killed two people who are more incredible than you'll ever be. You're murderers, plain and simple, no matter who foots your bill."

Those bright blues darkened for a millisecond. The commander scowled at Griffin. "Get out of my way."

Griffin brought up the small blade. At least he knew how to use it. "No."

"Now!" snapped the commander.

"No," Griffin repeated, his voice firm and unwavering. "Listen this time. She's not yours to touch. Not yours to look at. Most definitely not yours to fucking hurt."

He went completely still beneath my touch. "She's mine," he breathed so softly I wouldn't have been sure I'd heard him if I wasn't pressed up against him.

My eyes widened. My heartbeat sped up even more, till I was certain he'd be able to feel it through the fabric of his t-shirt, through his skin.

"What?" I whispered, the question slipping out of me. Hearing it aloud, I realized it made it sound like I didn't want that, didn't feel the same. Like I didn't want to be his.

Like I didn't want him to be mine.

"Have it your way," the commander said, his lips flattening into a line of irritation as he raised his gun and pointed it at Griffin's forehead.

As if my very soul were ripping free of my body, a haunted "Noooooooooooooo!" tore out of me.

In the seconds before the commander tightened his finger around the trigger, I shoved Griffin out of the way. Unprepared for it, he stumbled and fell, landing on his ass.

Immediately, he pushed up, scrambling to get his feet back under him, already reaching for me.

His eyes were a bright hazel, panicked and desperate. I met them, my entire face softening with acceptance.

No matter my desires, my wishes, my love for my crew, apparently death was still coming for me.

And if it was, I knew what I wanted my final words to be.

Holding the eyes of the man I loved more than I'd allowed myself to accept until that precise moment, I whispered to him, "I love you, Griff."

"Noooooo," he yelled as he brought the knife down and into the commander's shoulder.

The man flinched but didn't allow the injury to interrupt him from completing his mission.

I didn't look at the gun, only at Griffin. Agony transformed his beautiful face, the one I loved studying, that I could spend happy years memorizing, each day finding more to love about it.

His mouth twisted as he screamed again.

Brady shouted.

I neither heard nor saw the gun fire at my head.

Without any idea whether there would ever again be light, my life went dark.

About the Author

Lucía Ashta is the international-bestselling Argentinian American author of more than seventy young adult and adult fantasy and paranormal books including the Royals of Embermere, Smoky Mountain Pack, Witches of Gales Haven, Magical Creatures Academy, Witching World, and Six Shooter and a Shifter series. A former attorney and architect, Ashta lives in North Carolina's Smoky Mountains with her husband and three daughters. When she isn't writing, she's reading, painting, or adventuring.

Podium

DISCOVER MORE

STORIES
UNBOUND

PodiumEntertainment.com